BOOK FOUR OF THE STACY JUSTICE SERIES

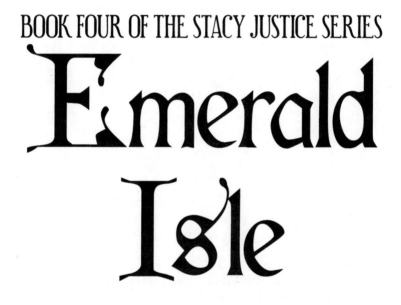

Emerald Isle

(IT IS HIGHLY RECOMMENDED
THAT THIS SERIES BE READ IN ORDER.)

Barbra Annino

Text copyright © 2013 Barbra Annino

Published by Thomas & Mercer
PO Box 400818
Las Vegas, NV 89140

ISBN-13: 9781477805848
ISBN-10: 1477805842
Library of Congress Control Number: 2013901627

For Mom

Prologue

Amethyst, Illinois. Twenty-nine years ago.

Birdie Geraghty stood in the vast bedroom of her childhood home, staring at the pile of beautifully wrapped presents with just one thought on her mind.

Today is the day.

She could feel it in her blood, smell it on the wind. Even her sleep had been disrupted all through the night by the excited chatter of a thousand generations of ancestors gone before her, whispering in her dreams, *She's coming.* Birdie couldn't recall the last time she had tossed and turned so much in a single evening when the moon wasn't full. Perhaps before she had divorced Oscar. That man could wake the dead with his snores. Of course, that was no longer a problem now that she slept alone and he was living across town.

She glanced around the room, tucked a crimson lock of hair behind her ear, and wondered if the house was lonely with fewer bodies to fill it.

But the decision about what to do with the Queen Anne home her father had built would have to wait. She had far more pressing matters at hand. Because today was the day she would become a grandmother. And the world would gain a gift.

Birdie finished dressing, careful to wear jewel tones so as to ignite imagination and inspiration in the child. She had to make certain that the infant felt a spark straight from the womb. It was important her granddaughter bond with the family bloodline as soon as possible. The little one would need a mountain of strength to face the challenges before her, and Birdie intended to help her build it. She wanted the child to recognize who she was born to be as soon as her little eyes gazed upon the world. No buttery yellow, sky blue, or bubblegum pink for her granddaughter. Certainly, soft pastels were quite soothing and necessary for other infants, but a witch who would one day be Seeker mustn't be sheltered from the wonders—or the cruelties—of this world and beyond.

Birdie smiled in spite of herself. She was practically giddy as she arranged the gifts into two large shopping bags. She couldn't wait for the council to accept the nomination of her granddaughter for Seeker. She knew it was only a matter of time, a mere formality. She knew it as sure as she knew her own name. And it was her task, as the mother of the mother of the only Seeker of Justice born in the New World, to protect the child at all costs.

She had a slew of gifts left in the closet, some for future milestones, some rewards for lessons learned in training. These were not meant to be given until the child was much older, but the one gift Birdie longed to give, the one she hoped would come in due time, wasn't hers to present. No, that gift—that precious talisman—would come only in a way Birdie herself didn't quite comprehend.

One day, the witch thought, *one day it shall be yours, Anastasia.*

Birdie picked up the quaint little card she had bought for her granddaughter's arrival and ran her strong hands over the embossed letters.

ANASTASIA
meaning: "resurrection"

It was the name she would call the girl. One more suitable for the woman she would become than the name chosen by her parents.

Birdie signed the card, stuffed it in an envelope, and slipped it inside one of the shopping bags perched on the bed. Just as she was about to rush to her sister's home, presents in tow, a light flashed and the black mirror in her room chimed, then filled with silvery mist.

Who would be bothering me now? She hesitated. *Perhaps Lolly or Fiona? Do they need something for the baby's witchening?*

She decided she should check. She set the bags near the door, crossed to the walnut fireplace, and tapped the gold-framed scrying mirror that hung above it.

As soon as that wretched Tallulah's taut face appeared, Birdie regretted answering the call.

"Birdie, darling. How lovely to see you." Tallulah's narrow head was wrapped in a turban with a teardrop diamond dangling from its crest. Every inch of her pale face was pinched tight and powdered. She looked to have been the victim of a poor plastic surgeon or a spell gone awry.

Either way, Birdie didn't much care. "Tabby, I don't have time to talk right now. I'm on my way out. What do you want?" The woman irritated her to no end. The best thing about Tallulah was that she was an ocean away.

Tallulah stuck her bottom lip out in a pretend pout and rolled her eyes, her false lashes giving the illusion of two spiders nesting.

"Well, now, is that any way to speak to someone who is only calling to congratulate you on the arrival of your granddaughter? Honestly, Birdie, you can be so ungracious."

How does she know already?

"Then you must know I am anxious to get to my daughter's side, Tabby, so if you don't mind…"

Birdie stepped forward to end the conversation by tapping the mirror three times.

Tallulah couldn't hide her irritation at the snub. She waved her hand before the connection was cut, and the mirror grew fuzzy, but retained a hazy image. "Birdie, I want you to know that I am aware of your plans and it will never work. She is not what you think she is. She is not one of them. I plan to file a formal protest of the nomination to the council."

Birdie didn't bother to ask Tallulah how she knew of her intentions. Witches were notorious gossips. Birdie stepped closer to the mirror, her unlined face taking on a few crossroads as she narrowed her eyes at the woman who had been like acid on her skin since the day they met all those years ago.

"Do what you must, Tallulah, but I assure you, she will be stronger than you can imagine. I wouldn't step into affairs you know nothing about, if I were in your shoes. This is for the good of all the clans. This has nothing to do with your petty insecurities."

"Ha! My insecurities? You are the one, my dearest Birdie, who cannot stand the fact that my son Pearce is twice the wizard your daughter is."

"You mean warlock," Birdie said, just to ruffle Tabby's feathers.

"That's a lie! Pearce never took the dark path. You withdraw that malicious accusation!"

"Fine, I take it back. Now, if you will excuse me, I have a Seeker to meet. Let's talk again when you have a grandchild."

This, Birdie could see before she cleared the mirror, infuriated Tallulah.

Sorry, Tabby. This time, I win.

PART ONE

The Awakening

You want your God to be wild and to call you to where
your destiny awaits.

—John O'Donohue

Chapter I

Birthdays are supposed to be a celebration of life, renewal, and endless possibilities. There's that little spark of hope you get, no matter what age, when you wake up in the morning on the day you came into this world and think, *This year will be different.* The last twelve months don't matter, because there's a brand-new slate to fill, a new *you* to find.

Some women rise to frolicking kids cooking breakfast. Some crawl out of bed to discover a sexy note left by a lover.

At this point, I would have welcomed a call from a radio disc jockey.

My grandmother Birdie was perched at the foot of my bed, and she wouldn't stop talking. She was incredibly excited, and because my level of enthusiasm before I've had my morning coffee is on par with that of a kid being whisked off to fat camp, I was not sharing her energy.

She didn't hide her agitation when she said, "You still don't understand, do you?"

"Not really, no. Come back later and tell me all about it."

I flung the comforter over my head and burrowed deep under the covers with my Great Dane, Thor. It was a sunny fall day at the end of September. Mabon, to be exact. The autumnal equinox, when the earth divides night and day in equal proportions and pagans honor the spirits of our ancestors. There are gardens to harvest, offerings to be made, rituals to perform.

It sucks sharing a birthday with a holiday.

Birdie sighed, as if the weight of the world rested on her lips. "I will explain it one more time."

She yanked back the covers, exposing my bare arms and legs, sending a chill across my body.

"Please." I put my hand up to stop her. "I need coffee first."

I swung my feet over the edge of the bed, wiped the sleep from my eyes, and stretched. Thor yawned in protest at being roused at such an early hour. He stood, circled the bed so his head faced away from the window, and collapsed onto a pillow.

Birdie offered to make the coffee and thankfully left my bedroom. As I rummaged through my closet, looking for a pair of sweats to throw over my shorts and tank top, I contemplated just what she was trying to tell me.

Which was, essentially, that I had not woken up the age I thought I would be today when I went to bed last night.

Of all the absurd conversations I had had with this woman over my lifetime, this was right up there with the dangers of garden gnomes.

You see, today was my twenty-ninth birthday, but Birdie was trying to work some sort of new math to convince me that I was actually turning thirty. This would not be that big a deal except that in my family—the Geraghty family, whose roots trace back to ancient Druids from Kildare,

Ireland—turning thirty was a whole lot more than a number. Thirty was a milestone. A momentous occasion. A commitment to being all you can be.

Simply put, thirty was the year that I was to grow into my full power as a witch.

And I wasn't quite ready yet.

Granted, I had been training these last few months. Honing my ability to communicate with the dead, mastering spellcasting and psychic defense, studying the history of my heritage, my Celtic people, even combat techniques. Plus, I learned six different formulas for potions that would knock a man out long enough to steal his wallet.

Not that I was a thief, but you get the idea.

At every milestone along the way, with every achievement earned and test passed, I received a small token from Birdie or her two sisters, Lolly and Fiona, as a reward. Some were wrapped in faded, dusty paper. They must have been in storage for years. I have to admit, despite digging my heels in for so long, reluctant to be what my family wanted me to be, I enjoyed all I had learned over the summer and appreciated all they had gifted me. My little cottage in the tiny hamlet of Amethyst, Illinois, was now filled with books, heirloom seeds, crystals, wands, and athames. Everything a good witch needs.

Or, in my case, Seeker of Justice.

I still didn't know if I bought that title. I certainly didn't *feel* like part of the intricately woven fabric of ancient Druid laws. What I did know was that all of this training was to prepare me to meet with the pagan council in Ireland that had imprisoned my mother over fourteen years ago. Her crime was murder. Her case was scheduled for review this Samhain, or Halloween, and Birdie insisted that they would release her then. She thought my involvement in protecting an ancient text from a homicidal couple last winter tilted the scale in our favor.

I hoped she was right. Because the man my mother had killed had intended to kill me. I was still a bit sketchy on the details. Not even Birdie knew exactly what had happened, because my mother had been taken abruptly and then denied all contact with our family. The man she had killed (my grandmother told me not long ago) had been a member of the very council I was soon to face for her freedom. So the lessons, the tests, the work I had poured into learning my path and my craft were more important than ever. There was no way to know if they would be put to use at the hearing, but I had a sense that the council across the pond might have a few tests in store for me.

It was important to be prepared for anything.

I stuffed my feet into fuzzy slippers and shuffled into the kitchen. My grandmother handed me a coffee cup dosed with cream and sprinkled with nutmeg. Just how I liked it. She watched me as I took one sip, then another, before she spoke. I climbed on top of a stool and put my elbows on the breakfast bar, giving her my full, caffeinated attention.

"All right." Birdie paced, her aubergine skirt waving behind her. "It's like this. The minute you take your first breath, the clock starts ticking." She began counting on her fingers. "You are born, essentially, at the age of zero, then you complete one full year and"—she spun toward me—"in society's eyes you are considered one year old." She held up one finger.

"I think that's how a calendar works, yes."

"But you are actually *entering* your second year of life on this plane." She paused, tried to read if that had sunk in. "Do you see? You have lived one full year."

Somehow, it made sense. "I'm with you."

"So." She rolled her hand in the air, coaxing me to come up with the correct answer.

I put my head on the smooth counter and mumbled, "So I am entering my thirtieth year on this plane."

"Precisely!" She smacked her hands together. "And upon its completion, you shall be fully vested as a proper witch."

Leave it to Birdie to find a loophole in basic math. "But I haven't even been studying that long. Surely, there's a lot more to learn. We've barely tapped the Blessed Book."

The Blessed Book, a written history of my ancestors and our theology, was filled with spells, potions, herbal remedies, rituals, and stories from generations past, as well as predictions for future generations. That's where Birdie got the idea that I was the Seeker of Justice in the first place. My great-grandmother Maegan had predicted that a Seeker would be born in the New World. Personally, I thought it just a coincidence that my father's last name happened to be Justice, but there you have it.

Birdie said, "You still have plenty of time before your mother's review. With your great-aunts' and my assistance, I think we may just get you fully vested before then." She beamed at me.

"That's just over a month away. I can't learn the whole book in one month!" Seriously, the thing was thicker than Webster's and Oxford's dictionaries combined.

Birdie rolled her eyes and said, "Hogwash. You learned it all years ago. This is just a refresher course." She patted my hand. She was in a suspiciously good mood.

I lifted my head. "What's going on with you? Why are you so…bubbly?"

"Am I?" She raised one perfectly arched eyebrow and winked.

"What's wrong with your eye?"

She leaned on the counter, directly across from me. "You know, I'm not all business. I can be fun too."

"Uh-huh." I sipped my coffee. Birdie turned and reached for the pot to top off my mug, adding more cream and nutmeg.

"I have a surprise for your birthday is all," she said quietly.

That woke me up. "No. No surprises, please. I hate surprises, Birdie, you know that. I've had enough surprises to last a lifetime." Insane relatives, incarcerated parents, dead bodies, ghosts that not only talked to me but touched me, zombie dogs—these were just a few of the surprises that life had lobbed my way recently. I just wanted to relax and enjoy my first Friday off in years.

I asked, "Is it a trip to a day spa?"

"No."

"Then I'm not interested."

"Don't be so cynical. You'll adore it." Birdie reached for her wheat-colored cape and headed for the door. "See you at dusk. Don't forget to tell Lolly what you'd like for your special dinner. And bring all your tools for the ceremony."

The ceremony. I'd almost forgotten. Mabon was a prime time of the year for a witch to rededicate herself, as was any birthday. Because I hadn't been practicing—or even interested in practicing since my father died, when I was a freshman in high school—Birdie thought I should be initiated again.

I slid the stool back and stood. "Birdie, shouldn't we wait until after Mom is home?"

My grandmother paused for a minute, her back to me. All I could see was a spark of copper hair poking out from beneath her hood. Finally, she turned and said, "This is your time. Your mother's revival will come when it's her time." She opened the door, tossed a smile at me, and left.

Had I known at that moment the surprise in store for me later that night, I would have crawled back under the covers with Thor.

Chapter 2

I finished my second cup of coffee, showered, and dressed all before Thor climbed out of bed. I was just pulling on a pair of brown leather boots over my new jeans when he sauntered into the living room and did a full-body shake, launching a glob of doggie slime onto the ceiling.

"Good morning, boy. Are you hungry?"

He tap-danced around the living room and barked, raising a paw in the air.

"Okay, business first, breakfast second."

I let my dog out the back door and reached into the cupboard for his stainless-steel bowl. I mixed him up a hearty portion of boiled chicken, pumpkin, and rice, laced with olive oil and a few vitamins. Thor had recently recovered from a nasty injury, and at our repeated visits to the vet, his doctor managed to convince me that cheeseburgers and pizza were not the best source of nutrition. There were no excuses for my ignorance on canine care, and I had to admit I was grateful for the fresher-smelling air in my house. Although every once in a while, we still indulged in a junk-food fix.

Thor let himself in the screen door a few minutes later by pulling on the handle with his teeth. The door slapped back and forth, and my giant familiar went to investigate what the morning's meal consisted of while I reached for a strawberry yogurt.

My phone rang as I was cleaning up the breakfast dishes.

"Happy birthday!" Cinnamon, my cousin, said. "I hope you don't have any plans today, because I booked us some girl time."

"Does it involve pampering?"

"It does."

"You rock."

Cinnamon laughed, and we made arrangements to meet at the Amethyst Oasis Spa at eleven o'clock.

I called Lolly after that and requested her famous balsamic chicken and fried zucchini for dinner with peach ice cream and apple cake for dessert. Her gift to me every year was a fabulous meal I didn't have to help prepare. As busy as she, Birdie, and their middle sister, Fiona, were running the bed-and-breakfast they owned (converted from the house their father had built), the three of them rarely took any time off. The last week of September was the one exception they allowed themselves. I wasn't sure if it was a happy accident that my birthday fell around that time, if they planned it that way to celebrate in private, or if they just welcomed the break between the busy summer and the even busier fall season. Regardless of the reason, I had no complaints. I helped out at the inn whenever they needed a hand, which was quite often, so no guests for them meant a break for me as well.

A short while later, I was in the car with Thor in the backseat, headed to the office of the newspaper where I worked.

We walked into the new editor's office at the *Amethyst Globe* just as he was wrestling with the printer. There was a wad of paper at his feet—crimped, crumbled, and generally strewn about in choppy pieces.

Before I could ask if he needed a hand, he started kicking the machine and a stream of colorful insults gushed from his mouth. "You worthless, archaic, made-in-China crap factory!"

I cleared my throat. "Need a hand?"

Derek turned around. "I hate this thing." He glared at the printer like it had just slept with his girlfriend.

"Allow me."

I walked over to the printer and turned it off, then on again, then off. I opened the paper tray, pulled out the jammed wad, and turned the machine back on, and it went about its business. Thor decided to nest in the pile of discarded refuse on the floor.

"Thank you," Derek said. "Tell me again why is it that I'm the editor and not you?"

I sat down in the chair across from his desk. "Because we both decided that you're much better at delegating than I am."

"Bull. You just don't want to be stuck behind a desk all day." Derek took a seat behind his desk.

"True. But you get shot at way less than I do."

"True." He fist-bumped me and I smiled.

Our old boss and my father's long-ago partner, Shea Parker, was convicted a short while back on several charges, including obstruction of justice, withholding information to defer an investigation, and tampering with a corpse. He was serving six months in a county jail. Parker was sole owner of the paper, having inherited the 51 percent my father owned when he died. Before going into lockup, he signed that 51 percent over to me. My grandfather, who had a small fortune, offered to foot the rest of the money so that I could own the paper outright, but that was the kind of responsibility I just couldn't take on right now. Derek's father, an East Coast investment banker, lent Derek the money to invest in the remaining 49 percent. So now we were partners.

Derek said, "So what brings you by? I thought you were taking the day off."

"I was, but I needed something from my office and I thought I'd pop in to see how things were going and to invite you to my birthday dinner."

Derek narrowed his eyes. "Is it at your grandma's house?"

"Yes."

"Then I'm busy."

"Don't be such a baby."

Thor was chomping loudly on a piece of paper to my left.

"I'm a baby? Are you serious? Now, hold up, woman. Even you have to admit that place is superfreaky. People getting killed. Murderers booking rooms. Dead men just walking away. Sheesh." He shook his head, shuffled some papers around. "I'm not a baby. I don't want my head chopped off is all."

I sighed. "First of all, the dead man was in the morgue when he walked away, not at my grandmother's house. And second, no one's head ever got chopped off. That was a complete fabrication. Quit believing everything the locals tell you." I stood up and said, "You should come. It'll be fun. Six o'clock."

"Come where?" a voice behind me asked.

I smelled her before I saw her. She was wearing a scent usually found in red-light districts.

I leaned toward Derek. "Please tell me she's placing a singles ad."

Derek shook his head but wouldn't meet my eyes.

"Help wanted?" I asked.

Another shake.

"I'm the new sex columnist, Stacy," Monique Fontaine said from behind me.

I went to high school with Monique. She dressed like a stripper, talked like a truck driver, and had all the personality of a used-car salesman. Individually, these traits might be annoying but bearable. Package them all up in a silicone-enhanced, overtanned body, and they made you want to poke her with a sharp stick.

I turned to face her. "No."

She folded her arms. "Derek already hired me."

I had to admire her bravery as she snapped her gum at me. Her choice of clothing, not so much. I was pretty sure she was wearing a Frederick's of Hollywood costume called Naughty Secretary. The skirt, although plaid, was hiked up to her hips, she wore long white socks with platform Mary Janes, and the buttons on her gray blouse were losing the war with her DD implants. I was thankful for the tie tucked into her cleavage.

"He did that without my approval." I glared at Derek.

He stood up. "What do you want me to do? You're taking a two-week leave pretty soon. I need to fill up some space."

"So give Gladys a column. She's been wanting to do more than just research anyway."

"Gladys has a hard time speaking the English language, let alone writing it. You know that."

He had me there. The sixtysomething was from Poland and spoke in broken fragments, but she would have been a better choice for our tame little town. People in Amethyst wanted to read about ice cream socials, church fund-raisers, and how to plant a sunset mum garden. Not how to give a hummer and still keep your lipstick intact.

I turned to face her. "Don't you have a bar to run?"

She shrugged. "Down and Dirty has slowed now that your cousin's place is up and running. I decided to close on the slow nights, pick up a part-time gig."

Cinnamon owned the Black Opal Bar and Grill, which had been a Main Street icon for eighty years. The place had recently received a makeover, thanks to a fire, but it was freshly renovated and fully functional again.

I looked from Derek to Monique and said, "This is a trial run."

They both nodded. I looked at the two of them and then at Thor. "I'll be right back. Don't slime anything."

Derek said, "He won't. He's a good pooch."

"I wasn't talking to the dog," I said.

My office was just down the hall. I hurried to retrieve the three muses sword my grandmother had given me when I landed my first job as a reporter. I was going to need it tonight for the ritual.

I climbed on top of a chair and unhooked the sword from the small triquetra that anchored it to the far wall. Just as I grabbed the hilt, my office door slammed shut, the lights went out, and a sharp jolt sizzled through me as my feet faltered. I toppled to the floor.

The wind was knocked out of me, so I lay there a few moments on my back, trying to catch my breath. The sword was hot in my hands.

That's when she appeared.

Chapter 3

Birdie Geraghty busied herself by shopping for supplies for the evening's ritual. Her mind had been racing a thousand miles a minute, and doing something so mundane as pushing a shopping cart through an uninspired, fluorescently lit structure calmed her thoughts.

She loaded milk, sugar, eggs, and cheese into the basket. There were plenty of herbs, spices, vegetables, and fruits harvested from her own garden back at the house, but there was only so much three old ladies could do on their own anymore. Truth be told, Birdie didn't miss the days of making candles, shearing sheep, or weaving cloaks. She rather liked leaving some of the work up to others. She did, however, miss the archer hunts, the fencing, and the psychic competitions.

But she had left all of that back at the Academy. It seemed like a lifetime ago now, as her knees protested a squat to reach the flour on the bottom shelf. A lifetime ago and a continent away.

Birdie's thoughts returned to the present day as she passed the wine aisle. They would need some for the ritual and perhaps extra should her granddaughter invite friends to her birthday celebration.

She ticked off several more items on her list. Orange, brown, and yellow candles, maize, a few extra gourds, as this year's crop hadn't yielded many, graham crackers, and molasses.

She stood in the fourth aisle of the grocery store, having added a jar of green food coloring to the cart for the Green Man tribute, checking the basket's contents against her list. A smile crept across Birdie's face as she scratched off the remaining items.

Today is the day she comes back.

It had been years since Birdie had felt connected to her oldest granddaughter. The little ball of energy had been filled with an insatiable passion for life and an enthusiastic understanding of her gifts from the time she could crawl. Birdie would watch the child scoot across the carpet, chattering in Gaelic to her ancestors, giggling and gibbering in that manner in which only the innocent can. By the time she was five years old, the girl was enchanting herbs, identifying gemstones, and reciting recipes. By ten, she was a master spell crafter and the dead were visiting her regularly. Once, the Samhain that Anastasia was thirteen, a dark spirit forced its way through the veil during the yearly ritual celebration that took place in the woods behind the Geraghty Girls' Guesthouse. It clung to the girl and followed her home. That night, Birdie's daughter had called to relay the story of how the young witch single-handedly banished the spirit back through the veil, binding it to harm none.

Then, one year later, after the girl's father passed, she turned her back on all of it. Her passion, her visions, her lessons, her very *essence* was extinguished. It was as if someone had reached right inside her soul and turned out the light.

There is always an emptiness that washes over an elder when a child reaches independence. Tragically, Anastasia's willfulness arrived far too soon in her young life, with the added burden of guilt and the weariness of loss. Guilt over not having been able to prevent her father's death, loss of her mother to imprisonment. Birdie simply hadn't been prepared for it. Nor had she been prepared for the secrets and the lies she was forced to tell to protect Anastasia.

Yet, somehow, rather than protect her granddaughter, the secrets had broken her.

It shamed Birdie to even think about those days. What she wouldn't give to turn back the clock. Perhaps she would be gentler with her granddaughter. Perhaps she should have told her what had happened to her mother. Except Birdie didn't have all the answers to that mystery herself.

Would it have mattered? Would it have reignited Anastasia's drive? Forced her to face her destiny once again? Or would it have only driven her mad?

Let the past lie in the shadows, Birdie, she thought. It served no purpose to shine light on painful memories. Tonight would be a new beginning. She had much to be thankful for. Both of her granddaughters were turning into such fine young women. Cinnamon was a wife, business owner, and soon-to-be mother. Anastasia was a truth seeker, reemerging as the powerful witch Birdie always knew she was. Both such strong young women. And soon her daughter would be home.

Yes, indeed, she had much to be thankful for.

The cart was nearly full by the time Birdie reached the checkout line. She began unloading her groceries onto the conveyer belt when suddenly a pang gripped her chest.

"Are you all right?" the young cashier asked.

Birdie clutched the edge of the cart and struggled to focus on his features.

The man's face blurred until it was completely gone, her breath with it.

The air in the room chilled, and I had a vague awareness of Thor barking as my breath came in stiff spurts. I was still flat on my back, and a bit sore from landing on my ass, but too scared to do anything about it.

I didn't recognize the woman. She was transparent. Nothing more than a pearly mist like a moonbeam, but the shape, and the wavy hair that floated around her head, definitely looked female. She didn't radiate the same vibe as other ghosts. As she hovered over my body, she didn't seem desperate to pass along a message, as the dead so often did when they revealed themselves to me.

She seemed pissed.

Finally, the illuminated apparition spoke.

"Tonight, the Seeker burns a path through history.

In the forest, may only humans be.

Choose your words wisely. Choose them well.

For words are only words until they create a spell.

Should you reveal weakness or a hint of fear,

They will come, and you will meet the Web of Weird."

Her eyes had the glow of blue marbles as her stare ripped through my soul. She hovered, waiting for…*what? Acknowledgment?*

I gave a faint nod, despite understanding none of the riddle. Then she was gone.

I scrambled to my feet in a coughing fit, as my lungs devoured all the air in the room. There was a crash down the hall—breaking glass—and the thunderous gallop of a Great Dane on a mission. Thankfully, the lights flicked on, the door flew open, and Thor charged into my office without having to demolish the door.

Apparently, Derek had not been so lucky.

"Dammit, Thor!" he said from behind my dog.

Thor came to me first, then, deciding I was fine, proceeded to inspect every inch of my office, snout twitching.

"He broke my door down," Derek said.

"What the hell was that?" Monique asked.

"A power outage," I said.

Derek eyed me suspiciously. "Are you all right?"

"I'm fine. I just took my sword off the wall. Lost my balance," I said. "I'll call Chance. He'll fix the door."

"A power outage wouldn't have slammed the door shut," Monique said, looking around my office. "Derek's door slammed so hard, we couldn't even open it."

"Thor took care of that, though. It's more of a passageway now," Derek said.

"Must have been the wind," I said.

Thor came over to me, and I leaned on him for a moment, still catching my breath. He didn't have a scratch on him.

Monique looked skeptical, but she didn't say anything. Her eyes were glued to my sword.

I put the chair back behind my desk and said, "Happy Friday. Sorry about the door, Derek. I'll pay for it."

As Thor and I left the building, the ghost's words echoed in my head, and one thought came to mind.

What the hell is the Web of Weird?

Paralyzed for what seemed like an eternity, Birdie finally felt her limbs relax and her sight clear. The young, smooth face of the cashier transformed into the lined, graying, distinguished head of Aedon O'Neil, the highest council member, as he took control of the cashier's body

"Birdie, I have been trying to reach you all day. I tried the house phone, the wall mirror, I even went on that FaceTime to contact you through your mobile, which you know I loathe."

The youngest Geraghty Girl was stunned. Aedon had been her closest friend at the Academy, and more for a time. Birdie knew he would never take such a high risk in contacting her in this extreme manner if it weren't urgent.

She checked her phone. She must have bumped the volume button while it was in her pocket, because it was turned all the way down. She made certain no one was near before she asked, "What is it, Aedon?"

"There's been a breach. One of the treasures is missing."

Birdie couldn't believe her ears. "Surely you don't mean what I think you mean."

Aedon said, "Yes, Birdie. One of *the* four treasures. I don't have to tell you how serious this is. Especially being so close to Samhain."

And my daughter's hearing.

"Which one is gone?"

Aedon said, "Best not to discuss it here. Go home and get on a secure line. I will call back."

With that, Aedon faded from view and the young cashier's face was restored. He stood there blinking for a moment, looked around as if he couldn't recall where he was. Birdie smiled at him and commented on the weather, and the boy shook off his stunned state. He rang up the groceries in silence. Birdie rushed to the parking lot, piled her purchases into the car, and sped off toward the house, hoping upon hope that the missing relic wouldn't impact her daughter's return.

Chapter 4

I took Thor for a long walk on a hiking trail before dropping him back at the cottage. I didn't have time to look up "Web of Weird" in the Blessed Book, but I made a to-do list and scribbled it on there along with *cleanse sword before rituals* and *write dedication spell*. All that had to wait, though, because I had no intention of being late for my pampering date with Cinnamon.

I slid into a parking spot on Main Street, eight minutes to eleven. The spa was playing soft flute music filtered through the sound of lapping waves as I entered. The woman who greeted me wore a brown smock and peach lipstick. She handed me a form to fill out and escorted me into a dimly lit room that smelled like lavender and grapefruit. A round table filled with bowls of fresh fruit, spring water, carafes, and assorted teas sat to my left, and two lush, vine-printed chairs stood to my right. The woman told me to make myself comfortable as I waited for my cousin.

Cinnamon arrived a few minutes later, while I was sipping a cup of steaming peppermint tea. She was only four months pregnant, so there wasn't a visible bump to her belly, but her face glowed with the aura of motherhood. She held a small gold and blue–wrapped package tied with a glittery ribbon as she came into the room. I stood up to hug her, and she handed me the box.

"What's this?" I asked. It was light as air.

"That's from Gramps. I stopped by his place this morning, and he said he wasn't sure if he was going to make your dinner tonight. He wanted to be sure you got your present."

"But he already gave me my present."

A couple of weeks ago, Gramps presented all of us—Cinnamon, Birdie, Lolly, Fiona, and me—with the newest cell phones. He'd gotten us a family plan and all the phones were connected to each other, complete with the latest technology, including face-to-face chat.

"I think that was just a Gramps thing. You know how he likes to do for us, especially when it comes to gadgets. This"—she tapped the box—"is just for you."

"Must be the heirloom my father mentioned in his note."

A few months back, I had discovered a note written by my father talking about some mysterious family heirloom I was to open my thirtieth year. It was kept in a lockbox, along with some incriminating papers my father had gone to great lengths to hide before his death in order to protect me. I had turned the box over to the police—or, rather, the chief of police, Leo. The papers contained key evidence in a murder investigation. Leo told me about the gift inside the box. My father had written in the note that he planned to give it to Gramps for safekeeping, but he was killed before he got the chance. So I asked Leo to do just that.

There was a card fastened to the ribbon. I flipped it open. It read, in a script I did not recognize: *For Stacy Justice. When the time is right.*

I put the present inside my coat pocket and told Cinnamon I'd open it later. Then we each sank into an oversized chair and waited for our day of pampering to begin.

Birdie sideswiped a mailbox halfway from the grocery store to her house. She wasn't a woman to run from her mistakes, but she didn't have time to make restitution at the moment.

Her brain fired off thoughts in rapid succession. Which of the four treasures gifted by the Tuatha Dé Danann was missing? Any of them would spell absolute disaster, not only for her people, but for the entire globe, should it be obtained by one whose heart was less than honorable. All of them had great power to protect, sustain, and defend, but also to destroy.

Surely it wasn't the Stone of Destiny. That was standing proud at Tara, and it hadn't spoken to a king in years.

Could it be the Spear of Victory, which promised conquest for any warrior who wielded it? Or was it the Sword of Light, from which no enemy could flee?

Birdie skidded her car into the driveway, threw it into park, and didn't bother to collect the bags as she hopped from the vehicle. She charged up the steps and twisted the antique handle, but it was locked. She rang the bell and pounded on the door, and after a moment, her older sister, Lolly, answered.

Lolly's lipstick was a golden coral, and she had used it on her cheeks, eyelids, chin, and nose. She blinked twice and said, "No vacancies." Then she slammed the door and locked it.

Birdie cursed herself for not spiking her sister's tea at breakfast. She ran around to the back door, found the spare key beneath the gargoyle, and slipped into the kitchen.

"Sisters!" She was out of breath by then. She leaned against the counter for a rest before she called them again.

"Sisters!"

She could smell a cake baking in the oven; the aroma of tart apples and warm allspice lingered near the stove. The Green Man mask was on the apothecary table, already anointed from the looks of it for the ceremony this afternoon. It was common to call on the spirit of the forest to thank him for the abundance of the harvest and wish him a peaceful slumber as the earth crept into hibernation for the winter.

Birdie wondered, given the conversation she'd just had, if they would have time to perform the traditional rituals the Geraghtys usually carried out on Mabon.

The back door opened a moment later, and Fiona stepped through the threshold, a basket of tomatoes and fresh herbs on her arm. She stopped short when she saw Birdie and said, "Oh, my. Birdie, are you all right? You look as if you've been in a footrace."

Fiona never had that problem. The middle Geraghty Girl always looked as if she'd stepped off the cover of a magazine. It was her most ethereal gift.

"Something has happened," Birdie said. "We need a strong elixir for Lolly. She must be at her sharpest."

Fiona didn't need to be told twice. She reached into the cupboard for a bottle of twelve-year-aged Jameson Reserve—the most powerful medicine to bring Lolly back to reality—and poured a shot.

Birdie called for her older sister, and Lolly came shuffling into the kitchen, her tangerine ball gown on backward.

"Take care of Lolly and then meet me in my quarters," Birdie told Fiona.

Birdie rushed up the back stairs and into her bedroom. She went straight to the scrying mirror. It was flashing, indicating three calls had been missed. While the mirror recorded all conversations, it was not equipped to retain messages. Birdie wondered if that technology existed in newer models. She went to her closet and pulled out the surprise she had made for her granddaughter—a small broom fashioned from the same twigs and branches as the first one Birdie herself had made. Which meant it also had materials from her mother's broom, her grandmother's, and her great-grandmother's. All three living Geraghty Girls had charged the piece she held in her hands, but it also held the power of centuries of witches.

It was to be a special surprise—the only surprise of the day—for Anastasia.

But the gods so often have other plans.

Fiona and a freshly coiffed Lolly came into Birdie's bedroom then and shut the door behind them, both looking concerned.

Fiona said, "Birdie, what's happened? What is it?"

Birdie paced as she spoke. "Aedon O'Neil contacted me. He said that one of the treasures is missing."

Fiona gasped.

Lolly sat on Birdie's bed.

"That is all I know for now. I'm about to call him." She looked from Lolly to Fiona. "Are you ready?"

Fiona said, "Are you? There's a lot of history between you two. Should we leave?"

"Don't be ridiculous. That was a lifetime ago." Birdie shifted her mirror forty-five degrees to the right, the angle programmed to dial Aedon's mirror directly. Then she waited.

Soon, the mirror sparked and sputtered, and in a flash of blinding light, Aedon O'Neil's handsome face appeared. He was seated at a long, carved table, surrounded by the rest of the council. Birdie could tell by the stonework, the oil paintings, and the light fixtures that they were in the forum room of the castle.

"Birdie, thank you for getting back to me so quickly. Now, as I mentioned before, one of the four hallows gifted to Ireland by the Tuatha Dé Danann has gone missing, specifically, the Cauldron of Bounty. I'm sure I don't need to remind you what happened the last time the cauldron was stolen."

Indeed, Birdie needed no reminding. The Great Famine was the reason her family had been forced to leave the Old World and come to America. So many of her people had suffered. Countless lives lost.

"Of course not."

Aedon nodded. "With the new year approaching and the veil so close to the transparent time, we feel it is of the utmost importance the cauldron be retrieved before Samhain."

Samhain, the day when this world and the Otherworld meet. The cauldron had a dual power and was also known as the Cauldron of Rebirth. In the early times, it had been a great source of resurrection and had breathed new life into many a fallen warrior.

In these times, that power could be very, very dangerous in the wrong hands.

"Do you suspect dark arts at play?" Birdie asked.

Aedon said, "Nothing is off the table at this point. We simply don't know." He looked at his council members briefly before returning to face Birdie. "We're contacting you, Birdie, because of the splendid job your granddaughter did in protecting the secret of the Book of Ballymote. We'll be calling on the Warrior and the Guardian as well."

Birdie kept her poker face, but inside, she was screaming. Not a quest right now. Not with her daughter's hearing so close.

"I have long known that she was the Seeker of Justice, despite protests of her nomination," Birdie said.

Aedon flicked his eyes to the left. To someone offscreen. "Yes, well, she certainly proved she has all the makings of a Seeker, but a true Seeker shall not be declared until he or she has reached full power, and even then, only on the old soil. It isn't as simple as confirming a Guardian or Warrior. There is much more power at stake where a Seeker is concerned."

Birdie shot a fiery look at her old friend. "She was declared, Aedon, months past, for the very task you mentioned not a fairy's breath ago."

"You and I both know that was a desperate, temporary situation. But she can still prove to be the Seeker. All she has to do is recover the cauldron. I understand her birthday is this very day. Has she performed a dedication?"

"Tonight she will."

"Good. And with twenty-nine years of your training, I'm sure, she's more than prepared. We would like her to leave as soon as possible." Aedon smiled.

Birdie didn't flinch. "She will recover the cauldron, Aedon, on one condition."

Aedon looked at Birdie. "We don't make deals, Birdie."

"You will if you want the cauldron back."

Aedon sighed. "Always so stubborn. Go on."

"Upon its return, you release my daughter and officially coronate my granddaughter as the Seeker of the age."

Aedon looked around the table. There seemed to be no objections. "All in favor, say aye."

Birdie heard several ayes.

"Opposed?"

"Nay."

Aedon looked past the screen to someone out of the camera's eye.

Birdie didn't have to see her. She'd know that icy voice anywhere.

"What is your protest, Tallulah?" Aedon asked.

"Stacy Justice is no more Seeker than I am Pirate Queen," Tallulah said.

That slithering snake. Birdie cleared her throat. "Aedon, I have the right to face the protestor."

Aedon's mirror shifted, and Tabby's face came into the camera's trajectory. She looked like a broken vase glued back together poorly. She was wearing a red satin hat the size of a toboggan.

"My grandson, too, has all the makings of a Seeker," Tallulah said. "I assert that he be allowed to search for the treasure as well. Whoever recovers it first shall be known as the true Seeker."

Birdie's anger took control of her voice. "You're on, Tabby."

Aedon looked at Birdie. "This is unusual, but perhaps an effective strategy."

He consulted with the rest of the council, and Birdie saw a sea of heads bob up and down. Her adrenaline had dissipated some, but she didn't dare waver. She was a Geraghty, after all. And Geraghtys showed no fear.

As the council agreed that two would be better than one for this mission, and Aedon's gavel slammed against the oak surface of the table, Tallulah shot Birdie a sinister smile.

Birdie spun the frame and cut the connection. She stood there, staring at the black mirror for a heartbeat or two.

Silently, she asked, *Dear Danu, what have I done?*

Chapter 5

Birdie turned to face her sisters.

Lolly simply stared at her, mouth agape, but Fiona was incensed. She crossed over to Birdie and said, "Do you have any idea what you have done?"

Birdie straightened out her skirt. She couldn't turn back now. "I have secured my daughter's freedom."

"At what cost, Brighid?"

Fiona never addressed Birdie by her full name, and it made her blanch.

"Stacy's training is not complete. She isn't ready," Fiona said.

Birdie said, "All she needs is to rededicate herself. The rest will fall into place."

Fiona shook her head. "No, Birdie. I respect your role as the matriarch of this family, but you have gone too far this time. You must call Aedon back and say it cannot be done. Tell him that she hasn't been training for twenty-nine years. She hasn't even been training half the years he thinks she has! He will understand."

Birdie knew Fiona had a point. A part of her wanted to retract her declaration, but another part—the slice of her soul that had known from the moment she laid eyes on her that Anastasia was born for bigger things, that the girl was part of something more important than all of them—couldn't leave the fate of the cauldron in anyone else's hands.

"And what if she doesn't go, Fiona, then what? The cauldron could be lost to the ages if the only one seeking it is that idiot grandson of Tallulah's. And then what will become of Ireland? Of the world?"

Fiona planted her hands on her curvy hips and said, "Is that what this is about? Tallulah and that ridiculous feud? Release it, Birdie. It was a lifetime ago."

Birdie shouted, "This has nothing to do with what happened at the Academy."

"Of course it does. You want to live through your granddaughter, Brighid. You're not thinking of the bigger picture," Fiona fired back.

Birdie slammed her hand on her desk. "That is all I'm thinking of. I want my girls back, both of them, safe and sound. Can't you understand that?"

"And in your desperate desire to reunite your family, you have put both of their lives in danger, Sister. What happens if the girl fails? Do you know what the council will do if you don't live up to your end of the deal? They may not set her mother free. And she will only blame herself!"

"Geraghtys do not fail," Birdie said.

"You did," Fiona shot back.

The two sisters stood face-to-face, heat radiating off them in angry waves.

Behind them, Lolly bellowed, "Enough of this!"

Birdie and Fiona turned to face Lolly.

She said, "I will not have this bickering today of all days. You are upsetting the woodland sprites and the earth deities. My great-niece is about to celebrate a very special birthday, and I won't have the two of you spoiling it with your nonsense. I am still the oldest in this family, and I can knock you both on your keisters." Lolly wagged a finger from Birdie to Fiona.

They each stepped back a foot.

"Now sit," Lolly ordered.

Birdie sat at her desk, and Fiona took a chair near the door.

"This is what's going to happen." Lolly paced as she spoke. "The three of us are going to perform all the rituals and spells for the holiday alone. We are going to tell Stacy that we thought she could utilize the extra time to prepare her spell and that she needn't arrive until just before dinner, whereupon I will present her with the beautiful maiden's dress I fashioned. Then we are all going to sit down and have a lovely dinner with Stacy and her friends. After the dinner guests have gone, Stacy will perform her dedication spell, and only then will we tell her what the council has proposed."

Birdie and Fiona exchanged a glance.

"And then what?" Fiona asked.

Lolly crossed her arms. "And then we let the girl decide."

Five hours later, I was plucked, painted, washed, dried, and styled. I felt absolutely amazing, but I was also sleepy.

I kissed Cinnamon good-bye, thanked her for the much-needed gift, and hopped in the car to go home.

Thor was waiting by the door when I opened it. He ran out to accost the shrubs and I went to grab the Blessed Book. I set it on the counter next to my list and flipped through the pages, but couldn't find anything on "Web of Weird."

My phone signaled there were messages waiting, so I hit the button to retrieve them while still turning the pages of the book.

There was a "happy birthday" voice mail from my sweetheart, Chance, with a promise to be on time for dinner, a message from Lolly telling me that she and her sisters would handle the traditional festivities, and that I should just arrive at five thirty to open gifts (yes! I really didn't want to ruin my manicure by digging in the garden), and an apology from Gramps explaining that he had a business dinner he couldn't postpone and asking if he could take me out for breakfast in the morning.

That reminded me.

I shuffled through my coat pocket, pulled out the gift Cinnamon had brought for me, and set it on the counter.

Thor knocked on the front door, so I let him in, fed him some dinner, and grabbed a bottle of water for myself that I chugged until it was gone. I took a few minutes to check e-mails and googled "Web of Weird," but still came up empty-handed.

Next on the list was cleansing the sword before tonight's spell.

There are several methods to consecrate and purify a magical tool, and most of them involve utilizing the four elements: earth, air, water, and fire. A smudge stick works well, but I can't stand the smell of burning sage. Some witches prefer a simple open flame to wave a wand or athame through, or they might bury their tools in the earth for nine days, then dig them up beneath the next new moon. Moonbeams will also cleanse a tool, especially gentle gemstones such as quartz, but that method works best if the item can be laid outside in an open field for the entire cycle of the full moon. Direct sunlight is another cleanser. I never used it personally, because I once set a crystal ball in a bright windowsill at the Geraghty Girls' Guesthouse, and Fiona's cat climbed up next to it and accidentally set his tail on fire.

It was not a pretty sight. Or smell.

My preferred method was the most powerful cleansing force in the universe—water. I kicked off my boots and socks, grabbed the sword and a few other items I would need, and padded into the bathroom. I plugged the tub, filled it with scalding water, poured in a handful of Atlantic sea salt from West Cork, added a few drops each of cypress and frankincense oil, then immersed the sword in the anointed pool.

Eyes shut tight, I imagined my body ensconced in bright white light and said:

"To the warrior goddess, fiercest of all;

see my vision, hear my call.

Charge this sword with your sacred power;

Badb be with me in the needful hour."

I repeated the chant three times, passing my hands over the steaming water in a flowing figure-eight pattern—the shape of the infinity knot. When I stopped speaking, the tub bubbled.

I opened one eye and saw that the water surrounding the blade was bursting with tiny explosions, as if a bath fizzy had been dropped under the faucet.

Which meant the consecration was working.

Smiling, I raised my palms to the sky to feel the energy flow from the water, through the sword, and into me. After several moments of breathing in the oxygen and herbs, I rang a bell to thank the goddess for her presence and stepped into the hallway to grab a fresh towel from the linen closet.

When I saw what was on the shelf, I screamed loud enough to wake the dead.

Chapter 6

Thor trotted over to my side. He cocked his huge head like I was a new species he hadn't yet encountered and wasn't sure what to do with.

The dog sat down as I lifted the blue and gold–wrapped gift from the linen-closet shelf—far from the counter where I had left it—and reached for a white, fluffy towel. I pocketed the present and sidestepped into the bathroom to lay the towel on the floor. The water was still steaming, so I turned on the cold faucet to cool it off a bit. Then I extracted the sword and wrapped it in the terrycloth. The tub gurgled as I knelt to unplug the drain.

The bell was still sitting on the bathroom sink when I stood up. It rang once, all by itself.

That's when I knew I wasn't alone.

Here's the thing about bells: They serve many magical purposes. They are used in cleansing rituals, to punctuate enchantments, and to open or close a sacred space. The soft ringing of one will banish negative vibrations, dissipate bad energy, invoke a goddess, or hail a spirit. They also represent the female form.

But you can't unring a bell. So just because you may have intended it to perform one function, there are no guarantees it won't do something completely different, like draw the attention of a dead woman who was maddeningly fond of limericks.

When I finally faced her, the cloudy ghost was flipping through the Blessed Book, frowning. I think. Her features were still pretty tough to make out. She looked at me with disappointment, crumpled up the piece of paper that was my to-do list, and bounced it off my head.

"Hey! What is your problem?"

She inflated herself so that her form puffed to twice its original size, covering most of the breakfast bar, and pointed to the crumpled ball on the floor. I bent to pick it up and smoothed it out, keeping an eye on the ornery spirit, wondering what I'd done in another life to send this loon my way.

On the paper, the word *Weird* was scratched out. Beside it was written *Wyrd*.

She crossed her arms and stuck her chin in the air.

"Seriously? You're mad because of a typo?"

She spoke then.

"A Seeker is born once a century;

Tracked by the watchful eyes of the She.

Do not falter in your dedication;

For that leads to misinformation."

Okay, now she was really annoying me.

"Can you please tell me in plain English what you're trying to say, Riddler?"

She rose up again, her sea-foam eyes glaring at me, but she didn't speak.

I sighed, looked at the clock. Thirty minutes until I had to leave. "Fine. Who is *she*?"

The ethereal spirit tossed her hands in the air as if to give up, then she flew toward the book and shuffled through the thick pages. She stopped near the end, and then flitted to the other side of the room.

I stepped forward and read the page.

Sidhe (pronounced She): The Sidhe are known as the people of the mounds or 'the Good People.' They are descendents of the Tuatha Dé Danann, the people of the goddess Danu, who brought the four great treasures to Ireland. They reside mostly in the Otherworld, but sometimes side by side with ours, cloaking their homes in magic. They interfere with our realm when called upon or when necessary to provide protection, guidance, healing, or teaching. These are not the Tinker Bell fairies of Western culture. These are noble beings of great prominence. They are fierce warriors, accomplished silversmiths, agriculturists, and intelligent beyond comprehension. They guard their homes and the entire fairy plane with pride, and rattle the walls of anyone who dares to destroy a leyline. These lines run the length and breadth of the homeland, and beyond. They serve as powerful sources of magic, and have been known to open portals to other dimensions.

I lifted my head to find the iridescent spirit hovering over me, staring straight into my eyes.

"Okay, got it. Don't piss off the fairies."

She seemed pleased with that conclusion. She gave me a thumbs-up, stopped to whisper in Thor's ear, and vanished.

Thor thumped his tail happily.

"Do you know that talking fortune cookie?" I asked him. He yawned and crawled onto the couch.

There wasn't a lot of time before I had to leave, so I got to work writing my dedication speech, careful not to say anything that would agitate beings from another dimension.

If only I had thought about the beings from this dimension, things might have gone a bit more smoothly.

There was just enough time to open the present from Gramps before I had to leave. I read the card for the fifth time, but for the life of me, I couldn't place the handwriting. It couldn't have been written by anyone in my immediate family, so then who? Perhaps my great-grandmother? Or my father's mother?

And what did *when the time is right* mean?

I carefully unraveled the pretty ribbon and set it on the sofa beside me. The paper was brittle, as if manufactured years ago, and it fell apart in my hands, revealing a royal-blue-velvet box. Inside the box was a gold filigree locket that appeared to be quite old, embellished with an infinity knot on its face.

I lifted out the beautiful piece by its long chain and held it up to the light. It pirouetted around my fingers, revealing a shield knot emblazoned on the back.

I clicked open the dainty latch and held the locket in my palm. On the right side was a watch face; the left side was plain gold.

When the time is right. Was it a pun? Or had it something to do with my birthday? If it was an heirloom, whom had it belonged to?

My phone chimed at that moment, reminding me it was time to go. I tucked the dedication charm into the locket, which I slipped over my head and under my sweater, then grabbed my cape, sword, and Thor, and headed out the door.

It was still bright outside, although a few clouds had rolled in, threatening rain. Someone was burning leaves the next block over, the smoke billowing around a giant maple whose own branches were nearly bare. Just as I approached the backyard of the Geraghty Girls' Guesthouse, I spotted Birdie and the aunts making their way out of the woods, each donning an autumn-colored cape.

The patio table was dressed in grapevines, with bowls of apples and pears, nuts, and candles scattered about. There were three wrapped presents in the center surrounding a painted plaque of the Green Man, the god of the forest.

Thor settled himself into a giant pile of leaves I had raked the day before as I watched the three Geraghty Girls approach, the air thickening with each step they took.

Something was wrong. Not one of them was smiling, which was unusual on any pagan holiday. They lived for these celebrations.

I heard Birdie say, "I can't believe you forgot the Green Man, Fiona."

Fiona replied, "Why must I think of everything, Birdie?"

"With all that's on my mind, you could have been more observant."

"You think you're the only one troubled? I'm concerned as well."

Lolly spotted me then and waved. She grabbed each sister by the earlobe, spun them around into a huddle, and bent down to whisper something.

What the heck is this all about?

The three of them swung toward me, each offering a false smile.

Lolly rushed over to kiss both my cheeks, reeking of whiskey—a sign that her mind was running on turbo power. Birdie and Fiona stepped in to hug me next, each of them warm to the touch. An enormous crow screeched overhead and landed on the table just as I broke away.

I took a step back and stared at the Geraghty Girls. "What's going on?"

Fiona said, "Whatever do you mean, dear?"

"Birdie?"

My grandmother shrugged her shoulders.

I tapped my foot impatiently. "Lolly, what's happening? I could cut the tension in the air with my sword."

"Oh, wonderful, you brought it," Lolly said, and clapped her hands.

They all three stood there grinning at me like I was a virgin they were about to toss into a volcano.

I crossed my arms. "I want to know what has you concerned, and I want to know now."

Fiona blurted out, "Birdie double-booked a room for next weekend."

Birdie glowered at Fiona. "We will make do. These things have a way of working themselves out."

"You shouldn't make promises you can't keep," Fiona said.

I said, "That's it? Why can't you just call the visitor center and book them a room at another inn?"

"Splendid idea. We'll do that in the morning." Lolly shot her sisters a look of warning. "Come, Stacy, open your gifts."

My oldest aunt glided toward the table, reached for the largest package, and motioned for me to join her. "This is from me."

I tossed one last glance back at Birdie and Fiona and walked over to where Lolly stood. The box was heavy. I shook it gently and smiled at my great-aunt. She stuck a tiara on my head.

"I hope you like it," she said.

I lifted the lid off the big box and brushed aside soft white tissue paper to reveal a purple brocade bodice, adorned with triquetras and crisscrossed with thin gold rope. I lifted up the garment, and out spilled a green and amethyst floor-length gown with billowing bell sleeves. "Oh, Lolly, it's gorgeous!"

"I thought you could wear it tonight. I stitched it from remnants of some of the finest ritual wear." She pointed out that the gold rope tied through the bodice was worn by Birdie one Samhain many years ago, the silk sleeves had attended Fiona's first hand fasting, and the emerald velvet patches were recycled from Lolly's own dedication gown.

"I will." I reached over to hug her. "Thank you."

Fiona stepped up and handed me her gift. "It belonged to your great-grandmother, but I had it freshly blackened and newly framed."

Fiona's gift was an hourglass-shaped scrying mirror, framed with three inches of etched silver.

"It's perfect. You'll have to help me hang it in the cottage," I said.

She smiled, and I thought I saw a tear in her eye.

Birdie was next. She stepped over to me and hugged me tight. Then she held me at arm's length and said, "I want you to know I'm very proud of you." Her eyes were shimmering as she held my gaze, but there was a cloud of concern in them.

"I know that, Birdie."

When she let go, a shiver danced down my spine, and another crow—or was it the same one?—swooshed over the table, squawked, and flew to the eave beneath Birdie's bedroom window. I watched it land and saw a bright light flash from the pane.

"What was that?" I asked.

"It's an old house. Old lighting," Birdie said, flicking her eyes nervously upward as thunder slapped the sky. "Open your gift."

Birdie's present was a broom.

"It took her ages to fashion," Lolly said.

Fiona nodded and said, "We all three charged it."

Birdie said, "It has the same branches from my mother's broom and her mother's and two generations before them."

It sizzled in my hand like kindling.

I hugged my grandmother and said, "I'll use it wisely."

She whispered in my ear, "Just remember, between destiny and duty lies faith. Keep your faith, and you won't go wrong."

I didn't have time to decipher that cryptic message, because a car door slammed, and another after that. The dinner guests had arrived.

Chapter 7

Fiona said, "Stacy, why don't you go change into your new dress and stash your gifts while we greet the guests?"

I wasn't planning to put the dress on until after dinner, but Lolly looked hopeful, so I agreed.

I slipped in through the back door and made my way up the far stairs to Birdie's bedroom. Someone was in the kitchen below, gathering dishes, as I shut the door behind me. I laid the gifts on top of my grandmother's bed, set the sword next to them, and disrobed.

The gown was stunning, like something you might see in a Shakespearean play. Even though I wouldn't get much use out of the gown unless I auditioned for one, I figured if someone offered you the opportunity to dress like a princess for a night, you might as well give it a whirl.

I climbed into the dress, tied the bodice, and fluffed out the skirt, wishing I had some glass slippers to go with it, but the boots would have to do. There was a full-length mirror across the hall, so I went to check out the whole effect. The dress made a whooshing sound as I walked, and it gave off the tiniest vibration, fortified, I suspected, with Lolly's energy. As I adjusted the waistline, I noticed there was a sturdy leather loop that hung on each hip and there was even a slot for my cell phone. Curious, I shuffled back into Birdie's room, grabbed the sword, and slipped it through one of the loops.

It weighed me down a bit, but the strap held. I waved my cape over my shoulders, tucked the phone in the pocket, shut the light off, and went to take one last look before dinner.

All I needed was an eye patch and a parrot and I would have made a badass-looking pirate. I shot a sideways look to the painting of Danu and asked, "What do you think?"

A blinding light flashed off the silver of the mirror. I whipped around.

Birdie's door was still open and the lights were off, but something chimed within the room.

Had I imagined the flash? Was it simply the front bell I heard ring?

I walked into the room, clicked on the light switch, and looked around. The curtains were drawn, so I went to the window for a peek. Chance stood in the yard, a huge bouquet of roses in his strong hands, talking to Fiona. Then that stupid crow flew into view and tapped his beak on the glass three times. I yelped and jumped back.

That's when I noticed the smoke seeping from Birdie's scrying mirror. I rushed over to it, fearing some sort of electrical fire. Perhaps it was positioned over an old outlet. I lifted the mirror gently but saw only wall space.

Until I let go. Then I saw a face.

If Big Bird had a mother, this was what she would look like. The woman staring at me through Birdie's scrying mirror had some sort of yellow-feathered hat on her head that bobbed up and down all on its own.

Unless it was an actual bird—I couldn't be sure.

I looked at my own scrying mirror, wondering if it too was equipped with Skype.

The woman snapped, "I need to speak with Birdie."

"She's not available right now. May I take a message?"

The woman leaned forward, studied me for a moment. Then her eyes pierced through mine and a chilling grin swam across her face.

I could not believe I was talking to a mirror while wearing a dress pieced together by recycled bits of other garments. I felt like Snow White meets Cinderella. And I had the sneaking suspicion that this woman was some kind of wicked.

I stepped back, startled by the malicious vibe emanating from her. My stomach lurched and that old familiar feeling gripped me.

Harmful intent.

She said, "Well, well, well, if it isn't the famous Stacy Justice."

Why did I get the inkling I was in for more than one surprise on my birthday?

I tried to appear a whole lot braver than I felt. "And who might you be?"

Her voice was coated with venom, as if she had just discovered a hundred Dalmatians and was itching for a new coat. "You don't know who I am?"

She waited for some recognition, but I had none. "Mrs. Peacock in the library with a wrench. Am I close?"

The woman's nostrils flared, and I was certain that fire was going to shoot from them. "You just tell your grandmother that I don't care what kind of privileges she thinks she has with the council. You will never find that cauldron before my grandson does, and when he does, not only will they know you are not the true Seeker, but your mother's chance for freedom will be lost forever. She will rot in that castle."

I had no idea what the hell she was talking about, but I got the sense that if I showed my confusion, she would feed off it like a vulture off a carcass.

"Over my dead body," I said.

"That can be arranged, my dear."

I thought about smashing the mirror, but decided to just flip it around to face the wall.

I paced around the room for a bit.

What did she mean, my mother's chance for freedom would be lost forever?

More importantly, what was all this about a missing cauldron? And what the hell had Birdie promised?

I stuck my head out the window and said, "Oh, Grandmother, may I speak with you a moment?"

And I'll be damned if that freaking crow didn't laugh.

Birdie had just set the corn muffins on the table outside. She was about to retrieve her granddaughter, when the child leaned out of Birdie's bedroom window and called to her. Birdie gave Lolly an odd look, as if to say, *What now?*

Lolly shrugged and poured some wine for Anastasia's suitor, Chance.

Birdie wove her way around the table, her grand-daughter's familiar at her heels. She had just reached the back door when Fiona bustled through with an herb-and-flower-petal salad.

"I've got the door, Fiona," Birdie said as Thor trotted through.

Fiona's emerald eyes grew wide, staring past Birdie, into the dark night.

"What?" Birdie asked, and twisted her head to follow her sister's gaze.

Instantly, she spotted it. A fluorescent-green trail snaked from the woods all the way to the house.

"Fairy fire," Birdie whispered.

Fiona asked, "Did you bring the Green Man back to the covenstead?"

"I thought you did," Birdie said.

The salad plate slipped from Fiona's hands and smashed to the concrete step. Both sisters looked up to the window where Anastasia was changing.

Birdie said, "We have to stop them."

Thor was already charging up the back steps.

I paced back and forth in the hallway in front of the painting of my so-called goddess, who, for one reason or another, never gave me a break. She was sitting in that chair with the lion's-head feet, sipping from the jewel-encrusted chalice, looking ever so smug.

"So not only did they all lie to me, but Birdie made some sort of underhanded deal with the stupid council to retrieve a freaking cauldron while my mother is sitting in a castle—Goddess knows where, because there are a gazillion bloody castles in Ireland—probably going out of her mind waiting for someone to unlock the damn door."

I couldn't stop moving. I wanted to punch something. I never wanted this, never wanted to be Seeker. And now, because of it—because of Birdie's incessant desire for me to be every bit as much a witch as she is—my mother might pay the ultimate price.

Would they really keep her imprisoned?

Could they?

I didn't know these people, didn't understand their laws, but I did know they wielded power over this family. Enough power to pull it apart.

"So now I'm a pawn in this stupid organization's games? I'm just another piece on their chess board?" I faced the portrait of Danu. "Is that about the gist of it? Well, Birdie and the council and whoever the hell else thinks they can play God can forget it. I'm not bargaining with my mother's life, and I don't give a flying fairy's fart who it hurts. Hell, I don't even know if the Tuatha are my people, do I, Danu?"

I put my hand on my sword, felt the heat there, the charge it held, and knew I had the strength to leave tomorrow and stand before the council, demanding my mother's release.

"That's it. No more of this Seeker nonsense." I reached into the bodice of my dress, opened the locket, and pulled out the dedication I'd written.

Behind me, I heard Thor, the only family member I could trust, galloping down the hall.

I crumpled the paper in my hand and spiked it at Danu's face.

That's when she stood up from her chair, tossed the cup, and yanked me right through the frame.

Chapter 8

Birdie moved up the stairs as fast as an old woman draped in a cape could move. Fiona kept pace directly behind her.

Fiona said, "All the emotion of the day, our bickering. It must have summoned them. And with today being Mabon and Stacy's rewitchening, well, it was the perfect playground—"

"We don't know that for certain," Birdie said. "Perhaps we aren't too late." She lifted her head. "Anastasia!"

Birdie reached the landing and rushed down the corridor, swinging open every door she passed along the way. Fiona's room, Lolly's room, the linen closet.

"Stacy!" Fiona called. She stuck her head into Birdie's bathroom and turned on the light.

Birdie searched her bedroom. "Anastasia, are you in here?" She flung open the closet door, yanked the duvet off the bed, and pulled the curtain back. There was no sign of her granddaughter.

Her sister called to her. "And where is Thor?"

Birdie clicked off the lamp and stepped out of her bedroom. She swung her head first to the right and then to the left. She stood there for a moment and tapped her foot. An eerie feeling settled in her gut as she did. As if they weren't alone. As if they were being watched.

Fiona joined Birdie. "What is it?"

Birdie put a finger to her lips, quieting Fiona. She lifted an eyebrow quizzically. "Something is off. Do you feel it?" the youngest Geraghty whispered.

Fiona cocked her head, trying to capture whatever sound or sense Birdie was picking up.

She met Birdie's eyes and nodded slowly. She felt it too. Fiona pointed over Birdie's shoulder, then reached around and hit the light switch to her sister's room.

Birdie whispered in her ear, "I checked already."

Fiona pointed again and said, "Look."

Birdie followed Fiona's line of vision to the scrying mirror. It had been turned around, and now the side used for divination was against the wall. Curious, Birdie stepped forward with the slightest hint of trepidation and gently lifted the mirror, righting it.

Tabby's scornful face stared back at her. "Lose something?" she mocked.

Birdie could hardly contain her anger. She was surprised the mirror didn't shatter from the explosive power of her emotions.

"What have you done, Tabby?" Birdie asked, her fists balled into tight white knots at her sides. She vowed silently that if this wretched woman had harmed a single hair on her granddaughter's head, she would personally make her pay in the most horrifyingly painful manner.

"Who, me?" Tallulah replied innocently. "Why, I haven't done a thing, Birdie. All I did was wish your charming little

witch well in her quest and said may the best Seeker win."
Tallulah frowned. "Although, I must admit, Birdie, she was
quite surprised by what I had to say. Almost as if she hadn't
heard a thing about it." She smiled, malice oozing from
her teeth like blood dripping from a lion's fangs.

Fiona said, "Meddling in family affairs, Tabby—honestly, have you nothing better to do?"

"Where is she?" Birdie shouted loud enough to shake
her old nemesis.

Tallulah looked genuinely startled for a beat. "What
do you mean, where is she? How in Hecate's name should
I know?"

Fiona cleared her throat and tapped Birdie's arm.
"Remember, Sister? Lolly was helping her adjust her gown.
I'm sure she's still in her quarters, primping. You know how
Lolly can be." She turned to the mirror. "Well, we have
rituals to attend to, Tallulah. I'm sure you understand."
Fiona didn't wait for a response. She tapped the mirror to
cut the connection, and whirled around to Birdie. "Birdie,
we must be very careful what we reveal to Tabby. She could
ruin everything."

Birdie nodded. "Yes, of course, you're right." She
tapped a few buttons underneath the mirror and played
back Tabby's conversation with Anastasia. It didn't reveal
where the girl had gone. Birdie stepped out of the room
and looked at the painting of Danu. "Do you suppose she
entered the chamber of magic?"

The chamber of magic was a secret room sheltered
behind the large oil painting of the goddess Danu. It could
be accessed only by visualizing a door, whereupon the
passageway to the room would appear. Fiona had taught

Anastasia how to gain access to the space a short time ago. It was where the Geraghty Girls kept their most powerful tools, talismans, spells, and secrets of the craft and family.

"It's possible," Fiona said with little conviction.

The two sisters walked toward the painting side by side.

When they reached the end of the hall, Fiona said, "What is this?" She stooped down to the burgundy carpet and picked up a wadded piece of paper. She unwrinkled it and read, a dark shadow creeping over her face.

"What is it, Fiona?"

Fiona looked at Birdie. "It's Stacy's dedication spell." She handed it to Birdie. "She must have been upset after speaking with Tabby."

Birdie pinched her lips, piecing together in her mind what had happened. Tabby had opened up her big mouth to Anastasia about the deal Birdie had made, and the girl must have become angry. Probably thought Birdie had no intention of telling her about it at all. "If anything happens to that girl, I will personally see to it that banshee suffers to the end of her days."

"So, then, do you think what we feared has happened? Do you think the fairy fire traced her steps? Do you think they used it to pull her into the Web of Wyrd?"

Fairy fire had led many a human astray, especially weary travelers, but it could also be used to pave a path from this world to the other, opening a portal that only the Fae could control.

Birdie said, "I'm afraid so, Fiona. If Anastasia's faith wavered and she was angry enough to turn her back on her destiny, then they will force her to understand destiny and free will can live cohesively within one's soul. They will have to exemplify it for her. Teach her the lesson that I so obviously could not."

Fiona patted Birdie's back. "You mustn't blame yourself."

A panic rose within Birdie. "Oh no." She looked to Fiona, grabbed her hand. "She could be gone for five minutes or five years. And by then, it will be too late. The council won't wait."

Fiona was worried too. "Time is not linear in the Web of Wyrd, not like in this dimension. She could circle backward or forward."

"Yes, and the web is altered by human actions. She could change not only the course of *her life*, but history itself. The ramifications could be monumental." Birdie held Fiona's eyes for a moment, then glanced at the painting. "We have to get her back. Because if we don't—"

Fiona finished her sister's thought. "She could cease to be."

Before I could soil my drawers at the realization that a painting—a freaking *painting*—of a woman I wasn't sure had ever existed had sprung to life and grabbed me, I felt Thor clamp onto my cape.

That was the last thing I remembered before waking up in a human-sized birdcage. That's right, folks. The next time you're having a shitty day, just say to yourself, *Well, at least I didn't wake up in a birdcage this morning.*

The cage appeared to be suspended from a tree I could not identify. Its leaves were a mystical shade of ebony violet, each as large as a pumpkin, and its branches stretched so high into the sky, I couldn't see beyond the canopy. I wasn't more than three feet off the ground, but the way the inky iron bars of my prison limbered in the wind, I was left with the eerie sensation that the tree holding me captive was *breathing* and, if it felt the urge, could drop me at any moment.

The other trees in the forest were covered in moss, their leaves a thick green, some with ivy squeezing their trunks. The ground, too, was a mixture of grass and moss, and seemed to form some sort of labyrinth. Straight ahead, a large pathway lay before me, flanked by wide-barked oaks that arched protectively over the grove to meet in the center, creating a kind of natural ceiling over the grassy space below, like fingers clasped together.

Nowhere did I see Thor. I called to him softly, then focused my mind on him, but my thoughts were jumbled and I couldn't concentrate.

A soft orange glow penetrated the landscape to my right, and I feared that darkness would set in before I figured out where the hell I was and why. My body felt fine, though my mind was hazy, but it seemed I was not hurt. No bindings on my hands or feet, so the first thing I did after assessing the area was look for the latch on the cage. I felt all around, from top to bottom, but there was no door. No key. Not even a twist tie.

A crow came along and pecked at my fingers as I pulled at the bars.

"Ow. Stop that. Go away."

I swear it was the same damn crow I'd seen outside Birdie's window.

Birdie. I'd almost forgotten about the woman in the mirror and what she had said. Something about a deal and finding something. It was on the tip of my tongue, but I couldn't conjure up the word. What did they want me to find? It began with a *c*, I remember that much. Canary? No, that wasn't it. Geez, had I eaten a magic mushroom? Swallowed some of Lolly's sweet-dreams tea? Because that would explain a lot.

The crow came back, squawked in my face, and pecked my thumb. Hard.

I flapped my arms at the bird. "Knock it off. Shoo."

It narrowed its beady little eyes and tilted its head as if I were the less intelligent species. Given the fact that I was the one swinging from a tree in a cage with no door, and he was free to fly, the bird had a point.

The mean little prick pecked me again. "Stop that. I'm not your competition, I swear."

Suddenly, the crow soared into the air, then swooped across the cage, flapping its wings gracefully, growing larger and larger with each pump. The wings expanded, the body elongated, and the eyes grew wider, fiercer.

Holy hobgoblin. This thing is going to eat me.

I ducked down, making myself as small as possible, crouched on the base of the cage, and covered my head with my arms. I had seen this defense mechanism used by a squirrel once when an angry hawk tried to make it his dinner. I prayed it would work.

The crow—or whatever the hell it was now—shrieked, and I heard rustling in the leaves above my head.

I stayed perfectly still. Another good defense ploy when faced with a predator, or so I'd heard. I'd never actually been in danger of being eaten before.

A woman laughed. The sound seemed to come from below.

Was someone else trapped? The forest could be full of other cages filled with tasty humans, for all I knew. *Dear Goddess, please tell me I passed out from drinking my weight in wine and this Kafkaesque nightmare isn't really happening.*

More laughter. Not just the woman. Children too.

Then a silky voice. "My competition? Ha! You should be so lucky to have such power, Stacy Justice."

Chapter 9

The doorbell rang and Birdie said, "Fiona, see to it the guests are comfortable. Try to stall them as best you can until I find a fetching spell to bring Anastasia back. I'll get the door."

Fiona nodded and rushed down the back stairwell.

Birdie strode down the hallway and unlocked the door that separated the private quarters of the house from the guest suites. She turned right down another hall and shuffled down the steps to the front foyer.

She peeked through the curtain and saw Leo, the chief of police, standing on her porch.

"What is he doing here?" she hissed to herself.

The man knocked. "Mrs. Geraghty?"

He must have seen her.

Damn!

She pasted a smile on her face and swung the heavy door open. "Hello, Leo. How can I help you?"

He held a package in his hand and offered it to her. "Just a little something for Stacy's birthday."

Birdie said, "How gracious. I'll see to it that she gets it." She gripped the handle and pushed the door forward, but before she could get it closed, Leo wedged his foot in the crack.

"There is one more thing."

Birdie rolled her eyes at the door. She stepped back and swung it open again. "Yes?"

"We received a complaint about you crashing into a mailbox." He thumbed behind him. "The homeowner recognized your car. There's a dent on the left fender."

Could this evening get any more complicated?

Birdie called on her most dazzling smile. "Oh, yes, that was me." She slapped her forehead. "I was in such a hurry to rush home for Anastasia's birthday that I'm afraid I took a turn faster than I should have. Then the time just got away from me, and, well, here we are. Let me just get my checkbook. I'm happy to pay for the damages."

Birdie held the door open, and Leo stepped over the threshold. She shut the door.

The chief of police sighed. "Actually, it's a bit more complicated than that, Mrs. Geraghty. The owner has filed a complaint, and since you didn't report the incident, and you just admitted you know you caused damage, I have to charge you with fleeing the scene of an accident with property destruction."

Birdie was shocked. "You're going to arrest me for hitting a mailbox?"

Leo looked as uncomfortable as Birdie felt. "I really have no choice. All it will amount to is a citation, and you can bond out right away. You'll be back with Stacy in no time."

From his lips, Birdie thought. "Leo, please, I have a dinner table full of guests. Just tell me who the homeowner is and I'll call to straighten this mess out."

Leo grimaced. "It's Bea Plough."

It was the last name she wanted to hear at that moment. Bea Plough was a burdensome, bigoted albatross. She was the wife of Oscar's best friend, Stan, so Birdie had been forced to endure the woman's presence for the span of her marriage. But when she discovered that Bea was substitute teaching at the school district years later—and preaching hellfire and brimstone in the classroom—Birdie was livid. So when Anastasia announced that her history teacher had taken ill shortly after assigning a big project, she helped the girl reconstruct the Hill of Tara, complete with the ancient Celtic pantheon at the helm. Bea had nearly had a stroke.

Fiona came sailing into the room then, donned in a frilly apron the color of a pomegranate, carrying a coffee cup. "Birdie, I wondered if you might have a taste of this soup. I think it needs a touch more curry. Oh, hello, Leo." She gave him a warm smile.

Leo said, "Hello, Mrs. Geraghty."

Birdie reached for the soup cup, but Fiona snatched it back.

"On second thought, Sister, I think I would prefer this young man's opinion." Fiona floated over to Leo and gently touched his sleeve. She said in a silky voice that no man could resist, "Would you be a dear?"

Leo smiled and accepted the cup from Fiona's soft hand. "Why not? I'm starving." He held the cup in the air, said, "Cheers," and gulped it down.

Leo looked at the empty mug. Fiona watched as he savored the soup.

"Hmm, pretty tasty. Are those chunks of appl—"

Fiona rescued the mug as Leo slumped to the floor.

I uncurled myself from the floor of my prison and stood to face the woman who'd just spoken my name.

She had hair the color of ravens' wings, but her skin was so pale, it was practically translucent. She wore a lustrous dress buckled at the waistline, with a high collar, and enough cleavage to nurse a small village. Her eyes took on an indigo hue in the fading golden glow of the sun as she stood there, laughing at me.

More children laughed too, although I couldn't see them. Just tiny fireflies popping around the forest, preparing for their evening flight.

A crow came and landed on the woman's shoulder, but he didn't peck at her, the bastard. He didn't morph into something out of *Jurassic Park* either, and for that, I was grateful.

"Wh-who are you?" I asked, because I couldn't think of anything less stupid to say.

More laughter.

She slinked around the cage, like a cat sizing up a parakeet.

"You don't recognize me?" The woman leaned into the bird and said, "Shocking."

The crow bobbed its head up and down as if that were the best joke he'd heard all week.

The dark-haired woman whipped her skirt around, sending feathers to the forest floor, and faced me. "Stacy Justice, I'm a trifle hurt that you do not know who stands before you on this cherished night. After all, you just spoke to me not a frog's spit ago."

A frog's spit ago? Who says stuff like that? Crazy people, that's who. She didn't look anything like the woman from Birdie's scrying mirror, and the only other soul I had spoken to was that irritating riddler ghost. But this woman looked very much alive.

She reached in through the bars and wrapped her sinewy fingers around the grip of my sword. Until that moment, I hadn't realized it was still with me.

Instantly, the weapon vibrated, and shiny sparks of light like splintered diamonds burst all around the blade, then circled up and over my body, sending shivers through to my core. I heard chirpy voices oohing and ahhing from somewhere off in the distance and felt the strength of a thousand warriors surge through my essence.

It was the most exhilarating experience of my life, and I made a mental note to find out exactly what type of drug I had been slipped.

The raven-haired woman released my sword, stepped back, and studied me for another moment. "Well? Anything?"

I racked my brain. *Think, Stacy.* Who was she?

A twittering came from the top of the tree that was holding me, and the woman shifted her stance and cocked her head, listening.

She turned back to me, crossed her arms, and arched one glossy eyebrow, questioning.

I shrugged. "I got nothing." She looked disappointed, so I added, "Sorry. Maybe if you gave me a hint."

Just then, the trees along the pathway uncurled them-selves one by one, and a wave of amber light flooded the cage, blinding me.

I heard squeaky whispers of "she comes" and "the queen," and I knew this situation was going to get a lot worse before it got better.

When the blaze of light subsided, I opened my eyes. Two things immediately struck me. The first was the sight of Thor rolling around in a patch of grass, fireflies flicker-ing all around him. The second was the staff of the woman standing before me.

I rubbed my head where she'd bonked me. "Ouch. What was that for?"

Her hair was a mass of flaming red waves, swept away from her face by a jeweled headpiece. Her eyes were a shade of sapphire sprinkled with specks of bronze that matched her draping gown.

She said to me, "That was for being incorrigible." She turned to the black-haired woman and said, "For all that is sacred, Badb, let her out. Honestly." She shook her head and walked over to a golden throne carved with lion's-head feet.

"Just having a little fun, Danu," the dark woman said.

Badb? The warrior goddess I had called on to charge my sword?

Danu? The mother goddess of the Tuatha?

This couldn't be real. This couldn't even be a hallucination.

Holy nutfugget, I thought. *I must be in a coma and Birdie's reading to me from the Blessed Book.*

That was the only logical explanation.

Chapter 10

Birdie stared at the still body of the Amethyst chief of police. "Was that necessary?"

"Absolutely." Fiona circled around to Leo's head, bent down, and secured a grip on his torso. "Grab his feet."

Birdie sighed and walked over to Leo. She stooped to lift his ankles.

Fiona explained. "Did you hear what he said? We don't have time for you to get wrapped up in red tape. Besides, we could use him." She pointed her chin toward Leo. "On three. One, two, three."

The two women lifted the police officer. Fiona's face reddened with the strain, and she grunted.

"He's heavier than he looks," Birdie said, gasping for breath.

They were inches from the settee when they heard a young man say, "Mrs. Geraghty?"

Both women dropped their cargo.

"The rug!" Birdie said.

Fiona ran to the edge of the antique wool rug and flipped it up and over Leo, kicking it snug.

It was Derek, Stacy's business partner, who was calling to them. "Excuse me, ladies, but your sister"—Derek looked nervously over his shoulder—"seems to be having some sort of episode. She's slow-dancing with Stacy's boyfriend and calling him Jack. We didn't think much of it when she took her shoes off, but she lost the dress about five minutes ago. All that's left is a pair of knickers and a sports bra."

"Thank you, Derek. We'll be right out," Birdie said.

The sisters smiled at Derek. He tossed them an odd look and walked out of the room toward the kitchen, mumbling under his breath.

"Lock that door," Birdie said.

Fiona produced a key from her pocket and hurried to the door that divided the house, locking it.

When Fiona turned around, Birdie asked, "What do you mean we could use him?" She thumbed over her shoulder to Leo.

Fiona said, "Do you remember the retrieval spell you created when you were a student at the Academy? The one you put so much time and effort into?"

"You mean the one Tallulah absconded with? Of course I remember it."

Fiona said, "That spell was genius, Birdie. I'm sure if we followed it precisely as it was written, we could unsnarl Stacy from the web."

Birdie frowned. "But I ripped it up, after that initial competition the first year of school. I knew if anyone found it, they would suspect it was I who cheated on the creative-spell-writing test." She tightened her jaw. "I feared expulsion. Not that it mattered in the end."

"That's true. But you see…" Fiona reached into her apron and pulled out a folded piece of paper. "I made a copy."

Birdie was stunned. She reached out her hand, and Fiona dropped a folded piece of notebook paper into it. Birdie uncurled the corners and read.

It was indeed the spell she had crafted more than fifty years ago. She looked at Fiona, incredulous. "But I don't understand. How? Why would you save it?"

Fiona said, "Because I was incredibly proud of my baby sister. Your talent has always been the force field of our family." She shrugged. "We visited that week, remember? I rescued it from the wastebasket."

Birdie felt a growing excitement. It could work. If Anastasia hadn't been pulled too deep into the Web of Wyrd, if she had only been sucked into one plane and not traveled through multiple dimensions—they could bring her home.

She threw her arms around Fiona and said, "Thank you."

Fiona squeezed her back.

There was a knock at the door that divided the house, and Cinnamon called, "Birdie? Fiona? Are you two out there?"

Fiona stepped forward and unlocked the door. Birdie pocketed the spell.

"There you two are. I just gave Lolly the last of the wine, but I have a case in my car I was going to drop by the bar. I sent Tony for a bottle, but you better get outside and bring some clothes before she catches pneumonia."

Birdie collected a hooded, full-length faux fur from the coat closet and handed it to her youngest granddaughter. "Give this to your aunt and we'll begin serving dinner momentarily."

"Where's Stacy?" Cinnamon asked, scanning the room.

Birdie and Fiona exchanged a nervous glance. "She was feeling a bit peaked, so I gave her a tonic and sent her up to a guest room."

"Really? She seemed fine this afternoon. Maybe I should go check on her."

Cinnamon started for the front staircase.

Birdie caught her arm and said, "I'm sure that isn't necessary, dear. She'll be down in a minute. You know those spa treatments rush all the toxins out of the body so quickly, it could cause anyone to feel woozy." She raised an eyebrow at Fiona.

Fiona picked up the cue and went to Cinnamon's side. She put a hand to the girl's forehead and said. "Oh my, you're looking a bit pale yourself, dear."

Cinnamon touched her cheek. "I am?"

"Certainly understandable. You are eating for two, after all," Birdie said.

Cinnamon nodded and said, "That's true. I am feeling light-headed." She glanced at the settee that Leo was near and said, "Maybe I should lie down too."

Fiona put her arm around Cinnamon and guided her to the doorway. "You need something to eat is all. How about some nice hot soup?"

Birdie asked cautiously, "Fiona, are you sure that soup might not be too…spicy…for a woman in her condition?"

Cinnamon said, "I like spicy food."

"Not to worry, Birdie. It's perfectly seasoned," Fiona said, and looked at her sister reassuringly.

A flash of light beamed from upstairs then, and Birdie's mirror jingled.

Cinnamon said, "What was that?"

"Motion light. Just had it installed," Birdie said.

"In your bedroom?" Cinnamon asked.

Birdie said, "Can't be too careful. Now be a good girl and go give your auntie the coat."

Cinnamon looked skeptical, but not enough to care, thankfully. She wasn't nearly as curious as Anastasia. She didn't have the need to understand everything all at once, just accepted things as they were.

Birdie was ever so grateful for that.

The girl shrugged and said, "Okay. Let me know if I can help with anything." She shuffled down the hall, struggling with the oversized coat.

Fiona called to her. "Be right out with that soup, sweetheart." She spun to Birdie and said, "I'll handle this. You see who's calling."

Badb, or the woman who called herself Badb, walked up to the cage. She winked at me, and with a wave of her arm and a shudder from the tree, the bars instantly melted into a thousand fluttering blackbirds that flew up into the evening sky.

I folded to the forest floor.

Hand on my sword, I called to Thor, who was still wriggling around on his back. The dog perked his ears, righted himself, and trotted over to me.

Danu took a seat on her throne, produced two ruby-encrusted goblets, and invited me to join her.

It was just the two women, Thor, and me. I saw no one else as I scanned the woods, and decided that my chances of escaping were pretty damn good. I tapped Thor on his backside and bolted in the opposite direction of the two women, pumping my legs toward the pathway and the light still shining through it.

I heard Badb say behind me, "You see why I trapped her?"

The fireflies wove through the trees. I had the sensation they were leading me to a way out of this nightmare, so I ran faster.

As soon as I reached the mass of tiny orbs, they burst into flames that showered down in front of me. I jolted to a stop.

And right before my eyes, the flames transformed into people. Fair-skinned, lithe, two-armed, two-legged people.

I think I passed out for a moment, because the next thing I knew, I was sitting in a drafty palace with twenty-foot ceilings, crystal-clear windows, and three bronze chandeliers anchoring the room.

Danu said, "There she is. Welcome back."

My mind was fuzzy again, same as before when I woke up in the birdcage. I moaned. "My head hurts."

Badb poured a yellow liquid into a pewter goblet and handed it to me. "Drink this. It'll clear the web from your mind."

"No way, Elvira. I'm not touching anything you want to offer me."

She rolled her eyes and turned to Danu. "Are you certain this is the one?"

Danu walked over to us and took the drink from Badb. "Have faith, maiden. The web is hard on the senses." She handed it to me, her eyes warm.

"Where's Thor?"

"Your familiar is fine. He's having a rest." Danu offered the cup again. "Go on, you'll feel better."

I took the goblet and sniffed. It smelled like May wine. Sweet honey and citrusy orange blossoms. I took a small sip, and instantly my thoughts cleared and the pain vanished.

I downed the whole cup and stood, feeling fortified. "What did you mean the web is hard on the mind? What web?" Was I trapped in the Internet?

Danu cocked her head and smiled. "The Web of Wyrd, of course."

Of course.

"So what you're saying is—" I started.

Danu cut me off. "Welcome to the Otherworld."

I turned to the woman with the jet-black hair. "And you are…"

She bowed. "Badb, warrior goddess of the Morrigan."

I flicked my gaze to the red-haired woman. "So that would make you…"

"Danu, mother goddess of the ancient island. And these"—with a sweep of her hand, the far wall fizzled away, revealing a cheerful scene of a village at work—"are my people."

It couldn't be. It just couldn't. "The Tuatha Dé Danann." I looked at her, incredulous. "This is a prank, right? A birthday gag? Did my grandmother put you up to this?"

Danu parked her hands on her hips. "Why don't you pinch me to see if I exist?"

Tentatively, I reached forward and she zapped me with some kind of electric current.

"Ouch!" I wiggled my fingers.

"Not very bright, today's humans," Badb said, reaching for an apple from the fruit bowl on the table.

I glared at her.

Danu circled around her throne and stood behind it. "I suppose you're wondering why I've brought you here, Stacy Justice."

"The thought did cross my mind."

"It seems that my cauldron has gone missing, and I want it found."

She stared at me, searching for a sign of recognition.

I said, "I heard something about that."

"You see, the Cauldron of Abundance was passed to my son, Dagda, but I encouraged him, before we departed for this land, to gift it to the island and her people." She frowned. "Had I known that you would be so careless with it, I wouldn't have suggested it."

"Sorry about that." I had no idea why I was apologizing. It's not like I misplaced the thing myself. Maybe because I was afraid the two of them would turn me into a hedgehog.

"Yes, well, it isn't the first time, and I suspect it won't be the last," Danu said. "Do you know what happened the first time the cauldron was stolen, Stacy Justice?"

I shook my head.

The woman worked her hands into a frenzy, circling her fingers round and round, faster and faster, until finally, a large bubble popped out from her palms and floated through the air.

I watched as the bubble puffed and expanded to the size of a Ferris wheel. It settled in the center of the room. Within seconds, a scene emerged, or rather several scenes all at once. Emaciated people, pale and gasping for breath; children crying as their mothers looked on desperately, helplessly; men in rags wandering the streets, begging for food.

"The Famine." My heart felt heavy and my stomach lurched as I watched all the pain and suffering.

"Precisely. We don't want that to happen again, do we?"

I shook my head.

The red-haired beauty smiled. "Good."

I looked from her to Badb. "But what does this have to do with me?"

Badb said, "Seriously, Danu, are you sure she's the one?"

Danu shot Badb a look. Badb shrugged and bit into her apple.

Danu rushed at me, grabbed my shoulders, and stared hard into my eyes. "It has everything to do with you, Stacy Justice, because you are going to find the cauldron."

She said it so convincingly, I almost believed her.

Chapter II

Birdie hurried upstairs to answer the call from her mirror. She hadn't expected to see the face staring back at her so soon.

"Aedon, what an inconvenient surprise."

"I know you didn't expect to hear from me so quickly, but the natives are restless, so to speak, and they are calling for swift action. I've arranged for a private charter to pick you up at the regional airport. You'll fly in to the west, to a private landing strip, where a driver will be waiting to transport your party to the castle."

"When?"

"They'll be expecting you on the plane by nine o'clock in the morning, your time."

Birdie was flabbergasted. "Aedon, you cannot be serious. That isn't enough time to pack and plan, let alone rest."

"This is quite serious, Birdie, and I put my tail on the line promising the council that you and your Seeker could complete the task. Do not make a fool of me. Should you fail, I cannot guarantee to keep my promise."

Birdie stiffened. What was she going to do? Anastasia was missing, her daughter was imprisoned, and there was a cauldron to find.

Her old fetching spell had to work. It just had to.

"I assure you, Aedon, we will not fail."

Aedon gave Birdie the rest of the transportation details. She jotted them down and cut the connection.

She exited her room feeling nauseous, nervous, and incredibly frightened for the first time in many years. The matriarch of the Geraghtys knelt before the huge painting that hung ceremoniously on the wall of her home, said a silent prayer to Danu, and fluttered down the back stairwell to prepare for the most important spell she would ever cast in her life.

Birdie bumped into Chance and Derek on her way through the kitchen. They carried the lumpy rug that concealed the chief of police.

"Jesus, Mrs. Geraghty, what you got in here, a body?" Derek asked.

Fiona bit her lip. "Don't be silly." She looked at Birdie. "Just having the rug cleaned. Careful, now."

Birdie watched in horror as Chance banged his end of the rug into the refrigerator. She was pretty sure that was where the chief's head was tucked.

"Just set it right by the back stoop." Fiona held the door open. "That's it. Nice and easy. It's one of a kind."

Derek tripped over the rug.

"Watch your step," Fiona said. "Now, everyone sit down and we'll bring out the soup. Stacy shouldn't be but a moment."

Birdie went back inside and grabbed a tray with five soup cups. She brought it to the stove as Fiona sashayed through the screen door.

"Would you like to tell me what that was about?" Birdie asked.

"It isn't my fault." Fiona patted Birdie's pocket. "Check the spell. We need nine loved ones present for the retrieval. I thought it best not to take any chances."

"You have no idea." Birdie filled Fiona in on the call from Aedon.

Fiona said, "Then there's no time to waste. You should know that Lolly is perfectly lucid."

Birdie reached for spoons as Fiona picked up the tray with the soup cups. The younger sister stopped, a cloud of concern crossing her face.

"Birdie, what is it?" Fiona asked.

Birdie took a deep breath, paused a moment. Then she shook her head slowly. "Something is wrong. I can't feel her."

Fiona's eyes widened. "She's gone deeper into the web."

Birdie said, "There's no time to waste."

The two women stood there, staring at me expectantly. I finally spotted Thor, snoozing softly near the fireplace, one ear trained on me.

Birdie never covered this in my lessons. There was no chapter in the Blessed Book on dealing with powerful hallucinogenics that conjured up visions of ancient talking goddesses who were unimpressed by your witchiness.

Of course, there was the possibility that they were the real deal. That I had indeed been sucked into another dimension just like that damn rhyming ghost warned me about.

Yet, knowing all the enemies my family had collected over the years, the chance that these two weren't goddesses, but simply powerful sorceresses who wanted to thwart my plan to bring my mother home, seemed far more likely.

"If you are who you say you are, then why can't you find the cauldron yourself? Why do you need me?" I asked.

The one who called herself Danu looked at me like she was the Great Oz and I was the scarecrow searching for a brain.

She stepped back, her eyes angry. "Have you not been listening? I told you it was gifted to your people and the fertile land that was once the home of the Tuatha. It no longer belongs to me." She stepped toward the bubble and tapped it. "It belongs to the island."

A gorgeous view of a lush green hillside came into focus. Then, with a flick of Danu's finger, the bubble spun and the scene changed to a waterfall cascading down a mountain. Another wave of her hand sparked the image of a vast forest, filled with towering pines. A slideshow followed then, and I saw a huge lake, dotted with islands and tiny fishing boats, then ocean waves gently lapping a sandy beach, giant cliffs perched along the edge of the sky, winding roads that passed castles and cottages alike, until finally, the bubble stopped spinning, coming to rest on an image of a huge stone protruding from a grassy knoll.

"The Stone of Destiny, planted thousands of years ago. It still stands at the Hill of Tara," Danu said. "Have you heard of it?"

"Yes. Legend says that it roared when touched by the high king."

Badb stepped forward to gaze at the picture. "Tara was once a place where heroes gathered. I aided many a soldier in the valley that is called Boyne."

"Felled many too." A mischievous smile passed Danu's lips.

I swung my head to Badb. "Really?"

"Yes, but they were all bad."

That wasn't much comfort.

Danu said, "If you know about the stone, then you must know about the other gifts."

Were they testing me? Were the council members considering my worthiness as a Seeker? I couldn't get a read on either of the women, emotionally or mentally. Normally, my intuition would tell me something about the intentions of a person. My body would send a signal—or a warning—but here, there was nothing, just numbness. I hadn't even felt the presence of a single spirit since I woke up here.

I felt naked without my intuition, helpless as a baby bird.

There was no point in dodging their questions until I figured out what they were up to. I rattled off what Birdie had taught me about the treasures of the Tuatha Dé Danann. "The Stone of Fal, or Destiny, which knows the heart of man. The Spear of Lugh, or Victory—it never misses its mark. The Sword of Nuada, or Light—none can escape its will, and the Cauldron of Dagda, or endless bounty and resurrection. The sacred gifts also represent the elements—earth, air, fire, and water, respectively."

"Most excellent," Danu said, and clapped her hands in a manner that reminded me of Lolly.

I suddenly missed my aunt terribly. I missed everyone terribly. I hadn't even kissed Chance yet, and it was my freaking birthday. People were waiting for me. There was cake to be eaten, dammit.

"Okay, ladies, why don't you tell me what I can do to help?" I figured the faster I appeased them, the faster I could get out of there.

Badb disappeared behind a curtain as Danu spoke. "A treaty was signed between the Tuatha Dé Danann and the first Druids to protect the four treasures. Throughout the ages, four people, or, as we refer to them, the four corners, have been appointed by the humans in charge to guard the hallows at all costs. We learn their identities only when they have completed a quest."

She snapped her fingers, and an image popped into the bubble.

"The Warrior."

It was a copper-haired woman on a ship in the heat of battle. She was fighting off six men with two swords—and winning. From her dress, the setting, and the way she fought, it could only be Grace O'Malley, Pirate Queen. She ruled the western banks of Ireland for forty years and protected her people and her land from foreign invasion, including the powerful British forces. She was known for expert navigational skills and her vengeful temper. Many a man was slaughtered in retaliation for crimes committed against Granuaile (her Gaelic name) and those she loved.

She was, as they say, a total badass.

Danu continued. "The Guardian."

There, on the screen, was Oscar Wilde lecturing before a classroom.

"The Seeker."

Joan of Arc.

Danu snapped her fingers again and said, "And the Mage."

Katharine Hepburn.

Aha! That's where they made their mistake. I knew all too well about the Warrior, the Guardian, and the Seeker, and their roles in serving the secrets of the old soil. Months ago, a young girl showed up on my door-step claiming to be my sister. Her mother was missing, and the clues the woman had left behind led the girl to me. She thought it was because we were related. As it turned out, we were connected in another way, a deeper way. Her name was Ivy Delaney, and she was a Warrior. Around that same time, the Guardian also showed up in Amethyst to help protect a sacred text from thieves. His name was John Mahoney, a police officer from Chicago, and we were all three descendents of the scribes who wrote that text.

But there was no Mage. It was a three-member team.

"Okay, ladies, I've seen quite enough," I said, stepping forward.

Badb emerged from behind the curtain, holding a golden chalice. Danu gave a slight shake of her head to Badb, then turned to me.

"So then you'll gather the corners and find the cauldron?" she asked.

"I don't think so. You see," I quoted from the Geraghtys' Blessed Book, "there are three only whose calling is a benefit to their people: the Warrior on the field of battle, the Guardian of sacred truth, and the Seeker of Justice, wherever she may be."

Danu rolled her eyes. "Who told you that? That is not true."

Badb said, "Danu is right. This"—she held up the cup—"is truth."

Danu said, "I'm not sure that is necessary, Badb. She will believe in her destiny if I have to shove it down her throat."

"My thoughts exactly." Badb smiled wickedly, moving upon me so fast, I was forced into a chair. She held the cup to my lips and gave a questioning look to Danu.

Danu thought about it for a moment. She said, "I suppose it couldn't hurt." She walked over to me. "Stacy Justice, since you know so much about the treasures—and just because you haven't secured a Mage in your time doesn't mean that corner doesn't exist—then you must know about us." She tossed a look to Badb. "Tell me what Badb represents."

Geez, would this nightmare never end?

I took a deep breath. "Battle. Sacrifice. Transformation… um…"

"Truth," Badb prompted.

"Thank you. Truth."

Danu snatched the chalice from Badb, offering it to me. "Either drink from the chalice of truth or we will find other ways to enlighten you."

I slapped it from her hand, spilling the liquid across the floor, and stood. "I want to go home. Now. I want to see my family."

Thor rose to his feet at the sound of the cup clanging against the wall.

Badb leaned into me, her hot breath melting my eyeliner. "You want to see your family? That can be arranged."

I heard Danu yell, "No!" just as Badb picked me up and threw me into the bubble.

Chapter 12

I could still feel the handprints on my arms where that bitch dug her talons into me, but I seemed to be unharmed. I found myself standing in front of a school, wearing a tea-length, belted dress, navy pumps, and a pillbox hat. My brain was scrambled again, which was beginning to worry me. What if I came out of this with permanent damage? I silently counted to ten, sang the alphabet song in my head, and tried to remember the name of my favorite sports team. I came up with the Chicago Cubs. Could that be right?

A gaggle of girls and a handful of boys rushed out the doors and lined up in front of me. They were at the tween age, perhaps twelve or thirteen, and smelled of porridge and hope. There were a dozen or so of them, and they stared at me with the inquisitive caution children exhibit when faced with a stranger.

"Maggie O'Brien," the first girl said.

"Nice to meet you, Maggie."

"Likewise." She stood there, waiting for something. After a moment she crooked her finger at me, signaling she had a secret to tell. I bent to lend her my ear and she whispered, in a thick Irish brogue, "You're supposed to mark *present* next to our names."

That's when I felt the clipboard in my hand.

"Right. Sorry, Maggie." I unclipped the pen from the metal fastener and scribbled *present* next to her name just as a bus pulled up.

The door made a hissing sound as the driver pushed it open, and Maggie hopped on, a purple satchel over her shoulder.

The next girl was Katie Byrne, and I did the same for her name, plus six more, until I heard a commotion near the end of the line.

I looked up and saw a tall, thin girl shove another.

"Hey! Stop that, right now." I said.

The tall girl sneered at me defiantly, then pointed at the girl she shoved and whispered something to the shy kid standing next to her. The neighbor laughed at whatever the bully said, although she seemed uneasy about it.

The blond boy in front of me rolled his eyes and said, "She's always like that."

"Yeah? Well, not on my watch."

I winked at him, made a note next to his name, Aedon O'Neil, and the next student's, and the next, wondering what this little jaunt was supposed to teach me. Junior high sucks? Mean girls exist on every plane?

Hell, I knew that.

The doe-eyed girl standing in front of me now was the one who had been shoved, but she didn't seem fazed. She seemed downright regal. I admired her moxie.

"Hi! Are you the new chaperone?" she asked, a bounce in her step.

Uh-oh. That must have meant there was a field trip in my future. "Well, I suppose I am. What's your name?"

"Brighid. Brighid Geraghty."

The clipboard clattered to the sidewalk as my hand let go, and I froze.

The girl smiled and said, "I'll get it." She scooped the clipboard up and held it out for me.

"Birdie?" I whispered. My head was spinning. All at once it hit me like a kaleidoscope. The clothes, the surroundings, the accents. I looked at the clipboard.

The Academy of Sorcery
Hill of Tara Field Trip Roster

"I prefer Brighid," my young grandmother said to me. "She was a powerful goddess, the daughter of Dagda, of the Tuatha Dé Danann." Her voice burst with enthusiasm. "Do you know who they are?"

I nodded, having learned that at the private school of Geraghty Girls. She continued, satisfied she didn't have to explain that whole gnarled mess of a family tree. "Brighid was so revered that the Christians made her a saint. There's a lot of stuff dedicated to her in Kildare. A sacred well, a statue, even a cathedral. It's where my people are from." She radiated pride.

Then the little shit behind her said, "She thinks she's so cool because of her name. Doesn't even sound good with your stupid American accent, *Brigit*."

The troublemaker pretended to accidentally bump into Birdie, and she stumbled forward, into me, dropping her notebook. It took all I had not to grab that kid by the ear and introduce her to an American swirly.

But Birdie handled it with aplomb. Her smile wavered just a bit, and then that ferocious resolve, which I both admired and feared, rose above the snide remark.

She turned to face her attacker, hands on hips. "Tallulah, just because your daddy is a member of the council doesn't mean you have what it takes to be a good witch. I suggest you spend more time on your studies and less time picking on me if you want to graduate."

I wanted to applaud, but decided against it.

Tallulah's face reddened so fast, I thought steam might shoot from her ears.

"Okay, girls, why don't you both get on the bus?" I said.

Behind me, a man's voice said, "Oh, wonderful! The agency sent someone to fill in for Miss Murphy. Thank you so much for filling in on such short notice."

I turned to face a wiry, middle-aged man who was losing the battle of the bulge. He looked as flustered as I felt. "Mrs. Doherty is right behind me. Everyone accounted for?"

I checked the clipboard. "Looks that way."

"Very good, very good."

He took a minute to speak with the bus driver and the students, then he hopped off, wished me luck in a tone that indicated I was going to need it, and disappeared back inside the building.

I looked at the bus, and my stomach suddenly felt like I had swallowed wet cement. I had absolutely no experience chaperoning children, let alone a dozen of them, let alone my own grandmother. Oh, and let's not forget they were witches and wizards in training.

Yep, I was in way over my head thanks to my big, stupid mouth.

Someone tapped my shoulder and said, "They can't leave without you, lass. Up you go."

I shifted my feet to face her. "Mrs. Doherty?"

The woman wore cat's-eyes glasses and a drab pantsuit, and was pushing the other side of forty. "At your service. Come on, now, Tara is waiting."

Birdie was sitting in the second seat on the right, so I took the seat across from her and Mrs. Doherty took the first seat on the left.

Doherty settled her things onto the bench and stood up, the scent of violets trailing her. "Listen up, class. Now, you are all here because you are a descendent of either a high king or an important scribe. I expect you to behave with the propriety and class of those noble men and women. The council will be expecting a full report, and believe me, you do not want your name in it." She gave a brief warning that spellcasting would absolutely not be tolerated, and suggested everyone sit back and enjoy the scenery.

I kept my eye on Birdie the entire bumpy ride. It was fascinating and disturbing at the same time to see this woman who had raised me, comforted me, guided me all these years, as an innocent, wide-eyed, hopeful kid. She wrote in her book most of the way, periodically lifting her head to take in the sights, and I wondered why she had never told me about this school.

Occasionally, I glanced back at Tallulah, who, by the end of the hour-long trip, had managed to come up with the nasty rhyme *Brigit is a dimwit, a stupid twit, an ugly zit.*

Others chimed in instantly. I stood and firmly said, "Stop," wishing I had paid closer attention to all their names.

The bus had come to a halt, and Mrs. Doherty was busy giving instructions to the driver, although she did glance back when she heard the taunt. She simply chose to ignore it.

So that's how it's going to be? Because Tallulah's father has clout?

I glanced at Birdie, who winced but lifted her chin to drink in the spectacular hill that was once the seat of the high kings of Ireland. I followed her gaze, and to my amazement, I saw flashes of battle scenes scattered across the landscape. I could actually smell the rich green hue of the grass carpeting the rolling hills, could taste the history and sacrifice in the air. Visions of men and women fighting side by side flickered before me. Warriors being honored, priestesses receiving crowns. I could hear rituals, dancing, and chanting all over the mighty knoll. I knew I was really in Ireland, not only because of the breathtaking landscape and the earthy scent of the land, but because I felt like I had come home.

"*Hmm-hmm.*"

The kids giggled, and I realized that Mrs. Doherty was waiting for me to exit the bus, reminding me that I was a chaperone, not a spectator. I stood up and quickly stepped off, then scooted to the side, waiting for Birdie.

Mrs. Doherty had other plans.

"Why don't you take one group over to the Stone of Destiny, and I'll start at the Mound of the Hostages, then we'll switch?"

"All right," I said, planning to pull Birdie into my group.

But that didn't happen.

"The children already know their assigned groups." She clapped her hands and said, "Boys and girls, attention, please. Will Group A please come with me? Group B, please follow Miss, er…" She said to me, "What is your name?"

"Justice." I can't say why, but I immediately regretted telling her my real name.

To my dismay, both Birdie and Tallulah gathered in front of Mrs. Doherty. I let her group go first, so I could keep on eye on Hades' Little Helper.

Tallulah was still snickering behind my grandmother's back, a few cronies playing along, but Birdie seemed to be handling it well. She was listening intently to everything Mrs. Doherty had to say, nodding, and writing in her book.

Aedon sidled up next to me. "Don't worry about Birdie. She'll be okay. She's really smart. And strong."

I turned to him and smiled. "Thanks, Aedon."

I knew all about the magic of Tara from my lessons. The stone was perched at the top of the highest hill, so I led my group up to it, discussing its legend, where it came from, and what it meant to the people of the land. We hadn't hiked too far when I spotted the stone protruding from the grass.

We formed a circle around it, and a few kids asked questions. Thankfully, I was able to answer them. After about fifteen minutes of the children chattering and touching the stone, pretending they were kings and queens, I let them explore a bit more of the hillside and I did as well.

I could sense them here. Danu, Badb, Lugh, Nuada. My gods and goddesses. I could feel the dynamic energy of the earth, the power of the wind, the presence of greatness. The landscape herself was beyond beautiful. It was intoxicating, and I knew then that they had sent me here. The redhead and the raven-haired woman were the real deal. I opened my arms wide and soaked in the essence of Tara.

That's when I heard Birdie say, "Give it back!"

I whipped around to see Tallulah hiding behind a headstone in the old cemetery at the bottom of the hill, holding a book. Birdie was trying to catch up with her, but Tallulah had three accomplices playing keep-away with her.

Mrs. Doherty was still absorbed in her lecture around the mound. I told Aedon to lead the group to where she was, yards away, and ran down to help Birdie.

Birdie said, "Give it back, Tallulah, please."

I had never heard her so desperate; her voice was on the verge of cracking, and my heart ripped.

I called upon the inner goddess of my core, wishing badly that Thor were here. He'd teach these little trolls a lesson. "Girls. Enough. Give the book back. Now."

The other three scampered away, but Tallulah remained still, shooting daggers at me with her eyes.

She stepped forward, leaves crunching beneath her feet. "Do you know who I am?"

Those words startled me, for some reason. Stopped me dead in my tracks. Her voice. The very tone she used reminded me of someone, but I didn't know who.

I shook it off and said, "I know exactly who you are, missy." Anger swirled in my belly. It was her turn to be surprised. "You're a bully. And believe me when I tell you, bullies get what they deserve, threefold."

As I will it, so mote it be.

The air whirled around her and a gust of wind blew in from the east as I focused all my energy on the book—Birdie's book—that was still in the hands of this stranger. I heard a crow caw, then another, and saw Tallulah look up nervously as a tree branch cracked over her head.

Her lip quivered for a moment, and she lifted her eyes skyward as a dark cloud tumbled in from the west. Her skirt flapped in the wind that circled around her. Her hair knotted into a nest, and I could tell she was having a hell of a time retaining ground.

She turned an icy glare to me, and then to my grandmother, who stood perfectly still, eyes only on her work.

Finally, as a sunbeam from the south nearly blinded her, and the wind whipped so hard it tossed Tallulah on her ass, she held up the book. "Fine! Take the stupid book."

My young grandmother reached for it, but before Tallulah passed it off, she tore out the first page and sacrificed it to the wind.

Birdie screamed. "No! My fetching spell."

Fat, rolling tears tumbled down her face as the paper twisted and flipped in the air.

I called to Birdie, "Stay here. I'll get it."

Birdie scanned the garden table. There were five guests slumped over their soup. Derek, Cinnamon, Tony, Chance, and Gus. Gus had come by looking for Leo, and since they needed one more person for the spell, they decided to include him. Leo was still rolled up like a burrito near the back step.

"Including the three of us, that makes nine," Fiona said.

Lolly was lighting the candles and gathering the herbs for Birdie's retrieval spell. She read the ingredients one last time. "I remember you speaking about this fetching spell, Birdie. You worked on it for months, did you not?"

Birdie nodded. She was adjusting the rug to make sure Leo had enough oxygen. "I began that my first year at the Academy. I recall it was on a field trip to Tara." She cocked her head. "Funny, I don't recall the name of the nice chaperone who assisted me with it."

Lolly frowned then and said, "I think I must need my reading glasses. I can't seem to make out the words very clearly."

Fiona joined Lolly and said, "The ink seems to be quite faded." She looked at Birdie. "Funny. It was much darker a few moments ago."

Birdie stopped fiddling with the rug she was adjusting. For the life of her, she couldn't recall why there was a rug outside in the first place. Her thoughts felt fuzzy.

Fiona said, "Birdie? Are you all right?"

Birdie said, "Yes, of course." She smacked her hands together. "Now then, what was it we were about to retrieve?"

Chapter 13

I chased the page as it curled through the wind, past the headstones, past a few trees, until it finally snagged on the branch of an ancient oak, twenty feet in the air.

"Damn," I said. "Now would be a good time to report to duty, Badb. Or at least send one of your soldiers."

Behind me, I heard a sniffle.

I turned to face Birdie, tears sliding down her puffy cheeks.

"Don't cry. We can get it."

"It's not fair. Tallulah spoils everything." She kicked the dirt.

I remember feeling like that when I was little. It was a horrible feeling, getting picked on for being different. Sure, everyone went through that kind of teasing at one time or another, for one prejudice or another, but knowing that didn't make it sting any less. I was the odd kid out because I grew up in a family full of witches. Birdie was being bullied because of her address.

"Brighid, my friend, you will meet people in your life who will test your courage, question your wisdom, and challenge your beliefs. You can't let those people squash your ambitions. They are not who defines us. But they are important. Do you know why?" I picked up a rock and tossed it at the branch holding the page. Missed.

She thought for a moment, then shook her head. She picked up a rock too.

"Because they teach us to value what matters. When the battle is over and those people fade into mere memories, you are left holding on to the most important thing of all. And it isn't fame, or conquest, or riches, it's personal truth. Stay true to yourself, my dear, and you'll never go wrong."

We tossed a few more rocks at the branch, to no avail. I whistled to a passing crow, hoping Badb had sent it, but it soared on by, the stench of river water floating alongside it.

Birdie threw her rock and hit a lower branch. "It doesn't matter. It was just a stupid fetching spell." She stared at the tree wistfully. "I probably wouldn't have used it anyway."

I faced Birdie, put my hands on her shoulders. "Hey, you shouldn't give up so easily." I lifted her chin to meet my eyes. "You know what my grandmother says?"

She shook her graceful head.

"My grandmother—who is a very powerful witch, by the way—says that between destiny and duty lies faith. If you have nothing to believe in, then you have nothing. Just believe, Brighid." I looked at the tree. "Now then, are you going to climb it, or shall I?"

As Birdie sized up the tree and her flat shoes, Mrs. Doherty screeched from beyond the graveyard. "Miss Geraghty! You are in big trouble, young lady! You too, Justice!"

Well, this can't be good.

"She sounds pretty mad," Birdie said, fingering her scarf.

"She sure does," I agreed.

Tallulah was marching right next to Mrs. Doherty, a satisfied smirk on her face.

I was so over this kid.

The teacher yelled, "You are going to get the licking of your life. I warned you not to practice magic!"

"I didn't." Birdie stepped back and positioned my body in front of her as a shield.

The woman couldn't be serious. "Does she mean what I think she means?" I asked Birdie.

Birdie whispered, "Disobeying a direct order is twenty licks, if you're lucky."

Oh no. No way was I going to let this bitch lay a hand on Birdie. Spare the rod, spoil the child was not a phrase in our book of child rearing. The Geraghtys used much more creative methods, which were far more effective, I might add. Like driving your granddaughter to school wearing a pentagram cape, and carrying a crystal ball to escort her to freshman English class.

"Badb, please help," I said through gritted teeth. "I know you can hear me. Probably watching from that floating HD monitor."

A raven came swooping down then, a piece of paper stuck on its beak. I pulled it off and scanned the writing. It looked like Birdie's spell. The bird flew to a low-hanging branch.

Not exactly what I had in mind, but I figured I'd take what I could get at that point.

I passed the paper behind my back to Birdie.

She whispered, "Oh, thank you."

Doherty was making pretty good time down that hill, and I wondered if I had misjudged her age.

Birdie clutched my skirt tighter, and a sickening thought occurred to me. *I may be able to help her now, but what about the next time, and the time after that?* If I was pushed back through the web, then who would protect Birdie? I suspected Lolly and Fiona had never gone to this school. That would explain why Birdie had taken on the leadership role for the family when her mother died. Or perhaps her sisters had already passed through and Birdie was the last one. The best one. But if they weren't here, that would mean she was all alone, with no one and nothing to count on except herself and her magic.

Magic. That was it.

Tracing a finger around my neck, I lifted the locket over my head and turned to face Birdie. I cradled the piece in both hands, put it to my third eye, and charged it with the power of Tara, the gods and goddesses, and the ancestors who wore it before me. I still had no idea of its function or importance, but I knew with every fiber of my being that I was supposed to give this heirloom to Birdie right now.

What had the card on the box read? *For Stacy Justice. When the time is right.*

So maybe the time wasn't right when I opened it. The ghost didn't tell me to open it. She just moved it so I'd pay attention to her.

"Birdie, listen to me."

The little girl my grandmother had been looked up at me with such fear in her eyes, I wanted to break the legs of whoever put it there. I slipped the locket over her head.

"I want you to wear this at all times, for protection. When you're feeling scared, or uncertain, just click it open"—I flicked open the latch—"look at the clock, and remember what I told you today."

She glanced down at the necklace. "Is this…?" She turned the locket over and gasped. "It is." She looked me straight in the eye for the first time, and a flutter passed between us. "I've only read about it. No one knows what it actually looks like, but it must be." She examined it closer. "This is a Seeker's amulet." Her eyes strained to memorize my face. "That means you must be—"

Doherty came around me then, and Birdie shoved the locket under her shirt.

As Tallulah laughed, the woman grabbed Birdie's arm violently. "Practicing magic, when I specifically restricted you from doing so, is grounds for dismissal."

"I didn't, I swear," Birdie cried.

In two strides, my hand was on the teacher's throat. "Let her go."

She did, and so did I.

Doherty swung toward me. "I will deal with you too, Justice, make no mistake!"

"Fine. So who will deal with Tallulah?" I asked. "She must be disciplined for stealing and intentionally destroying property that does not belong to her."

Mrs. Doherty straightened out her pantsuit. "I heard mention of no such thing. Only that Brighid cast a spell."

The children had descended the hill by then, so I stepped sideways and leaned in to speak softly. "You and I both know that is not true, now, don't we?"

She glared at me.

"Look, I understand the kid's father is some big shot, but don't you think—when Daddy's little girl gets herself killed because she has no clue how destructive magic can be when you don't know how to use it—that he'll trace her failure right back to this school? Back to those who were supposed to teach her. Back to you?"

Mrs. Doherty frowned. She obviously had not considered that possibility. She flicked her eyes to my young grandmother. "Brighid, go wait on the bus. We shall discuss this incident later."

I watched as Birdie made a wide loop around Tallulah, who stood there with an *aw, shucks* look on her face.

"Look, Miss Justice, we run a pretty tight ship around here."

"And a brutal ship, from the sound of it, just not a fair one." I stepped into her personal space. "This is how it's going to be, Doherty. Brighid and all the other kids will be treated with respect and diplomacy. You will not punish those who do no wrong, you will punish those who misbehave in accordance with the Druid triads and Celtic law, and that means Miss Tallulah. The kid's probably pissed off because her parents slapped her with that ridiculous name, so she'll need some positive guidance too." I narrowed my eyes. "That means no spankings, lashings, slapping, or any other bullshit you intend to rain down on these kids. You got me?"

She swallowed hard and nodded.

"And if I hear you laid a hand on any of them—especially Brighid—I'll be coming back for you."

Lightning split the sky then, and a thunderous cloud boomed over our heads.

Behind me, Tallulah started chanting her spiteful Brigit rhyme again.

With the image of Badb's crows in my mind, heat in my gut, and love in my heart, I waved my arms in a frenzied circle that brought no fewer than three dozen crows flying over Tallulah's head to soil her sweater.

She screamed and ran for the bus.

I turned back to Mrs. Doherty.

"Who *are* you?" she asked.

I spread my arms out wide. "I'm the Seeker of Justice, baby."

The black cloud parted, and out flew the giant bird—I suddenly realized it was Badb in shape-shifting form. She plunged toward the earth and scooped me up into the sky, her huge wings flapping gently toward the unknown.

Chapter 14

When I opened my eyes, I was wearing the gown Lolly had made me and sitting near the huge hearth in the palace of the goddess. The sword was at my side, and Thor was at my feet. The fire felt good, so I leaned in to warm my hands by the blaze. A tray next to the chair held a glass of water, soft bread, and a bunch of grapes.

Danu was standing in front of me, tapping her foot, a smarmy look on her face.

I rolled my eyes. "You proved your point. I am completely convinced that you are who you say you are, and I will do anything you ask, anything you need. Just please don't flash me back to babysit my great-great-grandmother, or introduce me to anyone who worked on the *Titanic*. I can't risk losing more brain cells, and the chances of my screwing up history are too great and too close to home," I said.

Then I thought about it and looked at her hopefully. "Actually, I might be able to help with the *Titanic*."

"No."

"Fair enough. So how do I find the cauldron?"

She snapped her fingers and the sphere floated forward. Badb came into the room then, loaded down with maps, which she spread out across a large banquet table.

I helped myself to the water and grapes as Danu explained to me that I needed to gather all four corners—Guardian, Mage, Warrior, Seeker—and head to the Hill of Summoning.

"While you are all responsible for the treasures as a whole, each of you has an intimate connection with a specific hallow. To the Seeker goes the cauldron. The Warrior is tethered to the spear. For the Guardian, it is the sword of light. The stone of destiny is tied to the Mage. The remaining three corners must connect with his or her treasure before you all approach the Hill of Summoning to find the missing cauldron. How that connection is satisfied is up to the individual; we do not govern the humans. Then, at the hill, you should be able to cast a spell to conjure an image of the cauldron. The strength of all of you combined leaves me no doubt that the cauldron will lead you directly to it. You just need to open your mind and follow the signs."

"Like what? What kind of signs?"

"You will know them when you see them. Or hear them. Or feel them."

"Thanks, that clears it up." A snapshot of the cauldron sputtered into view inside the bubble. I filed it into my memory bank. "Where is the Hill of Summoning?"

Danu tapped the bubble, and a picture of a grass-blanketed mound with a small opening appeared. "It's in the Boyne Valley."

The mound I was looking at wasn't Dowth or Knowth, the megalithic passage tombs of Ireland constructed five thousand years ago, but there were other mounds in that area; I just wasn't familiar with all of them. This one had stone steps embedded into it. A simple Google search would tell me where it was located.

"I can find it."

Badb called me over to her to view a map of the island. I gulped down the water, set the glass on the tray, and joined her at the table. "The green lines are the leylines that make up the Web of Wyrd. Those are the arteries to the Otherworld, where we reside. Should you need to recharge your energy, require a magical boost, or speak with us or any god, you must locate a leyline."

Most of them threaded around and through ancient sites.

Badb explained, "The leylines are guarded by the Sidhe, and they are extremely protective of their roads. You must be respectful and cautious when traveling over a leyline."

"They are a sensitive race, so whatever you do, don't offend them," Danu said.

Badb added, "And bring an offering. Milk, honey, cake, or anything shiny. Fairies love shiny things. They're like cats that way."

"We have assigned you a Fae fetch to guide you safely through the Otherworld, should the need arise," Danu said. She raised her voice. "Pickle, would you join us, please?"

A blond, wispy boy of about eighteen slipped through the door. His eyes were seashore blue and he was wearing a *Star Trek* hat.

"Pickle, I'd like to introduce you to Stacy Justice. She'll be performing a very important task, and I'd like you to guide her through the leylines should she call on you."

Pickle bowed before me and kissed my hand. Then he licked it and winked at me.

I yanked my hand back and said, "Don't get any lewd ideas, pal."

The poor thing burst into tears and bolted out of the room.

Danu barked, "Did I not just tell you they are sensitive? He was being friendly."

"He licked me. My dog doesn't even lick me."

Thor looked up from a bone he was chomping on and belched.

Danu said, "If you need him, all you have to do is whisper his name three times while standing on or near a line."

"Got it. Pickle, Pickle, Pickle."

He popped back into the room.

"Just checking," I said.

He left.

Badb said, "I've marked on the map previous locations where the cauldron was stored, and where it was taken when it was last stolen, as well as the location of the remaining three hallows."

There were several landmarks circled in red. One was Newgrange, a five-thousand-year-old passage tomb older than the Egyptian pyramids. The shape of the construction represents the female reproductive organs. Inside the inner chamber, a beam of sunlight illuminates the ground every winter solstice for exactly seventeen minutes. There was another circle around Cong, a quaint village on the west coast where *The Quiet Man* was filmed. Several stone monument formations can be found nearby, said to have been erected by the Tuatha Dé Danann to mark battle sites where they defeated the Fir Bolg, and to honor fallen warriors.

There was a blue circle around Trinity College in Dublin. Badb told me that was where the cauldron had been discovered after it was stolen in 1845. She pointed to another blue circle very near that. "The spear is on display at the Royal Irish Academy." Farther north, another circle indicated the home of the sword. Howth Castle, located on the edge of the seaside village, Howth. Legend has it that Grace O'Malley, returning from a long voyage at sea and low on supplies, approached the castle seeking sustenance for her and her men. The lord of the manor refused to open the gates, balking at the interruption of his dinner. The pirate queen kidnapped his son to teach the English lord a lesson in Irish hospitality. She refused ransom but insisted that an extra plate always be set for weary travelers. The lord agreed. To this day, the tradition stands.

"Now then, do you have any questions?" Danu asked.

I looked from one to the other. "That's it? That's all the information you have?"

"If we knew any more, we wouldn't need you."

Badb rolled up the maps and handed them to me. "Are you ready to return to your realm?"

"I guess so. Four corners. Hill of Summoning. Listen to the cauldron." I couldn't believe that was all they were giving me to help in my search.

Danu walked me over to the hearth. Thor stood up, and I held his collar. She looked at me and raised one eyebrow.

"Ready?"

I nodded.

She waved her arm in front of the opening.

Nothing happened.

She frowned. Waved it again.

Still nothing.

She looked at me, then at Badb. "Did you leave anything behind in the web?"

I didn't like the way she asked me that. I had a bad feeling about this. "I gave Birdie a locket. Why?"

Danu turned to Badb. "Uh-oh."

Badb shook her head. "The Seeker? Really?"

My stomach flip-flopped, and my lip was sweating. "What 'uh-oh'? Don't say 'uh-oh,' never say 'uh-oh.'"

Danu looked at me, worry painted on her face. "I'm not sure we can send you back."

Worst. Birthday. Ever.

I stared at the flames of the fire, wishing with all my heart that I could go home.

Birdie, if you can hear me, help.

Fiona shot Birdie a puzzled look. "You mean you don't remember why we are all outside? You don't recall the purpose of the fetching spell?"

Birdie was drawing a blank. She had the sense that this was important, however.

Lolly had been bustling around the table, but she stopped what she was doing when she heard Fiona's question. Birdie watched as Lolly approached, a shimmering hematite necklace in her hand.

Lolly said to Fiona, "Could it be the fairy fire?"

"Perhaps. She needs grounding," Fiona said.

"I have the hematite rope right here," Lolly said.

Birdie was growing annoyed that they were talking about her as if she weren't there. "Just tell me, please."

Lolly said, "As soon as we get this on you." She had to stand on her tiptoes to reach Birdie's neck. She was just about to slip the crystal necklace over her baby sister's head, when something caught her attention.

She hit the switch for the back porch light, nearly blinding Birdie.

"Turn that off. It's too bright," Birdie complained, shielding her eyes.

Lolly said, "Fiona, look."

Fiona rushed forward to see what had piqued Lolly's interest.

There, around Birdie's neck, was an intricate filigree locket dangling from a long golden chain. Fiona reached for it.

"Birdie, you weren't wearing this earlier. Where did you get it?"

Birdie looked down at the locket, then lifted her eyes to meet Fiona's. "I don't know. I've never seen it before."

The locket was long enough for Fiona to pull up to Birdie's third eye. In a flash of clarity, Birdie saw Anastasia, watched the conversation they had had that morning at the cottage unfold in her head. She felt the warmth of her love for the child, and the light of her granddaughter embedded inside this talisman. That's when she knew they were running out of time to rescue her.

"Anastasia. We must retrieve Anastasia."

Lolly and Fiona looked relieved, and the three of them rushed to the table. Lolly pulled the fetching spell from her coat pocket and read aloud, glasses perched at the edge of her nose.

"The love of nine works best for this spell, to fetch a witch caught in the fairy realm."

Lolly did a quick head count before she continued. Nine bodies were present. "A sprig of basil in each hand, and hawthorn root from the witch's land."

Fiona got to work prying open Derek's hand to tuck a basil leaf inside. Birdie did the same for Cinnamon and Tony, while Lolly worked the herb into the rug that was Leo's temporary home. Then she made sure Gus had one, and each sister grabbed a sprig for herself.

"The hawthorn is here," Fiona said, holding up a purple pouch.

Lolly read on. "A symbol of the town where she resides, and the hair of a harlot who was never a bride."

"What?" Fiona frowned. "I don't recall that last part. I have the amethyst crystal right here to represent the village, but where will we find the hair of a harlot?"

Birdie said, "Let me see that," and held her hand out. Lolly passed the page over to Birdie.

"I don't recall that part either." She looked up at Lolly. "Do we know any harlots?"

The two sisters stared at each other for a moment. Then, slowly, they both swung their heads to Fiona.

Fiona parked her hands on her hips. "Really, we're going there?"

Lolly pretended to swat a bug. Birdie feigned a hangnail.

Fiona said, "Fine. I'll give you this one, but I have been a bride, so you can't use my hair."

"What should we do?" Birdie asked.

"Where will we find a harlot at this hour?" Lolly asked.

None of them spoke for a few seconds, until Fiona snapped her fingers. "I've got it. There's a tavern in town called Down and Dirty. Apparently, the owner has quite the reputation. Birdie, you stay here and keep an eye on our participants. Lolly, let's go."

Birdie watched as her two older sisters raced off toward the driveway. She heard her car start and tear away.

If this works, she thought, *I won't force Anastasia to do anything she doesn't want to do again. I'll even call her Stacy. Perhaps.*

Birdie paced, nervously glancing at the clock through the kitchen door every fifteen seconds. She wondered how much longer her guests would sleep, how much longer Anastasia could survive the Web of Wyrd without losing her mind, and how much longer she could endure this night.

She caught a glimpse of the locket in the reflection of the back door as she passed it. She paused, focusing on what it could mean.

Where had it come from? She didn't recall owning any such piece. Gently, she raised the trinket to examine it more closely.

Why did it seem so familiar?

Birdie clicked open the latch and saw a watch face tucked neatly inside. Instantly, a sharp bell rang in her mind's eye. A far-off memory she couldn't quite pull to the surface, but it was there nonetheless.

This locket was important. But why?

Then, like a whisper on the wind, she heard the call of her granddaughter.

Birdie, if you can hear me, help.

The voice was urgent, desperate, and fearful. Birdie swung her head toward the forest. She inched forward, then walked her eyes all over the house. She saw nothing in the windows, no light, no sign of life.

No more voices.

Had she really heard it? Or was it a trick? More fairy fire to distract her from bringing Anastasia home? What did they want with her, anyway?

Frustrated, she sat down on the stoop hard, basil still clutched in her palm. She cradled the locket in both hands, put it to her third eye, and focused all her energy, all her strength, all her love onto this carved piece of metal. She concentrated. She envisioned Anastasia home, here with her.

Eyes closed tight, hands locked around the necklace, Birdie imagined the face of her granddaughter, the face of the Seeker, and whispered a prayer to the wind. To the stars. To the gods.

In the distance, a crow cawed.

Chapter 15

"What do you mean, you can't send me back? You have to send me back!"

Danu said, "You've disrupted the delicate fabric of your history. You caused a ripple in the web."

"So unripple it!"

Danu chewed her lip. "I'm not sure how."

"I can't believe this. You're not sure how? You're a goddess, for crying out loud." I flipped my frustration over to Badb. "And you think *I'm* not worthy of my title? Give me a break."

Danu said, "You don't understand—this has never happened before."

"Never happened before? Seriously?"

Badb said, "Well, there was that one time, Danu."

Danu's worried face took on a reflection of nostalgia. "Oh, yes." She looked at me. "She was a Guardian."

"Great." I slapped my hands together. "Who was it? What did you do?"

Danu looked away. "Her name was Amelia Earhart."

Amelia Earhart. The first woman to fly solo across the Atlantic, who disappeared somewhere over the Pacific in 1937, never to be seen or heard from again. "Oh my God. Oh my God." I was vaguely aware that the incessant repetition of words made me sound like a parrot, but I didn't care. I slumped against the wall. Thor trotted over to me and clamped his jaw on my skirt.

Badb said, "Don't despair. We can find a way, in time."

I marched toward her, wrestling myself away from the dog. "In time? You've had, like, five thousand years to iron out the kinks in this rabbit hole."

Thor tugged on my skirt again, causing my sword to jingle.

"Not now, boy." I turned to Danu. "How will I find the cauldron if I can't get back?"

"I suppose you wouldn't."

I started pacing, clutching the maps tight in my hand. *Oh, Birdie, I swear if you get me out of this, I'll be a better witch. I'll go on any ridiculous quest you ask me to.*

I stopped. A sinking feeling settled in my gut. "Mom," I whispered.

Thor barked impatiently and pawed at my skirt.

"Yes?" Danu asked.

"Not you. My mother. I have to get to her. If I don't show up at the council hearing, they won't release her."

Apparently fed up with getting the brush-off, Thor flung his head back, reared up like a stallion, and howled loudly enough to pierce an eardrum. The floor shook with force when he landed. Even Badb jumped.

I twirled to face him. "What is it?"

He looked at me like he wanted to whiz all over my shoes, then charged from the room.

Danu, Badb, and I glanced at each other. Then we shot after Thor.

We found him standing in the great hall of the palace—a room large enough to park a yacht in—in front of a larger-than-life portrait of Danu. It looked eerily similar to the one hanging in Birdie's house. Thor sat down, harrumphed, then cocked his head, as if wondering if I was smart enough to figure out what he was trying to tell me.

"Do you think it'll work?" I asked him.

He grumbled loudly, then pawed at the carpet. A display I deciphered as, *You got a better idea?*

I ruffled his ears, kissed his big snout, and said, "Good job."

He pranced up to the painting proudly and waited.

I turned to Badb and Danu. "You brought me here through the painting on our end; let's see if I can go home through it on yours."

"It's worth a shot," Danu said.

"I'll give it a go," said Badb.

I turned toward the huge frame and tucked the maps under my arm. I stepped forward, put one hand on Thor's collar, and glued the other to my sword.

Behind me, I heard the goddesses chant. My eyes were squeezed shut, my mind focused on home, and my thoughts trained on Birdie.

If anyone had the talent to bring me back, it was her.

Birdie's sisters, having returned from cutting the hair of the harlot, completed the spell and watched as Birdie brought the locket to her head for a third time.

This time, she chanted to the goddesses, still clinging to the image of her granddaughter in her head and the will to bring her home in her heart.

Then she heard a rustling in the woods.

I felt as if I had been stuck in a commercial dryer on the spin cycle for about three days. But whatever wormhole we had traveled through, one thing was certain when I opened my eyes.

I knew these woods.

Thor did too, judging by the manner in which he glee-fully pranced around, peeing on every branch that brushed against his hind legs.

I ran my hands up and down my body to make sure I was intact. Two hands, two arms, ten digits…wait…what was this?

The locket was hanging from my neck.

But how? I had given it to Birdie back in the Web of Wyrd.

Thor lifted his big snout high into the air, zeroing in on a whiff of something.

I sidled up next to him. "What do you smell, big man?"

Then I caught a hint of it too. The aroma of autumn—nutmeg, cinnamon, allspice, ginger—the scent of Lolly's award-winning apple cake.

It smelled like home.

I raced through the forest, Thor darting ahead of me. Dark as it was, I had years of experience navigating these woods day and night. It wouldn't be long before I arrived at the Geraghty Girls' Guesthouse. The trail I was on would eventually spill into a clearing that butted up against the boundary line. The emotions coursing through my body then left me fatigued. I was bursting with anticipation, euphoria, and the simple joy of feeling my feet on familiar soil. Where leaves were green, cages didn't fly away, and lightning bugs wouldn't grow thumbs. I was so elated, I actually stopped to kiss my favorite oak tree.

Which was a mistake.

When I turned to catch up with Thor, she was hovering right in front of my face.

"Ah!" I clutched my heart. "Don't do that. What is wrong with you? Don't you know you're not supposed to sneak up on people?"

The snow-white apparition fluttered a foot off the ground, her blue eyes communicating incredible disappointment in me. She just bobbed in the air like a buoy, waiting for me to say something.

"All right, look. You were absolutely spot-on about everything. I'm sorry I didn't heed your warnings."

She bloated her frame, and I could see that the area where her mouth was supposed to be was moving, but I couldn't hear a thing.

"Um, I can't hear you. If you're trying to tell me something, you should know there's no sound coming from your lips."

She cast her eyes down, annoyed, then spun around briefly. When she faced me again, I could hear her perfectly.

"The council awaits your arrival, in the castle you shall stay; but beware of the wrath of a rival, and the one who will betray."

Again with the maddening riddles.

"Who? Who is the rival? Who will betray? Is it one of the four corners? Is it the Mage? Who is the Mage, anyway?"

She seemed pleased that I was interested in her brainteaser this time, but it didn't do any good. She evaporated in a puff of smoke.

Dammit. What was her problem, anyway? Why couldn't she just get to the point like every other spirit who had a message for me?

I tramped through the woods for a few more minutes, until I saw the glow of the backlight of the Geraghty Girls' Guesthouse.

I spotted Thor leaning affectionately against Fiona. Lolly was setting up food and water for him near the back step, next to a rug that was rolled up on the lawn for some inexplicable reason.

And then I saw Birdie. She was searching for me with her eyes, scanning the field, the woods, and beyond.

My heart lurched at the sight of her. The concern on her face read like a road map to a painful place. A place where she had almost lost everything. It reminded me of the tortured little girl she'd been at the Academy. So very brave, yet so lonely in a world that didn't think she belonged.

But I knew better. And now, I knew her better.

I wanted to burst into tears, but I didn't dare reveal to her that I was relieved. That I had been, just minutes before, more afraid than I had ever been in my entire life. Because I knew now what she had been trying to teach me all these years. That it is important to be strong, courageous, and true to yourself, no matter what the rest of the world thinks. That the greatest mistakes in life are not the ones we make, but the ones that never get made because we are too afraid to try.

After my experience in the web, I understood that all she ever wanted for me was to believe in myself. To have the confidence to face life's obstacles head-on, because dodging them only makes the journey more treacherous. She knew the path I would travel long before I did, and she wanted me to be prepared.

My role in this family, in this world, was bigger than me. More significant than I had ever imagined. If I could use that role to make a difference—however great or small—in people's lives, then I had no other choice but to follow the path, wherever it would lead.

I took a deep breath, rolled my shoulders back, and straightened my sword.

Then I stepped out of the shadows and into my destiny.

PART TWO

The Reckoning

In old suffering that held you long paralyzed, you find
new keys. When your mind awakens, your life comes
alive and the creative adventure of your soul takes off.
Passion and compassion become your new companions.
—John O'Donohue

Chapter 16

Birdie Geraghty had never been so delighted to see anyone in all her life. She rushed forward, took her granddaughter in her arms, and squeezed until the child sputtered, "I can't breathe, Birdie."

She let go and inspected Anastasia. "Are you all right?"

The girl looked different. Felt different. There was a glimmer in her eyes that hadn't been there before.

"I'm fantastic."

Her sword gleamed in the moonlight, and she was carrying a pile of rolled-up papers under her arm. Then Birdie saw the locket, and as soon as she did, she remembered why it had seemed so familiar. It was the Seeker's locket. She had only heard rumors of its existence, but she had hoped it would be presented to Anastasia someday. And now here it was, around her granddaughter's neck. But how had Birdie possessed it just moments ago? And who had given it to Anastasia?

Birdie slicked her fingers over the design. "Where did you get this?"

Anastasia said, "It's a long story. One we don't have time for right now." She kissed Birdie on the cheek and hurried toward the house.

The girl halted when she saw the cast of her birthday celebration slumbering at the table.

She turned her head and cocked one eyebrow. "Do I want to know?"

"Not likely."

"Fair enough." She grabbed a slice of cake from the table, kissed her beau, and rushed inside.

Birdie followed, Lolly and Fiona behind her.

"What are you doing?" Birdie asked as Anastasia jogged upstairs.

"I need to get into the chamber of magic."

The three Geraghty sisters shared a look. They followed the girl up to the back hallway.

By the time they reached her, Stacy was emerging from the chamber. The mystical door fizzled away, replaced by the painting of Danu. A menagerie of enchantment tools and weapons weighed down Anastasia.

"Okay, here's what we need to do." She glanced back at the painting and said, "By the way, we're getting a real door for that room. One with a handle and everything." She waltzed into Birdie's boudoir and put the tools on the bed. "Birdie, I need you to call Gramps and see if he can get a hold of his friend Roger."

"The pilot? Why?"

"Because I need to get to Ireland sooner than expected." She was examining a box of crystals, lining up the stones on the duvet. She went to Birdie's closet and pulled out a duffel bag.

Birdie shot Fiona an uneasy glance. "Actually, dear, we wanted to discuss that with you."

"Discuss what?" She picked up a pair of nunchucks with her right hand and a five-bladed star with her left. She decided on the star and shoved it in the bag.

Fiona strode forward. "We understand that you spoke with someone on Birdie's scrying mirror."

"Yes, I did." Anastasia reached for a ball with iron spikes attached to a long chain. She whirled it over her head.

Lolly asked, "Are you going to fight a dragon?"

The girl frowned. "Hell, I hope not." She put the spiked ball aside and grabbed the broom Birdie had crafted for her. She shoved it into the bag.

Birdie said, "The woman you spoke to, Tallulah, what did she tell you?"

At the mention of Tabby's name, Anastasia bristled. Slowly, she turned to face the sisters. "What was her name?"

"Tallulah," Fiona replied.

Anastasia shook her head and laughed. "Oh, this is going to be fun." She picked up a vial of deadly nightshade and tossed it in the satchel.

"We were going to tell you everything," Birdie said.

"It's true," Fiona said.

"We just wanted you to have a nice birthday," said Lolly. "It was my idea to wait until after your dedication ritual."

Anastasia ran her hands through her hair. "Yeah, well, I don't think that will be necessary. Pretty sure I'm thoroughly dedicated." She turned back to the bag and put a wand inside. Then she lifted the scrying mirror Fiona had given her and gazed into it, a perplexed look on her face.

"So what did she tell you? What do you know?" Fiona asked.

Anastasia sighed. "Those are two very different questions, Auntie, but here goes. Tallulah told me her grandson is a Seeker."

"Lies," Birdie spat.

"I know, right?" The girl shook her head. "I mean, I'm the Seeker. And there's only one born every century, so how could he be one too?"

Birdie nodded, surprised by the girl's enthusiasm and knowledge. She was embracing her calling. What had happened in the Web of Wyrd? Birdie was hesitant to ask. She didn't want to interrupt the flow of the girl's frenzy.

Anastasia continued. "So then she said something about a deal, and my mother rotting in a castle, which, you know, I'm not going to let *that* happen." She picked up an athame and slid it through the belt of her dress. "Then I was angry, because I was worried about Mom, so I said some things I shouldn't have, and Danu threw a hissy fit and yanked me into the Web of Wyrd. And that's when I learned about the cauldron." She took a deep breath.

"Danu?" Birdie whispered, astonished.

"You met her?" Fiona asked.

It was too much too fast for Lolly. She sank into a chair.

Anastasia said, "Her and Badb."

"The Morrigan?" Birdie asked.

"Well, one of them. They really are three separate goddesses."

"And you know about the missing cauldron?" Fiona asked.

Anastasia nodded.

"The council specifically requested you find it," Birdie said.

"So did Danu and Badb, and let me tell you, those chicks are crazy, so I have every intention of following their orders. Now, what's this about a deal?" The girl crossed her arms.

After what her granddaughter had just endured, Birdie felt ashamed about making that deal with the council. She wished she could revoke the offer, but it was too late, the wheels were turning. She dug deep for her composure. "The council has agreed that should you find the cauldron, your mother will be set free."

Fiona pinched Birdie's backside, prompting her to expose the rest. "But if you don't—"

Anastasia raised her hand. "No. Don't even say it. Failure is not an option."

Birdie felt lighter just hearing those words.

Anastasia shoved a few more things into her bag and picked up her scrying mirror again. "You have to show me how to work this thing, Birdie." She patted her pocket. "For now, though, we'll stick with the iPhones to keep in touch when I'm gone."

"Actually, dear, we'll be traveling with you," Fiona said.

"You will?"

Birdie explained, "The council has arranged for our transportation. We leave first thing in the morning."

"Good." Anastasia glanced at the bag. "I was wondering how I was going to get all this crap through TSA and customs." She looked at Birdie. "I assume the council has ways around that sort of thing."

Birdie nodded.

"Well," Anastasia said, "I guess the only other thing I need to explain is the four corners."

The girl launched into a tale about how the Druids had signed a treaty promising that the four treasures of the Tuatha Dé Danann would be guarded by four people, called the four corners.

Anastasia counted on her fingers. "So I know the Guardian, that's John, and the Warrior is Ivy; I'm the Seeker, but we need to find the Mage. Can you call the council? Do you think they'll know who that is?"

Birdie shot a surprised look to Fiona. "Impossible."

Anastasia stared at them. "Why? Do you know who it is?"

Fiona was thrilled. "We certainly do."

"Who?"

Fiona beamed. "Your grandmother."

A sly smile crept across Anastasia's face. "Well, isn't this an interesting turn of events."

Before Birdie could process what that meant, Chance called from the hallway. "Mrs. Geraghty? Stacy?"

"In here, Chance."

He popped his head into the room and said, "Hey, baby, you feeling better?"

Anastasia rushed into his arms and kissed him. "Much better, thank you."

Chance said, "Glad to hear it. By the way, do you know why Leo is sleeping in a rug outside?"

Anastasia turned around, a bemused look on her face. "Really?"

Birdie simply shrugged.

Lolly said, "Looks like the charm has worn off. Let's eat."

Chance said, "What charm?"

Anastasia's phone chirped as everyone left the room. She paused, looked at the screen. "Did one of you cut Monique's hair?" she asked.

Fiona and Lolly fluttered away.

Anastasia trained her eyes on her grandmother.

"Who's Monique?" Birdie asked.

Chapter 17

I decided against telling Birdie about my encounter with her as a child. Ever. If she remembered it, she gave no indication, so I felt it best not to stir that pot. Or, in this case, the cauldron. I couldn't help but notice, though, the perplexed look on her face every time she glanced at my locket.

I tucked it into my dress when she went to brew the coffee. Until I knew myself who had given it to me, there was no point in discussing my new amulet.

Whatever charm the aunts had slipped my dinner guests had apparently left them with no recollection of the event. Leo kept looking around the patio, as if he had no idea what he was doing there. His hair was in shambles, his shirt rumpled, and I wondered why they'd felt it necessary to roll him up in a rug, but decided it best to question Birdie on that later. Luckily, we'd unwrapped him before he came to, and Birdie thanked him for joining us for supper the moment he opened his eyes, as if that had been the plan all along.

Derek couldn't stop fidgeting. He looked like a mouse caught in a maze. I wasn't sure what his voodoo aunt was into, but from the looks of him, it was some pretty freaky stuff. Gus cheerfully chatted away as Cinnamon devoured every last bit of the cheesy scalloped potatoes. Tony's adoration for his wife sprouted every fifteen seconds, or whenever she reached for something. I thought it was sweet. I suspected Cin found it rather annoying, the way her eyes narrowed when he asked if she needed anything for the umpteenth time.

And then there was Chance.

He had a shine in his eyes that night that made him even more dazzling than usual. They held mine for ages at a time, melting me into a pool of passion with each gaze. Despite all the warmth and love at the table, I wished everyone would just go home so I could curl up in his arms and get lost in his heartbeat until the sunrise.

I hated knowing that beginning tomorrow, I wouldn't be seeing him for a while. There was no telling how long I'd be gone. Days? Weeks? Only that I had to do this, and I had to do it without him. My independence was something he always appreciated, but would he accept me for who I was now? It would strain any relationship, this kind of pressure. As loving as Chance was, he was still a man of confidence and pride. Would he feel threatened by the role I'd inherited? Would he put up with my running off whenever the call came?

Jesus, Stacy, get a grip. You're not Batman.

A few hours later, after the presents had been opened and the dishes put away, Leo and Gus thanked us for dinner and left. I pulled Cinnamon aside to tell her about the trip.

"Don't worry about a thing. Mama, Tony, and I will keep an eye on the property. We'll check messages and arrange for any bookings that come through." She smiled at me and grabbed my shoulders. "You just bring your mother home."

"I will."

I had a quick discussion with Derek, explaining that my plans had changed. I made up a story about an incapacitated relative who needed help, which was mostly true. He said he'd just bump up the time frame on Monique's column, and I tried not to cringe.

I told Birdie and the aunts I would see them in the morning. Left the sword and the rest of the magical tools—both the ones I stashed in a carry-on bag and the ones I received as gifts—back at the house. Chance helped me gather the other presents, and we strolled the short distance to the cottage, Thor leading the way.

Chance unlocked the door. I unloaded the gifts from his arms and put them on the couch. There was a vase in the cupboard, so I pulled it out, filled it with water, and arranged the roses he bought me—twenty-nine plus one for good luck. Thirty total. Birdie would approve.

When I turned around, he was staring at me wistfully.

"What?" I asked.

"You're beautiful."

I looked down at my dress. Miraculously, I had managed to keep it spotless through everything.

"Thank you. Lolly made this for me." I twirled, and the skirt billowed around my legs.

He sauntered forward. "I'm not talking about the dress."

He picked me up, his arms sliding down the curvature of my body until my toes touched the ground again. His mouth found mine, and I curled my fingers through his hair, kissing him with all the intensity of a sailor about to be shipped off to sea.

Heat tingled through me as his hands found the cord that secured the bodice of the gown. Gently, he tugged. The knot unraveled, exposing my breasts. As his lips traveled the length of my neck, his hand found my nipple and gave it a gentle pinch. I cried out as the blaze beneath my dress exploded into a bonfire of ravenous wanting.

My hands explored his strong back, tugging at his shirt, unbuttoning his jeans. They found their way to his chiseled chest and lingered there until he scooped me up and carried me into the bedroom.

Slowly, Chance eased the dress off my shoulders, and it spilled to the floor. His shirt followed. Then he guided me to the bed, and his lips replaced his hands on my bosom. His mouth probed every inch of my breasts, as his fingers explored the depths of me until I just couldn't take it anymore.

I slipped him inside me and we moved together, our heat building until we reached a crescendo and exploded in each other's arms.

Afterward, we lay there in the darkness of my bedroom for a while, our hands clasped together, our bodies thoroughly satisfied. My cheek was resting on his chest, listening to the beat of his heart, when he said, "I heard you talking to Cinnamon."

I winced. Damn. I really wanted to tell him myself. "I was going to tell you. I just didn't get the opportunity."

He caressed my shoulder. "How long do you think you'll be gone?"

"I don't know."

He didn't say anything for a time. Then, "Is it dangerous?"

I sighed. I had never lied to him, not even when we were kids, and didn't intend to start now. Granted, no way was I going to tell him that there was a fairy named Pickle who'd be looking out for me and if things got really touchy, I could always summon up a goddess. After all, no one was that open-minded.

"It could be," I said, then rushed to add, "but I'll have Birdie and the aunts there to help."

He swallowed hard. "These people who have your mother. What if they lock you away too?"

"They won't, because I won't give them a reason to." I rolled over to face him, propped my head up by my elbow. "Don't worry. I always land on my feet."

Chance took my chin in his palms. "It's my job to worry about you. I'm in love with you, Stacy. I have been ever since I can remember. It's always been you." His voice was hoarse.

The intensity in his eyes and the seriousness of his tone startled me. My feelings for Chance ran deep, there was no question, but my life was such a mess, so unstable. Sometimes I thought it wasn't fair to hold on to him. That he should be with a woman who'd jump at the opportunity to become his wife, who'd give him three kids, cook pot roast on Sundays, and decorate the house for holidays.

But that's not the kind of woman I was. At least, not now.

I found his hand and kissed it, put it to my cheek. "I know you worry. I know you care. I can promise you that I'll be careful, and guarded. I promise I'll come home as soon as I can."

He sat up a bit higher in bed and looked at me. "That's all you have to say?"

I blinked a few times as he turned on the light.

"What else is there? I can't tell you there won't be more of these kinds of excursions, because I don't know that for certain. What I do know is that I have to bring my mother back."

Chance looked up at the ceiling and sighed. "That's not what I mean."

"What, then?" I sat up too.

He ran his fingers through his hair. "I just told you I'm in love with you. Don't you have anything to say to me?"

His eyes glimmered in the moonlight. Or was that mist?

My stomach twisted in knots and my pulse quickened. "Chance, you know how I feel about you." I reached for him, but he pulled away.

"See, that's just it. I don't know, because you never say it. Even now, you're about to fly halfway across the world and you won't say it."

"You're the best man I know."

He just stared at me for a few moments. Then he swung his legs over the bed and stood. Reached for his jeans.

"What are you doing?" I asked.

"I could ask you the same thing. Better yet, what are *we* doing?" He pointed from him to me.

"Don't do this. Chance, please."

He climbed into his pants. "I understood when you turned down my marriage proposal." Shrugged his shirt on. "I understood when you said you didn't want to live together." Grabbed his socks and shoes. "But dammit,

Stace, when the woman I love doesn't love me back, what's the point?"

I wrapped the sheet around me. "But I do. Chance, you know I do. Come on."

He left the room and walked toward the front door, grabbed his keys. I followed him. He turned, hand on the knob. "Then why don't you ever say it? I need to hear you say it."

"You're the most important person in my life," I whispered. "You're the only man I ever let in."

"But I'm not in, Stace. I'm standing on the porch in the pouring rain, waiting for you to open the door. I've been waiting ever since you left after graduation, ever since you came back last year. Even now, you've let me into your bed, but not into your heart. I'm still waiting."

How could I explain it to him? How could I make him see that in my world, when you got too close, knew too much, it destroyed lives? I couldn't allow that to happen to us. There was no telling where this path would take me now, and I couldn't let Chance get hurt because of something I was involved in. Hell, Ivy had been kidnapped, John's wife had been shot, my own mother was imprisoned. If anything happened to Chance, I would never forgive myself.

He said, "You know what I think? I think I'm a safety net for you. That it's just easy to be with me because of the years between us, and because I know all the secrets and I don't judge you by them."

"That's not true." Did he really believe that?

He looked at me sadly. "I don't want to be the guy on the sidelines anymore. I can't be that guy anymore."

As the door creaked open and I saw my closest friend about to walk away from me, I panicked. When your heart is racing, fear pumping through your veins, and you think you're on the verge of losing the only real thing you've ever had in this world, the truth rushes to the surface and demands to be heard.

I blurted, "They all leave." I struggled to keep composed, to restrain the tears bubbling behind my eyes.

He turned, questioning.

"Don't you see? My mom, my dad, my uncle, even Leo. The people I trusted, the people that were closest to me. Eventually, they just...go."

He paused. Then he said, "Stacy, what do I have to do to prove to you that I'm not going anywhere?"

I opened my mouth to say something, but nothing came out.

He sighed. "When you figure it out, please let me know." Then he left.

Chapter 18

I tossed and turned all night, hating the way Chance and I had left things, a knot of worry tangled in my stomach, not knowing what I could do to make things right, or if I would even have the time to do anything.

Why hadn't I just told him I loved him?

When the alarm finally pierced my ear at six a.m., I crawled out of bed and directly into the shower.

I quickly dressed and packed a week's worth of clothes, toiletries, and sundries, hoping that it would be enough. I shoved the Blessed Book on top of all that, slipped the amethyst necklace over my head, and put some bladder-wrack in my running shoe for safe ocean travel. Then I texted Gramps, asking if he could meet me at the cottage for our breakfast date.

The coffee was percolating, eggs scrambled, and toast poised to be browned when Gramps arrived twenty minutes later. Thor was still sleeping. His feet bucked, and small, whiney cries escaped his lips every so often, as if he were lost in a dream.

Gramps smelled of Old Spice and Irish Spring as he walked through the door. He gave me a big kiss, and I ushered him over to the breakfast bar, where the plates waited to be filled.

He said, "Sorry I couldn't make your birthday dinner, sweetheart."

I almost didn't make my birthday dinner, I thought. I waved my arm and said, "No worries, Gramps." I poured him a cup of black coffee and spooned some eggs onto his plate.

He thanked me. "Say, did Cinnamon give you that present?"

"Actually, Gramps, I wanted to ask you about that." I pulled out the locket. "Was this from you? I didn't recognize the handwriting on the card." I slid both the card and the locket toward my grandfather.

He reached into the inner pocket of his jacket and produced a pair of reading glasses, pushed them onto his nose. "No, it wasn't from me. Your father told me about the lockbox and the heirloom before he passed, but I didn't get it until the chief found it in his car. Said I was to hold on to it until you turned thirty." He met my eyes. "Frankly, I would have waited till next year, but when I spoke to your grandmother about dinner, she was going on and on about your thirtieth year, so I figured it must be a Geraghty thing." He winked at me, scanned the card.

"You figured right. So did my dad say who it belonged to or who it was from?"

The deep lines carved in his forehead crunched together as he thought for a moment. "No, I can't say that he did."

Damn. "What about the card. Does the script seem familiar to you?"

He glanced at it again and shook his head. "Sorry, honey. Can't say that it does." He sipped his coffee. "What's this about?" He passed the card back to me, and I slid it to the end of the counter.

I explained that we were all leaving that morning for Ireland, and that when we came back home, his daughter would be with us.

Gramps slowly set his coffee mug down. The rosy glow that usually colored his cheeks instantly faded.

"You mean you know where your mother is?" His voice was incredulous.

The question took me by surprise, as did the baffled look on his face. He didn't know where my mother was? Oh no. What did that mean? Birdie had kept it from me all these years—the slaying of the council member, my mother's incarceration—but I had never dreamed she would have withheld that information from Gramps.

Why would she do that?

I had the nagging sensation that I had just opened a can of worms that was meant to be sealed shut a while longer.

Gramps stood up, kicked the chair back, and threw his napkin on his plate. "Never mind. It's not your fault. It's hers."

The word "hers" clung to his lips like a bitter cocktail onion.

"Gramps, calm down. I'm sure she had her reasons."

Even as I said it, I didn't believe it. Hidden truths and untold secrets seemed to make up the very fabric of my grandmother.

Although now I had secrets of my own.

Gramps kissed me on the cheek and said, "This is between me and your grandmother, Stacy. Don't worry yourself over it."

He tried to smile, but it morphed into a grimace. He left me there staring at cold eggs and cloudy coffee, feeling like the kind of jerk who tells a kid there's no such thing as Santa Claus.

I rousted Thor and fed him the remainder of our breakfast, turned a few lights on in case Cin didn't make it over here before nightfall, grabbed my bags and dog, and hurried out the door.

Chance was sitting on the porch when I stepped outside. Thor greeted him with a delirious wag of his tail and a nuzzle on the chin, then ran off to chase a squirrel.

"Hi," I said.

"Hey."

He smiled at me, but he still looked forlorn. Even the adorable cleft in his chin that I found irresistible seemed to droop.

"I know I should have called, but—"

I said, "No, I'm glad you came. Look, Chance, I—"

He put his hand to my lips, whispered, "Shh. Me first, okay?"

I nodded.

"I don't know why I got so upset. I did a lot of thinking last night, and I had no right to put you on the spot like that." He pulled me onto his lap. "I know you, I know what you've been through, what"—he shifted his eyes to my suitcase—"you're still going through. I just wanted to tell you that I'm sorry, and that I'm here for you, if you'll have me."

I kissed him, then I pulled back and studied his face. He had the most sincere eyes I'd ever seen. I thought about Birdie and Gramps, about my mother and father and all the untold truths, the hushed shroud that lingered over Geraghty relationships like a plague just waiting to devour them.

And I realized that with Chance and me, there were no secrets. Or at least none that I could otherwise explain.

I said, "I trust you more than I trust my own family, you know that?"

"Well, they don't set the bar real high." He smiled at me, a silly, playful smile. The kind of smile shared by people with a lot of history. As I smiled back, a jolt of comprehension surged through me. Why I couldn't tell him I loved him, why I was afraid of falling too deep into each other.

"Chance, you're my best friend. If I ever lost that, if I ever lost you…" My voice cracked, unable to complete the thought.

He embraced me, his arms dancing up and down my back. He said softly, "That won't happen. Not ever. Even if this doesn't work out and we're married to other people in twenty years, you'll still be the cool chick who likes baseball, carries a sword, and can summon a boatload of fish just to cheer a guy up."

That was the day his grandfather died. We went fishing to get away from the veil of sadness hanging over his house, and the fish weren't biting. So I used one of Fiona's spells to rollick them. He loved it.

"I can't believe you remember that. We were what, twelve? Thirteen?" I asked.

"Somewhere around there."

I heard the back door slam at the Geraghty Girls' Guesthouse, and Fiona and Lolly emerged with their luggage.

Chance tossed his head to the side. "I'll go help them."

"Thanks."

As I watched him trot over to relieve Lolly of her hat case, I murmured, "I love you."

Then I saw a second-floor window open—Birdie's bedroom—and Gramps's hat flew out. I ran to the house, praying the rest of him wouldn't follow.

The suitcases were folded open on Birdie's bed, and she was doing a final inventory when that ex-husband of hers stormed into the room.

She didn't need to turn around to know it was him. The man was as predictable as gravity. He'd been using the same soap, the same shampoo, and wearing the same cologne for fifty years.

"Oscar, you lost the privilege to barge into my home when you signed those divorce papers thirty years ago."

"Brighid, I've never hit a woman in my life, but I swear you'd test the patience of Jesus."

Something in his voice forced her to turn around.

His face was beet red, and a large vein throbbed in his temple.

"Oscar, you don't look so well. Perhaps you should sit down. I'll get a glass of water." She pivoted to head to the bathroom, but he cut her off.

His frame blocked the door, and he kicked it shut behind him.

Birdie had never seen him so angry. Well, perhaps once, when she made his mother cry by refusing to marry in her church, but not since.

"What?" She threw her hands in the air. She really had no time for this. Thankfully, she had already spoken to John the evening before. The council would arrange for his transportation as well, and Ivy was already in Ireland, at the Academy. "What are you so upset about? And make it fast, because I'm in a hurry."

"Well, my darling, I wouldn't want to interrupt your schedule. Where exactly is it you're off to?" He shot a glare at her luggage.

He knows, Birdie thought. *It's about time he showed some interest.*

She crossed her arms. "I refuse to play games with you, Oscar. Speak your piece or go."

"Fine. How could you possibly refrain from telling me that our daughter is alive and well?"

Birdie looked at him, dumbfounded. "You can't be serious. I did tell you. I told you over and over. I've been telling you since the day you asked me to marry you."

Oscar shook his head, wagged a finger. "No, no, no. Don't try to pretend that those"—he used air quotes, and Birdie wanted to break his hands—"feelings, spells, and magic-mirror meetings had anything to do with her disappearance."

Birdie put her fists on her hips and cocked her head. "You know, Oscar, for such an intelligent man, you can be a ripe idiot. Not to mention a jackass." She advanced on him, forced him into a chair near the bedroom window.

"Now, you sit there and listen to me," she demanded.

She paced the length of the room, wringing her hands, wondering where to begin. She thought she had given him all the proof he needed, back when they were young, when they were in love. She had performed spells to enhance their lives, intensify their bond, even to boost success in his business endeavors. He probably wouldn't be nearly as wealthy or respected as he was if it weren't for her.

In the beginning, Birdie's young groom had given the impression that he believed, that he understood who she was, and that he accepted all of it, no matter the consequences. *I love all of you, Birdie, every recess of your soul,* he had said. But it didn't take long—perhaps until their fifth year of marriage—before she realized that Oscar was just patting her on the head to appease his bride as you would an imaginative child. He didn't truly believe, which meant he would never be supportive of the lifestyle, and it cracked Birdie's faith in him. In all men, truth be told. She had no use for that kind of nonsense.

Oscar was a good person, a decent man who adored his family and worked hard to provide for them. But the mate of a witch was required to be much more than that, especially the mate of a Geraghty.

The kind of man who doted, who wanted to solve his sweetheart's every problem, who "fixed" things, was the worst kind of man for a Geraghty woman. For as noble as they were, they sucked the power from a witch, made her weak, dependent—vulnerable to attack.

A man who loved a Geraghty woman had to be loyal, trustworthy, receptive, and confident enough to live in the shadow of her strength. He had to embrace her independence—encourage it, even—especially when she felt needy, when she wanted him to take the reins and guide her through the storm. He had to be masculine enough to understand that those were the worst times to do so, that she could stand on her own only through the challenges that tested her resolve.

Fifteen years after it started, Birdie's marriage was over. She stopped trying, stopped caring, hoping that one day their children and their grandchildren would enlighten the man.

But alas, that had not been the case. He was sitting in her bedroom like a virgin on her wedding night, expecting answers. But Birdie didn't have the time or the patience to explain everything she'd been explaining to him for decades.

Then she got an idea.

She snapped her fingers. "I've got it." She directed him to twist his chair to face the scrying mirror. While the mirror did not accept messages, it did record all conversations between two parties.

She pressed a button on the bottom of the scrying mirror, tapped the options a few times, and played all the conversations of the past day and a half.

Oscar sat in the chair, statue still, until the last message ended.

Birdie looked at him expectantly.

"This is a gag, right? You're punishing me because I didn't make it to Stacy's birthday dinner."

Birdie strode over to him, snatched the hat off his head, opened her window, and tossed it out. Then she yelled, "Get out." Pointed to the door.

Oscar stood up. "Now, just hang on a minute, Bird, give me a goddamn minute to process what you're telling me." He dragged his hands through his hair.

"You've had nearly fifty years to process what I am telling you. You chose not to."

He sank back in the chair, stared at the floor. "So this council, have they been treating her well?"

Birdie told him all she knew about their daughter's arrest and captivity, which wasn't much. She explained that contact had not been permitted.

"And this was because Stacy was in danger. The man she killed, I mean. He was going to kill Stacy?"

Birdie nodded.

Oscar stood again and looked out the window. "But doesn't that mean that Stacy may still be in danger? I mean, there must have been reason behind his intentions, correct? What if that reason still exists and someone else decides to act on it?"

Birdie scooted next to him, to see what caught his attention out the window. Anastasia was rushing toward the back door. Chance met her halfway, relieved her of her luggage.

Birdie hadn't considered what Oscar was suggesting. She had always believed that the man had come after Anastasia because he felt he was a Seeker, and with her out of the way, he could secure a point for nomination for the role. There were three stages at which one was brought to the attention of the council. Birth, one's teens, and one's thirtieth year. Only then could the confirmation be deemed official. But many Seekers faced tasks along the way, which only enhanced their chances of proving to the council who they truly were. After that, it was rumored, the locket would be presented.

Except Anastasia was already wearing it.

Or perhaps Birdie had been mistaken. Maybe it wasn't the Seeker's locket after all, but a piece of jewelry given to the girl by a friend for her birthday.

"Birdie?" Oscar said.

Birdie snapped her head his way. "I don't know. It's possible, I suppose."

"Then no." Oscar shook his head. "I can't let her go. I've lost so much, Birdie. I can't lose her too." He walked to her, placed his arms on her shoulders, and held her gaze.

The stale scent of remorse hung in the room. Echoes of loss, regret, and what-might-have-beens vibrated the walls.

But Birdie had no time for nostalgia.

She wriggled free of him. "It's the only way, Oscar. You don't know these people. We have to follow through with our promise."

"We can go to the police, tell them everything."

She railed at him. "Tell them what? Think, Oscar. This is a world that conflicts with the one you know. If you do anything of the sort, there is no telling what they will do to both our girls." She narrowed her eyes, slicing the air with her assertion. "That's not an option."

Oscar slapped his knees. "Well, then, there's only one thing left to do."

Birdie looked at the father of her daughter.

"I'm going with you."

He strolled out of the room, cell phone in hand.

Birdie's mouth hung open as a wave of Old Spice followed Oscar out the door.

Chapter 19

Chance was loading my bags into Birdie's car when my grandfather banged through the screen door.

Gramps winked at me. I was about to say something, but he held up a finger. That's when I noticed the phone covering his ear.

"Yeah, Roger? Listen, buddy, I need a favor." He slipped around the burning bush and disappeared behind the house.

Birdie soared through the door next, her head swinging every which way. She saw me and said, "Where is he?"

Not knowing what was going on, and not wanting to get bumped farther up Gramps's shit list, I said, "Who?"

Birdie waltzed toward me. "You couldn't have waited until your mother was home, hmm? You had to tell him?"

"Whoa." I put my hands up, blocking her aggression. "I had no idea he didn't know about Mom. I can't imagine why you never told him, Birdie."

"What?" She prickled, smacked her lips together, then sucked in some air. "I did tell him, but you don't know the man like I do. He's bullheaded, and…"

She must have seen the confused look on my face, because she flung her arm in the air and said, "Never mind. I'll explain later."

Couldn't wait for that conversation.

She rushed off toward the front of the house. I silently rooted for Gramps.

Chance jogged over to me. "Birdie have any bags?"

"Upstairs, I'm sure. I'll help you."

We came down with Birdie's suitcases a few minutes later, and walked into a heated argument.

"You are not coming." Birdie looked as if fire would shoot out her ears at any moment.

"Yes I am. It's all arranged." Gramps pivoted to Chance. "Hey, Chance, set those down and give me a hand with the bags you put away, will you? We won't be taking Birdie's car."

Chance started for the Cadillac.

Birdie said, "You will do no such thing, young man."

Chance hesitated, looked from one to the other.

Gramps pooh-poohed Birdie with a flick of his wrist. "Pay no attention to her."

Chance trotted forward and opened the car door.

"Chance, who do you think could disrupt your life more?" Birdie asked this from where she stood on the back patio.

Poor Chance didn't know what the hell to do. His gaze darted to my grandmother, and then beyond. My guess was he was looking at the back step, probably recalling Leo wrapped up like an egg roll the night before. He shut the door.

"Come on, boy, you're not afraid of an old lady, are you?" This from my grandfather.

All three Geraghty Girls reeled at Gramps. It was fifty degrees and overcast, but Chance started glistening like he was sitting in a sauna.

I waved an imaginary flag. "All right, that's enough. All of you." I headed for Chance, passed a stern look from Birdie to Gramps along the way, and hissed, "You two ought to be ashamed of yourselves."

Chance shook his head and smirked.

I reached up to kiss him. "I appreciate you helping out at the asylum, but I think they all need a medication adjustment. Probably best if you go."

"You sure?" He shifted his eyes past me. "You're outnumbered."

I laughed. "Yeah, I've got this."

He squeezed me tight, said he'd miss me, and I told him I'd call as soon as I was able. I watched him head down and around the driveway of the bed-and-breakfast and toward the cottage where his truck was parked.

He waved as he drove off.

A stretch limousine rolled into the driveway then. The driver got out and said, "Pickup for the airport?"

"We'll just be a few minutes." I tilted my head toward Birdie's car. "But you can grab the bags in the backseat." I ran back to the house.

Birdie and Gramps were still bickering.

"Someone want to tell me what's going on?" I asked.

Gramps jumped in to plead his case before my grandmother had a chance to open her mouth. "I've arranged for transportation for all of us to go to Ireland."

Birdie crossed her arms, darted her eyes to Gramps. "You're not going." Her eyes slid to me. "He could jeopardize everything. There's no telling how he could bungle this."

I wasn't sure why Birdie objected to Gramps's tagging along, but I suspected I didn't want to know, that it was between the two of them.

"She's my daughter too," Gramps said.

The hurt in his eyes was heartbreaking, but there was determination there too. Was it redemption he was chasing? For what? He couldn't have prevented what had happened to my mother any more than the rest of us, my father included. It wasn't right to leave him in the dark on this. Gramps loved us—all of us—and he'd always been there, whenever or wherever we needed him.

Birdie said, "He knows nothing about the council, about how any of this works."

I rolled my eyes. "To be fair, Birdie, neither did I until a few months ago."

"I have money. You never know when that will come in handy," Gramps said, flapping a wad of bills in front of Birdie's face.

"He has a point there." Bribe money. Hell, maybe we could buy Mom's freedom if things went sour.

Birdie said, "That won't do us any good."

Gramps remained composed. He looked like a man sitting on a royal flush. "Well, then how about a plane navigated by a pilot guaranteed to have no affiliation with the people who kidnapped our daughter? Not to mention the nut who came for our granddaughter."

That clinched it for me. Having been hunted more times than I cared to count, I was all for flying friendly skies and getting to the island with all functioning body parts still attached. I looked at Birdie. "He goes."

I whistled to Thor, who galloped to my side. Gramps decided to quit while he was ahead and strutted away.

"Excuse me? What makes you think you get to decide?" Birdie poked my shoulder.

I shrugged. "Easy, Grandma. I'm the Seeker. I've got a sword and everything." I grinned and kissed her cheek.

"Well, I'm the Mage, and you need me too. All four corners, right? So what if I decide not to go?" She raised one threatening eyebrow.

Fiona piped up, "Actually, Birdie, you aren't technically the Mage."

I whipped my head around. "What?"

Birdie glowered at her sister.

"Who is?" I asked.

"Technically, it was Tallulah who was confirmed," Fiona said.

Birdie flashed Fiona an inflamed look.

I was flabbergasted. I stepped directly in front of Birdie. "Oh, come on, are you going to tell me that you'd let that bitch take your place?" I grabbed the purse from my grandmother's shoulder. "Please." I trekked toward the limo.

"I still don't like this," Birdie called from behind me.

"Protest noted," I said. "Now get in the car."

Except for the driver's rigid disapproval of traveling with a dog the size of a pony, the ride to the airport was quiet and uneventful.

Birdie made a few phone calls, explaining the change in plans to whomever it concerned. She jotted down notes here and there and made assurances that we were still on schedule, whatever that meant.

Gramps was silently watching the scenery fly by, and Lolly and Fiona were indulging in the minibar.

Over an hour later, the sun was shining brightly as the limousine wove around a bend and into the small airport parking lot. Gramps went inside to "take care of paperwork," and Birdie followed. I clipped a leash on to Thor so he could drain his breakfast.

A man came to collect our bags. I dug around for the maps Badb had given me. I didn't want those in the belly of the aircraft. I was hoping to learn more about the council, the cauldron, Tallulah, and her grandson—perhaps even formulate some sort of plan—while we were in flight.

I also couldn't wait to hear the Mage story. If Fiona insisted it was Birdie, yet the council had appointed Tallulah, what had happened?

As much as I was dreading this trip and the daunting task that lay ahead of us (because it was the only thing standing in the way of my mother's freedom), I had to admit I was looking forward to a showdown with the almighty Tallulah.

I suspected perhaps Birdie was too. That boosted my confidence, knowing that we were on the same side, had the same goals in mind, even the same enemies. It wasn't just my quest this time, it was a family affair.

A custodial twinge clawed at my ribs, a need to safeguard my grandmother from the demons she might face as she confronted her past.

How would she handle it?

How would I?

The engine of a plane rocketed to life, bursting my thought bubble, and I watched a small jet drift down the runway, nudging its way into position.

Gramps came out of the building and said, "Everybody ready?"

Birdie and I shared a look.

"Yes," we said.

Chapter 20

An hour into the flight, both Thor and Oscar had fallen asleep, upside down, with their tongues dangling over their cheeks. Birdie, her sisters, and her granddaughter were huddled around a table, maps spread out in the center. Birdie was enraptured by the transformation in her granddaughter. The girl seemed energized, but there was something else. It took Birdie a moment to discover what it was, but then she knew.

The light that had been switched off so long ago was back on.

Anastasia was explaining what the goddess had told her. "So the red circles indicate where the cauldron had been sheltered over the years, peacefully, and this"—she pointed to the location of Trinity College—"is where it was taken when it was last stolen, just before the Great Famine."

The girl grabbed a bottle of water from the table and swigged it. Then she questioned Birdie and her sisters. "So what do you guys think? Any chance it's there again?"

Fiona said, "I suppose anything is possible, but it was a professor who stole it then. A madman, really. He moved it often, hiding it all around the campus, disguising the cauldron in plain sight."

"Blasphemous," Lolly said, sipping a whiskey sour.

Fiona continued, "He even put it on display for a time in the library."

"So what happened?" Anastasia asked.

Birdie stood, stretched. "The Seeker of the era was nearly worn out, when she finally tracked him down."

"What do you mean?" Anastasia asked, looking nervous.

"It was a long journey, six years total," Birdie said.

Lolly said, "Many lives lost."

Anastasia swallowed hard. "That long. Why?"

"For starters, he was the Mage," Fiona said.

"And he had managed to convince the Guardian and the Warrior to join forces with him in his despicable plan," Birdie said.

Lolly said, "Only the Seeker remained true to her cause."

"Is that why there's no mention of the Mage in the Blessed Book?"

Birdie sat back down. She clasped her granddaughter's hands. "Yes. That was your great-grandmother's way of locking up the most painful stretch of her life. You see, it was her cousin who was Seeker. The entire ordeal ravaged your grandmother. The eviction from her land, watching her neighbors, loved ones, wither away and die, the emigration from the ancient soil—it was a lot to bear."

Anastasia looked at her shoes. Kicked the table. "Six years." She stood, went to gaze out the window.

Birdie felt her heart tug at her granddaughter's obvious worry. She wanted to tell her that everything would be all right, that she was strong, that her destiny dictated she had to be. But the girl had to come to that conclusion on her own.

"She wasn't you, Stacy," Fiona said.

"But she was a Seeker," the girl replied, her back to them.

"That is all she was. You are much, much more. Your talent, your abilities, surpass any I have ever seen," Lolly said.

"Plus, you have mastered the gift of necromancy, become a leader for your familiar, honed your spell crafting. The visions, the dreams, you understand them now, even learned to tune in to the physical alerts your body sends to you." Birdie paused to see if that had sunk in.

"I haven't had any visions or dreams lately, and only one spirit has visited me."

"Hecate's skirt, child, you've been too busy summoning the goddess. Literally." Birdie watched as the corners of her granddaughter's mouth curled up.

Anastasia turned, smiling. "I guess I did do that, didn't I?"

The Geraghty sisters nodded.

The girl stepped forward. "What I don't understand is why the Mage stole the cauldron."

"Greed," Birdie said.

Fiona elaborated. "Ireland was a conquered country. It fell under the rule of the British government, became a member of the United Kingdom in 1801."

Birdie said, "The Celtic grazing lands, held by the same families for centuries, were seized, colonized, and carved up by the new government. Lofty rents were enforced, along with exorbitant taxes."

"And the money," Fiona said, "was spent on England."

"Farmsteads shrunk as middlemen began managing properties for landlords," Birdie said. "More parcels meant more money to line their pockets."

Lolly said, "And more tax dollars sent to the crown. Six million pounds in 1842 alone."

Anastasia gasped.

"Evicted from their pastureland and forced to farm smaller patches, the Irish searched for a more suitable crop that would feed their families in tighter quarters," Fiona said.

"So they turned to the potato," said Birdie. "It became the sole source of nourishment."

Anastasia said, "And then disease struck."

The three Geraghty sisters nodded.

"I still don't see what the professor's goal was in stealing the cauldron," the girl asked.

Birdie explained. "He saw what had been happening to his countrymen ever since the Act of Union. Farmers and the working classes were stripped to a shameful level of barrenness. So he accelerated the decline of an already impoverished populace by inciting a famine. He thought he had the key to riches. He was certain that the cauldron would fetch a hefty price from anyone who cared about the island and her people. He first approached John O'Connell, a politician who was born of wealth, but that backfired because the O'Connell clan had also been ripped from their homestead. He tried others, but he soon realized that there was no coin in Irish pockets. So then he approached Lord Heytesbury, lieutenant of Ireland, and his plan failed there as well."

"What happened?" Anastasia asked.

Fiona interjected. "He underestimated the cruelty and apathy of the government. England, you see, was exporting crops from the land even during the harshest years of the Hunger."

"The globe's richest empire was systematically murdering the native people of the world's most fertile land," Birdie said.

"So why not return the cauldron if he couldn't get a price for it?" Anastasia asked.

"Because by that time, the council had a bounty on his head. The fact that only he knew where it was located kept him alive," Fiona said.

"Until the Seeker found him," said Lolly gravely.

The girl looked at her grandmother, wide-eyed. "I hope you don't expect me to…"

"We don't do that anymore," Birdie said.

"Good to know," said Anastasia.

The girl took a deep breath and hunched over the map again, pointing out leylines and describing a Fae person named Pickle who would help navigate them for her. She explained the instructions given to her: that their best bet was to gather all four corners and head to the Hill of Summoning.

"I know what it looks like, they showed me a picture, but do you know where that is?" Anastasia asked.

The sisters exchanged glances, confused.

Fiona said, "Why don't you describe it, dear?"

Anastasia described an ancient mound in the Boyne Valley, with steps planted in the grass that led to the top.

"It looked like it was in a rural area. More remote than Newgrange," she said.

Birdie was grateful to hear that. Newgrange, while a spectacular example of the Tuatha Dé Danann's knowledge of astrophysics, was a tourist mecca. The fewer people around, the better, for what they were up against.

Fiona said, "Could it be Fourknocks?"

Birdie pointed at her sister. "That's it. I'm certain of it. I cannot recall another mound carved with stone steps."

Anastasia was pleased. "Great. So then all we have to do, after each corner connects with its treasure, is meet there, stand at the top, and weave an enchantment. Danu said the cauldron will lead us to it."

Fiona nodded, as did Lolly.

Birdie smiled, an anxious quiver pinching at her nerves.

She had the disturbing sense that their quest would not be so facile.

It was dark when we arrived in Ireland. There were no houses or businesses that I could see from the light cast by the plane. Just a hilly landscape that swelled and dipped for miles. The nose jerked and jutted for a few brief, terrifying moments before the wheels mercifully bounced down and we finally skidded to a stop on a stretch of pavement the size of a postage stamp.

There were no vehicles, no planes, no airport terminal. Nothing except green grass, a few looming trees weary from carrying their aging limbs, and a handful of painted sheep in the distance.

"Where are we?" I peered out the window opposite my seat.

Birdie said, "We're in Connemara. A driver is scheduled to meet us here to take us to the castle in Cong."

Birdie pulled Gramps aside to have a few words with him. He nodded and went to the cockpit to speak with Roger.

All I could think about, as we were led off the plane and Roger helped us collect our luggage, was that I was one step closer to seeing my mother.

My heart leaped at the prospect.

Thor pranced around the dewy grass, inspecting this strange new land. Lolly had packed sandwiches for us to eat on the plane. Since he had slept most of the way, I fed him his share now. I asked Birdie if we were going to pass a store on the way to the castle. Told her I needed food for Thor. She said we weren't stopping, that we were headed straight there, and that there would be more than enough food and drink to feed all of us for a month.

"Let's hope that won't be necessary," I said.

Gramps said, "What do you mean we can't stop? I don't have any clothes."

Birdie snapped at him. "You should have thought about that before crashing our soiree."

Soiree? Really?

Lolly tapped him on the shoulder, kicked open her trunk, and flashed plenty of men's slacks, shirts, and undergarments. She unzipped a side compartment to expose a shaving kit.

Gramps hugged her and said, "Ever the sister-in-law. Thanks, Loll." Then he smirked at Birdie.

The mysterious workings of Aunt Lolly continuously amazed me. I used to marvel at her superpower of knowing exactly what to pack for any given occasion. Now I just admired the accuracy of her projections. The irony that half the time she could hardly dress herself, however, was not lost on me.

As that thought threaded through my mind, it dawned on me that I was the only one not swathed in the finest evening wear.

"When did you all change?" I asked, dumbstruck.

Fiona was applying ruby-red lipstick. "On the plane, dear." She was wearing a strapless, nude cocktail dress overlaid with black lace.

Birdie's gown was a swirl of russet tones, highlighted by a beaded, one-shoulder neckline. "We tried to wake you," she said.

I didn't even know I had fallen asleep.

Lolly said, "Not to worry, Stacy. You can change outside the castle." She adjusted the peplum on her dress. It was the color of blackberries.

I couldn't believe it. We were here to find a cauldron and get my mother back. What the hell were they dressing up for? My suitcase was stuffed with sweatshirts and jeans.

"Change for what?" I asked.

They all three looked at me as if I had just picked my teeth with a fork.

Birdie spoke first. "You don't just show up to a castle in travel clothes. You enter its halls draped in elegance."

"It's a sign of respect," Lolly said.

"Not only to the castle, but to the men and women who defended it with their lives." Fiona smacked her lips in the mirror of her compact.

"Not to mention the council." Birdie fluffed her hair with a comb.

Uh-oh. How to bring this up? I sighed. "Here's the thing. I didn't pack any special-occasion clothes."

Fiona snapped her mirror shut and plopped it back in her purse. "That's all right, sweetheart. Just wear the dress Aunt Lolly made you."

Oh, geez. "Great idea, Fiona."

Lolly grinned, pulled out a flask from a garter strapped to her thigh, and took a swig.

"And I would, except I didn't pack that either."

Birdie rolled her eyes and groaned. "Do you mean to tell me you planned on meeting the oldest secret society on the planet in sneakers and dungarees?"

"Nobody calls them dungarees anymore, Birdie."

Gramps leaned in and said, "Great idea. Poke the bear." Then he disappeared behind some bushes.

Headlights shone in the distance.

"Honestly, Anastasia," Birdie said.

"No one told me," I said.

Seriously, how was I supposed to know it was prom night?

"Just get your bags. Perhaps one of your aunts will have something suitable for you to wear."

Lolly cringed, "I don't think she would fit anything I have. She's at least two sizes smaller than me." She looked at Fiona.

The middle Geraghty Girl shrugged. "I only brought the one dress."

Birdie said, "Just get your bags, all of you. The car's coming."

I jogged over to where my bag was propped near the plane. Just before I reached it, I slipped on the slick grass and skidded into a pile of sheep dung.

Well, this oughta help, I thought.

Chapter 21

Lolly had a package of wet wipes, and I used the whole thing to scrape the crap off my jeans. I wanted to change, but Birdie wouldn't allow it.

"No time for that," she said.

So now I was sitting in the front seat of a Cadillac Escalade next to a guy who looked strikingly like Cinnamon's husband. His name was Gary, and I tried to make small talk, but he was none too happy about being stuck with the stinky girl. Kept answering me in grunts, so I gave up.

Thirty long minutes later, the SUV snaked its way down a winding road lined with gnarled, medieval oaks. A mist had settled in for the night, and the trees seemed to be draped in gossamer, as if waiting for us to pass so they could continue weaving a veil for a phantom bride. Occasionally, a pair of glowing eyes penetrated the brush.

Gary slowed down as we came upon a thick river flowing beneath a narrow footbridge. Spotlights shone along the route then, highlighting two massive rock towers outfitted with arrow loops, a set of threatening iron gates between them. The gates reluctantly unfolded as we approached. The towers that flanked the bridge were each forged with battlement walls that joined forces with a barbican clutching iron spikes.

Beyond that, the castle punctured the night sky.

I wasn't sure what I had been expecting, but it wasn't this.

The stone structure sprawled across the landscape, its walls, towers, and turrets reaching out from its belly like bold tentacles marching across the ground, proudly claiming the land as its own. The waning moon hung low in the sky, a jewel in the crown of the castle. A dusting of clouds slowly rolled in, strangling the pinnacles of the tallest tower.

I felt my jaw go slack at the intimidating size of the place. It had to span three football fields, at least.

The driver maneuvered the car around a circular brick driveway and cut the engine. He jumped out, unloaded all of our belongings, and sped off, probably in search of an all-night car wash.

A few narrow steps, guarded by menacing gargoyles, rose up to meet an impressive door with a Celtic-knot knocker and an iron handle the size of a baseball bat.

I jumped when it yawned open before anyone knocked, half expecting Herman Munster to charge out.

Instead, the slight woman who stood before our group resembled Tinker Bell.

A shag of blonde hair framed her pale face, and I was willing to bet she couldn't reach those amusement-park signs that say YOU MUST BE THIS TALL TO BOARD THE ROLLER COASTER.

"Welcome to the castle of the council. My name is Elizabeth," she said in a voice way too loud for her body. "I trust your travels were comfortable?"

Birdie affirmed they were, and the woman ushered us all inside as an owl screeched through the forest.

I dropped my bags on the navy carpet, and Thor sat down next to me with a harrumph.

The ceilings of the foyer reached higher than the trees we just passed. If it weren't for the Gothic archways that divided the space into smaller rooms, it could have housed an Olympic-sized pool. Four sets of stairs enticed guests to explore different wings of the castle. Two were near the front, two pushed to the back.

Elizabeth walked past a white statue of a god and goddess clinging to each other near a marble-topped desk. She picked up the telephone receiver that sat on the desk, said a few words I couldn't make out, and then hung up.

"Aedon will be with you momentarily." She opened a drawer and pulled out a stack of papers and a handful of keys.

We were still clustered in a semicircle near the door as she handed each of us a folded map. "I'm afraid it's a bit late for a tour, but this map will guide you to your rooms. I've made it a point to label each with your names beside the rooms you'll be assigned, as well as marking the important areas that you'll need to find, such as the Great Hall, the Dining Room, the Library, and, of course, the Court of O'Conor."

"O'Conor?" I asked.

She wrinkled her nose, either at the stench wafting off me or at my stupid question—I couldn't be sure which.

"Turlough O'Conor, king of Connacht and high king of Ireland." She gestured to the space all around us. "The castle was built for him in 1120."

I nodded.

"Shall I send for someone to collect the luggage?" she asked.

"We can manage, thank you," Gramps said.

"Very well." She pursed her thin lips, nodded, and clicked off down the hall and around the corner.

Aedon. The name rang a bell. "Birdie, who is Aedon?"

"An old friend."

"Is there anything I should know? Anything you want to tell me before he gets here so I don't look foolish?" I asked.

Elizabeth had seemed put off by my lack of knowledge of the castle's history. I didn't want to make the same mistake with Aedon.

"I'm afraid that ship has sailed," Birdie said grimly, eyeballing my attire.

"Are you going to hang that over my head the whole trip?" Footsteps sounded from a short distance away, so I dropped the subject.

A silver-haired man with an air of distinction and the scent of juniper entered the room a moment later. He smiled at my grandmother and stepped forward to kiss her, his crisp suit refusing to wrinkle. "Birdie. It's been too long."

Gramps shifted uncomfortably.

The man shook my aunts' hands, introductions passed, and then he turned his sights on me. "And you must be Stacy."

I nodded.

He cast me a dubious look, flicked his eyes at Thor, and said to my grandmother, "Why is she dressed like a vagrant?"

Birdie flashed a *kids—what are you going to do?* look.

"Hey," I protested.

He leaned in to shake my hand, then hesitated.

"You smell like a barnyard animal."

"I'm aware."

"This is the Seeker? Are you sure?" Aedon questioned Birdie.

Why does everyone keep asking that?

He turned back and decided to take my hand anyway, and instantly a vision pierced my mind. The school. The bus. Hill of Tara. This man was the boy from the field trip. The one who assured me Birdie would be okay, despite Tallulah's taunts.

A jolt passed between us, and something in Aedon's eyes said he felt the power surge too, maybe even recollected the memory of that trip. Of me.

I jerked my hand back. If he did remember, or if he were to grasp a vision of me from that day, he might tell Birdie. After what happened in the Web of Wyrd, how the goddesses couldn't send me home, I wasn't sure that was a good idea. I had no plans to mess with the space-time continuum ever again.

Aedon was frozen in front of me for a split second. Then he snapped out of it, clapped his hands together, and said, "Well, then. I'm sure you are all exhausted. You've had a long day, probably want to get to your room, relax, wash up."

That last bit, aimed at me.

"Just some housekeeping notes first." He pivoted slightly to address the group. "Help yourself to anything you find in your suite. Every refrigerator is fully stocked. There are robes, towels, toiletries, extra blankets, and pillows. Should you need something, make a note of it and I'll alert the staff in the morning."

Fiona thanked him.

Aedon continued. "We expect the Guardian to arrive shortly, so we are fully prepared to conduct business first thing in the morning. The Warrior will join us virtually. Nine o'clock, in the Court of O'Conor room." He glanced around. "Questions?"

We all shook our heads, and Aedon disappeared through one of the archways.

My family and I said our good nights and parted ways, in search of warm beds and hot showers.

Or maybe the shower wish was just me.

The map Elizabeth had provided indicated that my room was up the far back staircase, to the left, and down a long corridor. I walked past several richly paneled walls until I came upon the stairs. Before I ascended them, I cast one look behind me. Birdie was doing the same. She winked at me once, from the first step of the staircase on the right, near the front half of the castle.

I nodded and began to climb.

At the top of the landing, a stout fireplace anchored the rounded nook. There was a chair next to it, with a pair of reading glasses tossed on the seat beside an open book, pages down, waiting for its reader to return.

I looked at the spine. *A Witch's Guide to Astral Projection.* I glanced at Thor. "Interesting reading."

He whinnied and moseyed down the corridor, past a portrait of a woman with ferocious eyes and wild hair.

As I edged by it, I got the spooky feeling those eyes were following my movements. A shiver raced through me.

Thor glued his nose to the ground, implanting every step into his brain. I was grateful for that, because I was pretty sure—map or no map—that not even a trail of bread crumbs would help me find my way out of here.

After an eternity of brocade wallpaper and endless knights of armor, I found the room.

I dropped my bags, slipped the key into the lock, and opened the door, not sure what I would find.

The relaxing scent of lavender greeted me, but most rewarding was the sheer luxury of the suite.

The bathroom was bigger than my entire cottage, equipped with double sinks, a walk-in shower with steam jets, a Jacuzzi, and a sauna. The sitting room had a flat-screen television, a writing desk, two sofas, and a wet bar. Beyond that, a mammoth bed, drenched in a cloud of pillows, was positioned near a window. A twin bed butted against the far wall, and there was still enough space for a walk-in closet.

I grabbed my suitcases and carted them into the bedroom.

Moonlight spilled through the large window as I set my luggage on the bench beneath it. A bouquet of gardenias was perched on the nightstand, lending a sweet aroma to the space.

Gardenias. My mother's favorite. I drank in the fragrance while Thor leaped onto the larger bed, circled around three times, and nestled his snout into a big, fluffy pillow.

I went to have a look out the window. The back of the castle was as majestic as the front, with more towers, turrets, and corbels jutting out from the main body. There was a courtyard down below, a gushing fountain pinned to its center. Above, a wall walk capped the castle, waiting for an armed sentry to pound the platform in search of encroaching enemies. A seagull screamed in the distance, and I noticed a lake claiming several islands as prisoners.

I closed the curtain and turned around, and the ghost was bobbing in front of me.

I swear my heart skipped six beats.

"Haven't we been through this? Stop doing that to me." I slapped at her, touching nothing but air.

She shrugged an apology, said, "Keep the locket safe, guard it well. When you most need it, time will tell," and vanished.

"Wait. Please don't go, Riddler. What does it do? Tell me why it's important. What does it mean?" I called, frustrated.

Thor lifted his head, yawned, and went back to sleep.

I sighed, crossed the room, filled up a sink full of water in the bathroom for Thor, and used the facilities. As I washed my hands, there was a knock at the door. I poked my head out, expecting to see Birdie or one of the aunts, but no one was there.

Maybe I'd taken too long to answer.

I stepped outside the room and ventured down the hall, past another suit of armor, hoping to find Birdie's room.

The hall was quiet, the only illumination supplied by a stained-glass lamp hanging in a corner where the hallway curved. The glow from the glass pattern cast odd shapes along the walls, like tiny dragons trying to claw their way to freedom.

The hair on the back of my neck stood up then.

Someone called my name.

I whirled around.

Vacant. I hurried back toward my room, toward my familiar, toward my weapons.

Just before I reached it, I was seized from behind. An unyielding, cold hand clamped my mouth shut.

Chapter 22

Why did I never have my sword when I needed it?

I couldn't scream, so I kicked, elbowed, stomped, and flailed, managing only to bang up my own limbs, because what was holding me was that damn suit of armor.

Then I heard, "Pipe down, sweet cheeks. It's me."

That voice. I knew that irritating South Side twang. "John?"

He loosened his grip, raised his face guard, and wiggled his eyebrows.

Jackwagon.

I slammed the mouthpiece shut and pounded on the helmet with a closed fist.

"Ah! You trying to make me go deaf?" he squeaked.

I let go and he removed the helmet, his dark hair shooting out from his head like a sparkler.

"Why are you wearing that? And why the hell are you trying to give me a heart attack? I've got enough on my plate without having to deal with your annoying ass."

"Easy, sister, it was a joke. Lighten up."

"It wasn't funny, and I'm not your sister. What do you want?"

"I wanted to touch base with you before that meeting tomorrow." His voice took on a serious tone. He quickly scouted the hallway. "Listen, something stinks around here, and it ain't just you." He made a face. "What did you do to yourself, anyway? Roll around in horse shit?"

"Close. Sheep shit."

"Why?"

I waved my hand in the air. "Can we hurry this along? I need to burn these clothes."

"Sorry. Anyways, I can't put my finger on it, but something about this whole thing—the cauldron, the meeting, the fast track of gettin' us all out here—it's fishy, you know?"

"How so?"

John frowned. "Well, since when do we need a meeting to do a job, you know what I'm sayin'? And they got us spread out all over the place. Why? Why not clump us all together? And that Tallulah, did you meet her?" He whistled. "I thought her dad was harsh when I met him at my confirmation, but boy, is she a piece of work."

"Can't argue with you there. What about Ivy? Do you know where she is?"

"That's another thing. She's at the Academy, training, see? It's an important year for her. She's up for another nomination point. Anyways, they don't mind doin' a virtual meeting with her. Why her and not us? She's all the way on the east side of the island."

"I think I can shed some light on that."

I explained to him about the Hill of Summoning, and how it was located in the Boyne Valley, and what we needed to do to find the cauldron. Everything except where I had acquired the information, because although he was a Guardian, I thought the Web of Wyrd might be too much for John. I was hoping he assumed that my source was my family's book of theology. He had his own, so he understood that each Blessed Book was unique.

I said, "We'll be headed that way. We can collect Ivy on the way to the mound."

He nodded, contemplating that tidbit. "I guess that makes sense." Then he groaned, "Man, I do not want to work with that Tallulah."

"You won't have to," I said.

He gave me a curious look. "She's the Mage. I thought you just said the four corners would be working on this."

"That's true, except Birdie is the Mage."

"Your grandmother? No shit?" He looked at me stealthily. "Wow. Two in one family. Don't happen too often." John met my eyes. "Just be careful. That's all I'm sayin'."

"Will do."

He winked, wrestled his helmet back on his head, and clanked away.

I locked myself in my room, indulged in a hot shower, and crawled into the bed utterly exhausted.

As I lay there listening to the wind slicing through the water, images of the riddler ghost, the castle, and my mother flashed in my mind.

Before I drifted off to sleep, someone called my name.

A ringing, like an old-fashioned telephone's, startled me awake.

"What is that?" I mumbled.

There was no phone that I could locate anywhere in the room. I climbed into a velvety robe and warm slippers and shuffled into the sitting room, then the bathroom.

Still no phone, but the ringing stopped. I grabbed a bottle of water from the fridge, went back into the bathroom, and turned on the sauna. I set the water down and did my morning routine.

Ring! Ring!

I rushed out of the bath, armed with a towel.

By this time, even Thor was annoyed. He hopped off the bed, thundered into the sitting room, and jumped at the television set.

"Thor, no!"

Instantly, it fizzed into action and I saw Birdie.

Thor grumbled at me and lumbered into the bedroom. I heard the mattress springs squeak as he climbed back into bed.

"Good morning, Birdie."

"Good morning, Anastasia."

"So, is this like a scrying-mirror thing?" I pointed to the television.

"The council is much more advanced than we are. This is just an inter-room connection. You simply dial the person's room number. The instructions are in the console."

I filtered through the drawer beneath the TV and found a booklet. "Thanks."

My grandmother was dressed in a simple pantsuit, her hair blown into sultry waves, her makeup expertly applied. She was radiant.

"You look beautiful."

She smiled. "Thank you. It's the island. All that fresh sea air is good for the skin."

From somewhere behind her I heard, "Ha!"

Sounded like Fiona.

"What does she mean by that?" I asked.

Birdie shot Fiona a rueful look. "Nothing. Your aunt thinks she knows me better than I know myself."

"When it comes to affairs of the heart, I do," Fiona said.

That tickled my curiosity. "You and Gramps?" I smiled.

An uneasy look crossed Birdie's face. Like that of a trapped animal.

Fiona didn't say anything more.

"Sleep well?" Birdie awkwardly changed the subject, and I decided my grandmother's romantic life did not concern me.

"Yes. What time is it?"

"Seven. We must prepare for the meeting. Get dressed and come to my room within the half hour." She clicked off the screen.

I shuffled back to the bedroom and unzipped my bag.

That's when I saw her.

She was strolling through the courtyard, a basket in her hand, gathering herbs. She stopped to pluck a sprig of rosemary, and her auburn hair cascaded all the way down her back.

I threw open the window, stuck my head out, and screamed. "Mom!"

She glanced in my direction, just as I heard a rattling from above. I looked up in time to see the rope snap on the old pulley window. I yanked my head inside a split second before the pane came crashing down. The glass splintered but didn't shatter.

When I looked back, she was gone.

Behind me, I heard the deep, menacing growl of a giant dog. I turned to find Thor standing on the bed, his head bent low, canines flashing, muscles tense. His anger was aimed at the window.

"It's okay, buddy. It broke, that's all."

He let out one long, deafening roar that would have made me wet myself had I not known him.

I waited. Watched him.

A moment later, Thor relaxed. He settled onto the bed, ears still alert, and I patted his huge tan head.

There was no time for the sauna, so I flipped it off and twisted the dials for the shower instead. I snapped a plastic cap over my head, grabbed the spa products that were tucked into a pretty silver basket, and discarded my robe.

As I soaped up, I wondered if I had been hallucinating. Was the woman in the garden really my mother? Or had I imagined her because I so desperately wanted it to be so? The crater in my heart carved by my mother's disappearance would never be filled until I saw her, spoke with her, touched her. If the redhead was Mom, did that mean she wasn't under lock and key? And if she wasn't, why hadn't she visited me? Did she know I was here at the castle? Perhaps Birdie would know the answer to that question. Maybe her friend Aedon would allow me to see my mother. After all, we had dropped everything to rush here per his request. That should count for something.

I was rinsing soap from my eyes when the bathroom door creaked shut. The frosted glass of the shower was foggy, so I rubbed the condensation away with my palm. "Is someone there?"

Birdie, impatient as always, I thought, but I saw no one.

I twisted both knobs, shutting off the water, and grabbed the towel that hung over the door. I was nearly dry when the hot water blasted on again.

"What the hell?"

I turned the handle to the off position once more. Then the steam jets screeched to life at full throttle, scalding my skin.

I screamed and pushed on the shower door, but it wouldn't budge. I heard Thor trying to claw his way to me from the other side of the bathroom door.

The nozzles fired on again, and no amount of tugging or twisting would shut them off. Then both spigots began shooting scorching-hot water my way.

My skin turned pink, then red. Felt like it was boiling.

I grabbed the towel and jumped onto the tiled bench. It wasn't in direct range of the jets, but my legs and feet were still getting pummeled. I wrapped the towel around my fist, tight as I could, closed my eyes, and delivered a left hook to the glass.

It shattered into a billion pieces. The entire bathroom was so steamy, I could hardly see a thing. No time to contemplate where the toilet was, the towel rack, or the wastebasket. I leaped as far as I could, hoping to avoid the glass (although it was tempered, thankfully), and crumbled into a soggy heap. My head scraped against the vanity, and a trickle of warm blood oozed down my temple.

My skin was on fire, so I rushed barefoot to the sinks, hoping for relief. I spun the knob for cold water and tentatively stuck my fingers beneath the stream.

It was cold.

I called to Thor, who was still beating away at the door, and told him I was all right.

There was a pile of washcloths neatly rolled on a shelf to the right. I grabbed one and soaked it under the chilly water.

The steam jets and the showerheads all shut off at that moment. Carefully, I dabbed the moist terrycloth on my skin. Then I blotted away the blood.

And I saw what was in the mirror.

Chapter 23

Birdie knew better than to engage Tabby, but the woman loved to push her buttons.

Minutes after Birdie had disconnected with Anastasia, Tallulah called, trying to goad the Geraghty Girl into an argument.

Presently, it was working.

"Birdie, darling, why don't you just call off this whole silly thing and admit that you only want to believe your granddaughter is the Seeker so that you can redeem yourself and the Geraghty name?"

Tallulah was wearing another one of her stupid hats, and Birdie just itched to rip it off her head and shove it down her throat. This one had a pink bow dangling from it, tilted absurdly on her pointy head, just above her mole. Boys used to find that mole attractive when they were younger. Now that it had a two-inch hair trailing from it, Birdie suspected that was no longer the case.

She sent Tabby a saucy grin. "Afraid of a little competition, my dear?"

Tabby rolled her eyes. "Please, Birdie, you were no match for me, and your granddaughter will be no match for Ethan."

Birdie snapped on a glove, thinking Ethan was a ridiculous name for a Seeker. "I think you have that backward, Tabby. It was you who could not compete with me, as I recall."

Tabby's eyes widened mockingly. "Really? Well, if that is the case, then why am I the Mage and you couldn't even graduate from the Academy?"

"Because you cheated and I'm the one who was blamed. Which is why I was expelled, which is why I could never accept a nomination, let alone get confirmed," Birdie shouted.

Fiona gently squeezed her sister's shoulder.

Tabby examined her nails. "Sour grapes."

"Is that so?" Birdie planted her hands on her hips. "So you didn't steal my spell books every year? Just like you didn't steal Aedon?"

Tabby said, "Oh, please, I hardly stole Aedon. The poor boy was following me around like a lost puppy—what could I do? Besides"—she adjusted her skirt—"that's all water under the bridge. It was over and done with years ago. There's a new man in my life."

Birdie was stunned. She had never known Aedon and Tallulah had parted ways. She assumed Ethan was Aedon's grandson. Behind her, Fiona squealed softly.

"Kudos for you, Tabby. Now, if there is nothing else…" Birdie reached to click off the television screen, as a door opened in Tallulah's room.

"Just a minute, Birdie. I'd like you to meet my fellow."

After a pause, Oscar's head popped into view. "Hey, Birdie," he said.

Birdie heard Lolly gasp and topple off the bed.

The true Mage of the four corners looked at her ex-husband. She didn't even blink. All she said was, "Oscar, you stupid, stupid little man."

Scrawled in the fog of the mirror were six words.

Return the locket or die tonight.

I flung open the bathroom door and stormed the suite. "Who's here?" I whirled around, Thor keeping pace behind me. "Show your face." Checked the closet, behind the curtain, under the bed. Nothing.

"Did you see anyone?" I asked Thor.

He yodeled what sounded like a negative response.

I grabbed only the essentials from my suitcase—jeans, a V-neck top, and my athame—dressed quickly, and ran from the room barefoot and commando, smacking straight into a guy eating a scone.

I slammed my left forearm into his chest and forced him to the wall. Pointed the athame at his throat with my right hand.

"What are you doing out here?" I demanded.

His hands were raised. "Stacy Justice, I presume?"

I pressed the knife to his skin. "How do you know my name?"

"They said you were a nutter."

"Who said?" I narrowed my eyes at him, my head throbbing from knocking it against the marble moments ago. "Who are you?"

"Ethan O'Conor. I'm supposed to challenge you to duel, or something equally absurd."

O'Conor? As in the high king for whom the castle was constructed?

I eased up on the blade, and he took a bite out of his pastry.

He raised one eyebrow at me. He looked a lot like Colin Farrell.

I heard Thor panting behind me, waiting to see if I needed backup.

This guy wasn't sending me any shaky vibes. I didn't have that nauseous feeling I usually experienced when someone wanted to harm me.

Then again, I didn't have it in the shower either.

I kept my arm pressed to him. "Why are you lurking outside my door?"

He flicked his eyes to the left. "I wasn't lurking, Princess Paranoid. My room is just down the hall. You can check if you like. There's a map in my pocket. My name is next to the room number."

"Which pocket?"

He smiled mischievously. "The front pocket."

I rolled my eyes. "Just get it."

He produced the map. *Ethan O'Conor* was scribbled next to a room down the hall. Tallulah's grandson. But that didn't mean he wasn't dangerous.

"So you weren't in my room just now?"

"No, but I'd like to be." His voice was low, sexy.

I was suddenly very aware that my shirt was wet and the outermost points of my body were saluting like soldiers. I lowered the athame. I hugged my arms close to my chest. "Why should I believe you?"

"Press up against me again, and I'll show you." He glanced down.

"Ew!" I jumped back, disgusted. "That's not what I meant."

If it wasn't he who'd written on my bathroom mirror, then who?

"May I be excused, or would you like my assistance toweling off?" Ethan asked. "My grandmother is expecting me, and she hates when I'm late, although I'm willing to risk the wrath if you'd like to continue this conversation."

I waved the blade. "Go."

Ethan gave a slight bow. "Thank you." He turned and whistled. "Gretchen."

I shook my head. What a jerk. Couldn't wait to see the kind of woman who came running when a man whistled.

Gretchen rushed around the corner and beelined directly to Ethan's side. Her big brown eyes regarded him lovingly, eagerly, awaiting his next command. Her curly locks shone in the morning light from the window at the end of the hall, and I couldn't help but admire her grace.

Thor admired it too, and said so by sitting up a bit straighter, his huge snout inspecting the air to catch the scent of her.

"Until we meet again." Ethan turned to saunter down the hall, Gretchen by his side. The sway of her hips thumped, as if to the beat of a drum.

She gave a shy glance back, and I could feel Thor vibrate with anticipation.

"Don't get any ideas, pal. She's one of them."

He whined miserably and sulked back to the room, poking his head out for one last look at the cream-colored Irish wolfhound.

Back in the room, I tossed a towel over the broken glass in the bathroom and dried my hair in the sitting room. Then I put some clean clothes on, undergarments included, slipped into my running shoes, and held up the locket.

I dangled it in front of the light for a moment, inspecting it as the chain draped over my wrist, trying to catch a vision from the intricate piece of jewelry.

"What is so important about you?" I asked.

Suddenly, the five-bladed star I had packed spun out of my suitcase. It whipped through the room, linked with the locket, and punctured the wall.

Thor charged the wall, growling and barking.

I sensed something—a masculine presence. Heavy, sinister air swirled around me. I snatched the locket, held it tight, and pocketed the star.

I called to whatever or whoever had left me that message on the mirror. "This was a gift. I didn't steal it. I don't even know who gave it to me." I wrapped the chain around my head and tucked the pendant under my shirt. Then I grabbed my sword. "If you want it so badly, why don't you show yourself, you coward!"

The room chilled so drastically that my breath came out in frosty bursts. I gripped the sword, shifted my stance, Thor at the ready next to me. One raspy word zapped my brain. *Mine.*

And as quickly as they came, the presence and the cold broke and retreated into the walls.

I looked at Thor. "Let's get out of here."

Fiona looked at Birdie, concern clouding her eyes. "Tallulah must have put him under a love spell."

"Probably one of mine," Birdie spat.

She was so furious with Oscar, she couldn't sit still. Why had he insisted on coming along if he was just going to be a burden? Now she would have to weave a remedy spell, and she simply had no time for this nonsense. She had a meeting to attend, a cauldron to find, and a council to appease so she could spring her daughter from the depths of this castle—wherever she was. Aedon hadn't mentioned if Birdie could visit her child, and she thought it best not to press the issue. She had to stay focused, and that meant keeping everyone around her sharp and on task, including her sisters, Anastasia, and—Hecate help her—that idiot she used to be married to.

She wanted to scream, she wanted to shed her poise for one freeing moment, but she didn't dare. Not here, at least, not within the confines of these all-seeing walls. The castle was a fortress, to be sure, but it was also a place of highly concentrated energy. As if the walls themselves could breathe, the windows could see, and the floor could feel her footsteps.

As if, at its own discretion, the castle could weave its entrails around her and swallow her whole.

There was a knock at the door then, and Birdie sensed her granddaughter. In fact, ever since the fetching spell had unsnarled the girl from the web, Birdie felt a bit more attuned to her. She liked the sensation.

Anastasia did not wait for anyone to open the door; she burst through it like a flamethrower, vexed about something, and hauling the bag of magical tricks she had brought.

Her familiar seemed to be spirited as well.

Birdie looked at her questioningly, as her two sisters stood.

"The castle is trying to kill me," Anastasia said. She didn't wait for a response, just went about stuffing crystals and herbs into the pockets of her hoodie. Then she lifted the hood over her head and tightened the strings.

Birdie stared at the girl. "What on earth are you talking about?" She noticed the sword hanging at the girl's side, and the chain from the locket hugging her neck.

Birdie still couldn't fathom how she had gotten hold of it.

Anastasia ripped into some outlandish story about showerheads firing up on their own, doors slamming shut, and her own tool going rogue on her.

Then she filtered through her gemstone pouch. "Is it onyx that severs a tie?" she asked.

Lolly said it was, and Anastasia pulled out a polished black stone, examined it.

It wasn't a moment ago that Birdie had been thinking that this place was enlivened, but she didn't actually believe it had a pulse. It was just that the grounds, the structure, was thousands of years old, and she could feel the history, the battles, the defeat and victories of warriors who'd protected it with their lives flowing through each crack and crevice. There was residual energy here, to be sure, of spirits passed and some who refused to pass over.

But the place didn't actually have a soul, or a brain.

"Anastasia, listen to me." She crossed to the girl, grasped her shoulders. "You become emotional when your car doesn't start. It's one of the things I wanted to discuss with you before the meeting. You must ground yourself at all times here, and everywhere on the island. Emotions make you vulnerable, and vulnerability leads to carelessness. I can only imagine the twists and turns your heart has taken being in this place, being close to your mother."

At this, the girl perked up. "Have you seen her? She is here, isn't she? I could have sworn I saw her out the window."

Birdie shook her head. "I don't know, but I will tell you it is highly unlikely you saw her. They would never let her wander about unsupervised under these circumstances."

Anastasia's face deflated. "So then I imagined her?"

"It's possible, or you may have conjured up an image of her. An impression from her energy. Your mother was tethered to you from the moment you were born until her arrest. She could have been in the garden, but if you were both thinking of each other at the same time, you could have also spawned a connection."

Doubt flashed over the girl's face.

Birdie continued. "I think, too, perhaps that's what happened in your suite. A powerful necromancer like you can electrify a space with this much history. The spirits, while harmless, can be sent into a tailspin."

Anastasia shook her head. "No. I'm telling you, Birdie, this was real, deliberate. And far from harmless." Then she added, "By the way, I hope you didn't give them a deposit for the room, because you can kiss that good-bye."

"The dead can't hurt you, child. I've told you time and again."

Anastasia stuck out her chin and planted her hands on her hips, looking so much like her mother that Birdie's heart lurched. "Oh, really? Do you see this?" She lifted her strawberry-blonde hair, pointed to a cut on her head. "Does this look harmless to you? I'm telling you, Birdie, if it isn't the castle, then it's a really pissed-off ghost with a chip on his shoulder."

Fiona asked, "Well, what could you possibly have done to provoke him, dear?"

Anastasia tapped her foot a moment, clearly contemplating her response. Finally she said, "I think it might have something to do with this." She reached into her blouse and pulled out the locket. She explained that while one spirit guide had warned her to keep it safe, there was also a threat to return it, from another, malevolent presence.

"The problem is, I don't know where I got it, what it does, or even who I would return it to," she said.

"Birdie said, "What do you mean you don't know where you got it?"

Anastasia furrowed her brow. "Gramps said it was a family heirloom. He said my father talked to him about it, asked him to keep it in his vault until my thirtieth year."

Birdie couldn't believe her ears. *Oscar, just wait until I get my hands on you,* she thought. Then she wondered, *Who gave it to Stacy Senior?*

The girl was studying Birdie's face. "I take it you have no idea where it came from either."

Birdie looked at Fiona and Lolly.

"I have an idea what it is. But I don't know what it does, or how your father received it," she said.

"So what is it?"

"It's the Seeker's locket. Passed from one Seeker to the successor every hundred years or so."

Anastasia looked down, fingered the piece. "Who was the last Seeker?"

Birdie shrugged. "Only the council knows. And only the Seeker knows its powers. When you are confirmed, its powers will be released. Its will bound to you."

"So what do we do? Someone's obviously after it. Someone's willing to kill for it."

Everyone thought for a moment.

After a while, Lolly said, "I have an idea."

She was looking at Thor.

PART THREE

The Tempest

On this journey, you begin to see how the sides of your heart that seemed awkward, contradictory, and uneven are the places where the treasure lies hidden. You begin to become true to yourself.

—John O'Donohue

Chapter 24

As we made our way downstairs to the meeting, the spicy aroma of oatmeal-raisin cookies wafted through the hallway. They were my favorite treat growing up, and my mother often made a batch on chilly weekends.

I flicked my eyes to Birdie. Could she smell the cinnamon? If she did, she didn't seem to notice. She was preoccupied with the meeting, I guessed. We hadn't had a lot of time to prepare, since my near-death experiences had become the focus of our powwow, but I had been given a very strict warning.

"Let me do the talking," Birdie had said.

Thor strutted alongside me, proudly displaying the decadent vest Lolly had fashioned for him from one of her ball gowns. The locket was sewn into the lining. I wasn't certain about this strategy, but Birdie had convinced me that it was too dangerous to keep it on my person, that I shouldn't even be in possession of it, and if anyone found out—friend or foe—we would all be on trial come Samhain. I was hesitant to agree. Thor could certainly hold his own when up against most other animals and humans. It was the ghost with the bug up his ass that concerned me.

We were ten minutes early, so I found a door to let Thor out to do his business quickly before the meeting was scheduled to begin. There was a breakfast spread just outside the room, so the aunts and Birdie helped themselves to coffee and muffins, while I loaded up a heaping plate of bacon, eggs, and potatoes for Thor. I grabbed a yogurt and an apple for myself. We all ate in silence, and someone came to clear our plates just as a clock chimed in the common area.

Gary appeared at the doorway. He ushered us all to our seats and offered to take my sword.

"No, thanks."

He shuffled nervously. "You'll get it back as soon as the session is over. It's protocol."

I looked at him. "I appreciate your position, but no one touches my sword."

It was still infused with Badb's force, and I really didn't want anyone else's imprint on it.

Someone kicked me. "Ouch!" I grabbed my shin as Birdie glared at me.

I shook my head vigorously.

The guy mumbled, "Oh, for the love of Pete." He whipped his sports coat off and laid it on the bench next to me. "Keep it covered." He walked off, shaking his head, and resumed his post by the door, clasping his hands in front of him.

The O'Conor courtroom, or whatever the heck it was called, was large enough to play a full-court basketball game in. It was dripping with richly paneled walls and indulgent trim. The floor was laid in a crisscross pattern of smooth hardwood, the ceiling elaborately painted with ancient battle scenes, gods, and goddesses. Wooden benches filled much of the space, all of which faced a long, rectangular platform, elevated a foot off the ground. Above that were photographs of council members past and present. I noticed that many of them were O'Conors.

I covered my sword with the guy's coat and sat down next to Birdie. "What should I expect?"

"I would imagine they'll ask for the plan on locating the cauldron."

"Will you tell them everything? I mean about the Web of Wyrd."

She shot me a horrified look. "Of course not. They'd crucify us. Remember what happened to Jesus? Would *you* believe everything you've told me about meeting the goddesses?"

"Hey, I was there, and I still don't believe it."

Birdie spoke softly out of the corner of her mouth. "We'll just tell them we found the instructions in the Blessed Book. That the ancestors left clues for us to find the cauldron based on what happened the last time it was stolen, and the steps taken to recover it."

"Good. What if they ask me a direct question?"

"Don't say a word. I'll answer all their questions."

John stepped through the door then, wearing a turtleneck and jeans, a satchel slung over his hip. He nodded at me as the driver-turned-bailiff escorted him into the room. I nodded back.

John was directed to a row behind us. I could smell the mint gum he liked to chew as he swaggered past.

Ethan came in next, Gretchen at his hip. He winked at me and I looked beyond him, shaking my head. He was led to the row opposite us. Thor drooled as his new love interest batted her impossibly long lashes at him. He sat erect, sticking his chest out to show off his new duds.

I nudged him with my foot. "Stop that. You're embarrassing yourself."

He grouched at me and aimed his perfectly regal profile at the Irish wolfhound.

A moment later, a door opened behind a huge platform and one by one, people filed into the room, each taking a seat at the table perched on the platform.

To my utter shock, that flappy-faced Tallulah was one of them.

I pinched Birdie's arm and whispered, "You didn't tell me she was on the council."

She wrestled her arm away. "I thought she told you when you spoke that day in my bedroom."

I shook my head. Birdie snapped her eyes forward as Aedon called the meeting to order.

A sickening feeling fell over me. If that catty woman was on the council, there was no telling what kind of power she held.

Or what she could do with it.

As I sat in that room, surrounded by friend and foe, the words of the rhyming spirit filtered through my mind.

The council awaits your arrival, in the castle you shall stay; but beware of the wrath of a rival, and the one who will betray.

I had a pretty good idea who the rival was. But who would betray?

Birdie Geraghty was not an envious woman, but as she stared at the nine council members, she couldn't help but feel cheated as Tallulah took her seat.

That should be my chair. And if it were, none of this would be happening. She knew in her heart of hearts that her daughter had been well within her rights to defend her family. It had been a preemptive strike, pure and simple, despite the fact that the man hadn't actually come in contact with Anastasia. He had obviously found the girl's mother, and she had thwarted whatever attack he had planned. If Birdie had been on the council, she would have appealed to their reason. She would have pointed out that saving a would-be Seeker was an act of heroism, not a crime worthy of punishment.

Not knowing was the worst. Not knowing what the man had been after or why. Birdie hoped that when this entire nightmare concluded, she would have her answers.

Aedon shuffled some paperwork and read through the preliminary meeting notes. He explained about the missing cauldron and the duties of the watchers sworn to protect it. He then explained that the Warrior, Ivy, would be joining the session virtually. Birdie watched as Tallulah's son Pearce punched in some buttons on a remote control.

The screen behind the platform sizzled to life, and the bubbly teenager with cherry-red hair appeared.

Aedon asked if Ivy could hear him, and she said she could. When he turned his back, she waved to Anastasia. To her credit, Birdie's granddaughter smiled back at the girl without drawing attention to herself.

Finally, Aedon addressed the court. "John, as the only watcher of the treasures who has been officially confirmed, would you like to explain your strategy?"

Birdie tensed, but quickly relaxed as John launched into the plan about the four corners heading to Fourknocks Mound, or, as the goddess referred to it, the Hill of Summoning.

Tallulah looked frightened at the prospect of being sent on a mission.

As well you should be, Birdie thought.

Aedon sat back in his chair, the wheels squeaking across the stage. "Interesting." His beard twitched as he thought for a moment. "I don't recall a Mage ever being appointed as a watcher, let alone participating in a quest. Where are you drawing your information from?"

Birdie held her breath.

John said, in a fluid voice like a saxophone, "From the Blessed Book of my clanspeople."

Aedon asked if he could view the passage, but John explained he had felt it too risky to bring the book. That it was locked away in a vault, but he had taken notes.

Aedon turned to Ivy. "Young lady? Are you prepared to assist in the mission?"

Ivy said, "I am. But we have exams today, and the headmistress refuses to grant me passage until tomorrow."

Next to Birdie, Anastasia tensed, wild-eyed.

"Very well," Aedon said. "The mission begins tomorrow at the break of dawn."

Anastasia squeezed Birdie's hand so tight, she felt knuckles crack. Then, after Aedon turned back to face the audience, Ivy flashed a cell phone and held up a thumb.

Anastasia sighed in relief.

Aedon pointed his head toward Anastasia. "I presume you are prepared, Miss Justice?"

The girl nodded.

Aedon looked at Ethan. "And you, son?"

"Aye," Ethan said, slouched on the bench.

Birdie couldn't help but notice the young man looked bored.

"Good. Directly after the session, you will meet your first challenge."

Ethan didn't look too thrilled about that. Stacy squeezed Birdie's hand again.

"Challenge?" Birdie questioned.

Aedon looked up from his notes. "With two Seekers vying for the role, we need to assign a leader and a qualifier."

Anastasia was so tense, she was practically vibrating. The girl was ready to burst, and Birdie feared what would happen if she did.

"I'll be the qualifier," Ethan said.

Tallulah shot him a death stare. "Always the joker, Ethan." She turned to Aedon. "Splendid idea. The usual challenges? Archery? Falconry? Jousting?"

"Jousting?" Anastasia quietly hissed. "Birdie, do something, for gods' sake."

"Absolutely," Aedon answered Tallulah. He jotted down a few notes.

Birdie whispered, "It'll be fine."

Anastasia whispered back, "There's no time for this crap. I'm not staying another night in this house of horrors. Remember, *return the locket or die tonight?*"

Aedon looked up. Smiled. "Miss Justice, would you like to address the council?"

Birdie stood up. "No, she wouldn't."

Anastasia stood too. "You bet your ass I would."

Aedon chuckled. "I admire your verve. Proceed."

Birdie tugged on Anastasia's arm, but the girl shrugged her off.

"Well, Your, er…Highness…it has recently been brought to my attention that there is another Mage in our midst. As a potential Seeker with multiple nominations under her belt"—Ethan scoffed at this—"I feel it is my duty to present her to the court."

Aedon looked at Tallulah, whose face had darkened into a scowl.

He turned back to Stacy. "Another Mage? Who is it?"

Birdie yanked Anastasia's shirt so hard, the girl coughed, but it didn't do any good. "Brighid Geraghty, my grandmother."

Birdie couldn't decide if she should gag the girl or kick her feet out from under her.

Tallulah shot up, fuming. "This is outrageous. Brighid was expelled from the Academy years ago. My father signed the papers himself. And only graduates are qualified to become Mage."

Aedon said, "That is true." He cocked his head, tapped his pen. "But your father's passed over now. Despite the fact that you were confirmed as Mage, Birdie has the right to contest her expulsion and, ultimately, the withdrawal of her Mage nomination. The rules have changed since he was in power."

Anastasia grinned.

Aedon looked at Birdie's granddaughter. "She'll need a nomination."

Birdie said, "That won't be necessary."

"I nominate her," Anastasia said, hand raised.

"I second it," said John.

Aedon asked if there was a third, and Ethan said, "Aye."

Both Birdie and Anastasia turned to him, astonished. He shrugged. Birdie couldn't help but smile. Tallulah had her hands full with that one.

"Well, then," Aedon said, "looks as if there will be multiple challenges today." He slid his eyes to Tallulah. "Are you up for that?"

Tallulah sat and crossed, then uncrossed, her legs. "Of course."

Birdie cringed. She hadn't participated in a contest since she was a girl. What if she made a fool of herself? What if—and this thought terrified her—she lost to Tallulah? She would be humiliated, mortified. The one thing she had held on to all these years—the notion she clung to in her darkest hours—was the idea that she knew she was better, that Tabby's deception didn't mean anything in the end, because Birdie had her truth.

But what if she was wrong?

Anastasia leaned in, whispered in her ear. "Don't worry. I have a plan."

Birdie winced. She wasn't sure why, but she didn't like the sound of that.

Chapter 25

Aedon pounded the gavel, concluding the meeting, and one by one, the council members filed out through the curtain from whence they had come.

Tallulah snarled at me right before she left.

That's right, sister. Geraghty Girls play hardball.

I picked up the coat covering my sword and jogged it back to its owner, thanking him.

Birdie was on me the minute I turned around.

"Have you lost your mind?" she demanded. "Do you have any idea what you've done?"

Actually, I had no idea what I'd done, but I figured if I had to play Wipeout, my best shot at winning would be with Birdie on my team. She knew all about this stuff, she had been to the Academy, and she relished every minute of it, I was certain. The little girl I met in the Web of Wyrd took pride in her studies, in her heritage, in herself. She could kick Tallulah's ass with one wand tied behind her back.

"What are you so upset about? You finally have the chance to prove that Tallulah has been lying all these years.

After the way she treated you, I thought you'd be happy to put her in her place."

Birdie gave me a confused look. "How do you know that? I never told you anything about Tabby."

Uh-oh. That's right, she hadn't. I knew because I was there.

Before Birdie's wheels could spin any faster, Fiona stepped in. "She's right, Birdie. This is your chance to redeem the Geraghty name, to put an end to any lingering doubts anyone might have about what really happened at the Academy."

"What do you mean? What happened?" I asked.

"Another time." Birdie looked torn; she tilted her chin to the ceiling. "I haven't practiced any of it in ages."

I grabbed her hand. "We'll get through it together."

She wrinkled her brow. "You do realize that the challenges of a Mage and those of a Seeker are completely different."

The thought had never crossed my mind. "So we won't be teammates?"

Birdie said, "Honestly, I'm not quite sure how the games will be structured."

"It doesn't matter." I lowered my voice, scanned the space. We were alone. "Look, I'm not waiting until tomorrow to go after the cauldron. We can signal Ivy in through her cell phone—the magic will still happen. I've seen it done through a training class, Witch in the Modern World, I think it was called."

"Tallulah will never agree to that. She wouldn't disobey Aedon," Birdie said.

I said, "Then we ditch her."

Birdie pondered that option. "Agreed."

Just then, Lolly jumped up on the bench and pulled her dress over her head, indicating it was time for more tequila.

I told Birdie I'd be up to her room shortly and to get used to it, because I wasn't stepping foot back in mine. She said she'd call housekeeping to send someone for my things.

They left, and I grabbed my sword. Thor wasn't where he'd been a moment ago. I called to him, but he didn't come trotting over to me as expected.

I searched the expansive room and finally spotted him in a far corner, nuzzling Gretchen.

"Thor! Bad dog. Get over here," I said sternly.

"Ah, give him a break. He's just having a bit o' fun," Ethan said behind me, in a thick Irish brogue. He was holding two cups of coffee, and offered me one.

"No, thanks."

"Not a drop of poison in the cup. I swear on my grandmother."

Thor completely ignored me. There was a bit of spittle glistening in the corner of his long jowl, and I could have sworn the dog was flexing his bicep.

"That's not saying a whole lot." I tilted my gaze toward Ethan. "You don't seem to like her very much." I took the cup, sniffed it. Smelled like Cafe Vienna.

"What makes you say that?"

"Nominating my grandmother as Mage, for starters."

Ethan guffawed. "Come on, now, I was just having a lark." He sipped his coffee. "All this rubbish about Mages and Seekers and cauldrons. She takes it so seriously, she deserves to be put on now and again."

I adjusted my sword, moving it off to the side, out of view.

Ethan stared at me for an uncomfortably long moment.

"Oh, blimey. You too!" He pointed at me, laughed. "You actually believe these loons and all their hocus-pocus." He stepped closer, slung an arm around me, and said conspiratorially, "You know, with our combined powers and my family heritage, we could storm this castle. Claim it as our own and live happily ever after. Bespell the entire monstrosity with a lusty potion. What say you?"

For the first time in my life, I heard what I had sounded like to Birdie all these years, and I felt ashamed.

Ethan hadn't seen the things I had. Probably hadn't experienced the heartache or pain that came with growing up. I suspected, like Tallulah, life was made easy for him.

Then he drew a heart in the air and mimicked it throbbing.

Ugh. I flung his arm away. "How *old* are you?"

"Twenty-six, but I like ripe women." He wiggled his eyebrows.

"You aren't even old enough to be confirmed, then."

"That's right, lass. Being an O'Conor has its advantages." He stood up a little straighter.

It sure did for his grandmother. And mine suffered for it. I said in a singsong voice, "Ah, yes, the workings of the privileged class. Where Mummy and Daddy see to it that little Junior has everything his heart desires. And then Junior grows up to be a wanker who can't fend for himself." I flashed my eyes to his groin. "And probably couldn't even satisfy a blow-up doll."

His eyes flooded with anger, and he stepped forward.

"Ethan!" a man called from behind us. "Your grandmother is expecting you."

Ethan didn't turn around as he called, "Coming, Father." Then he hissed, "See you on the battlefield."

"Wouldn't miss it."

My challenger downed his coffee, crumpled the cup, and tossed it on the floor. Then he whistled for Gretchen and she trotted after him, leaving Thor heartbroken. My Dane howled as his crush slipped out the door.

"You're better off, Thor. Bitches be crazy." I ruffled up his ears, and he rested his huge head against my hip, blew out a forlorn sigh.

I picked up the crumpled cup and headed out.

The man Ethan called "father" watched his son leave the room and met me near the door.

"Hello, Stacy, I'm Pearce. I'm an old friend of your mom's." He stuck out his hand.

I tossed the coffee cups in a wastebasket. I was hesitant to grasp Pearce's hand, but in the end, I figured the more information I could collect about these people, the better. His grip was warm and intense, like an electric blanket on a cold day. My brain was firing, trying to capture an image, but it floated to the surface without developing.

I eyed him suspiciously. "She never mentioned anyone named Pearce."

"We were school chums. A long time ago."

The Academy, I presumed. "Have you seen my mother?" I was still holding his hand, still trying to read him.

He smiled, sensing my motives, I guessed, but he didn't break free. I noticed his eyes were warm too. He didn't seem to fit the O'Conor mold.

"She's fine. This isn't like a real prison. She's treated well, fed well. She gets to listen to her favorite music, reads lots of books. She goes outside. She's even permitted to practice magic, within reason."

Relief, like I had never felt before, washed over me in a tidal wave. I was so happy to hear my mother wasn't caged like an abandoned animal that I didn't even think to ask why he was telling me this.

An oversight I would soon regret.

A huge bouquet of red roses bobbed in through the foyer, carried by a man much too old to be acting like a jackass.

Her sisters fell to the wayside as Birdie stopped her ex-husband in his tracks. She couldn't believe, on top of everything else, she had to deal with this absurdity. She wouldn't give a flying fig if it weren't for the fact that she had no idea what Tallulah was up to—or what Oscar would reveal to her that might jeopardize the entire mission.

"Oscar, what do you think you're doing?"

He lowered the bouquet, his eyes two huge puddles of puppy love. He looked pathetic.

"Hello, Birdie. You're looking lovely today." He liberated a rose from the cluster and handed it to her.

She accepted, then proceeded to throttle him with it.

"Hey, cut it out."

Birdie said, "Oscar, I want you to listen to me very carefully."

He stood there, grinning like an imbecile. "I can't thank you enough for letting me tag along. I'm having the most wonderful time." He leaned in, whispered, "I met someone. I think she may be the one."

She's the one, all right, Birdie thought.

"Oscar, do you remember why we are here? Do you remember what this is all about, what I told you back at the house?"

"I certainly do. We're here to rescue our daughter and bring her home," he recited like a robot. "I may bring someone else home too." He winked.

Birdie wanted to poke his eyes out. "She hexed you, Oscar. You cannot trust anything Tabby says."

Oscar reeled back in utter disbelief. "How dare you speak like that of the woman I love."

Birdie rolled her eyes. "You are not in love, you nitwit. You're bewitched."

His eyes hazed over again. "She is bewitching, isn't she?"

Birdie tossed a glance at Fiona. Fiona, the sister who was an expert at casting love spells, was at a loss for breaking one. She shrugged.

Birdie stepped close to Oscar and pulled a lily from her pocket. The flower was known for reversing love spells if worn by the enchanted person for at least an hour.

She was just about to slip it into Oscar's lapel, when Tabby flew in out of nowhere. The insufferable woman snatched the lily. It wilted in her hand.

She smirked at Birdie, then turned to Oscar and said, "There you are, darling! I was wondering where you'd gotten off to."

"I just stepped out to get you some flowers." Oscar presented the bouquet to Tabby.

She batted her false lashes and said, "For me? How incredibly thoughtful." Then she kissed him, leaving a huge red mark like a tomato splattered on the man's face. "Let's put these in water, shall we? Then we can take a stroll, get some privacy." She tossed Birdie a triumphant look. "It's rather crowded in here."

Oscar nodded his head, looking like a dog in heat. He started up the stairs.

Tabby hung back and said, "You'll have to do much better than that, Birdie."

"Count on it," Birdie said, seething.

Tallulah trailed up the stairs, locking arms with the grandfather of one of the most powerful Seekers of all time.

Birdie looked at her sisters. "Can you believe it?"

Lolly had somehow gained access to a sword and was challenging an empty suit of armor to a duel.

Fiona said, "We should go."

Birdie had just wrestled the sword away from her oldest sister when Elizabeth called to her.

"Birdie? May I have a word with you?"

Fiona said, "Go. I'll take care of Lolly."

Birdie walked over to the diminutive woman. She towered over Elizabeth by at least a foot.

"Aedon has requested to speak with you privately."

There was a flutter in her heart, but Birdie instantly extinguished it. *No time for nonsense*, she told herself.

"Of course." She tried to say it with authority, but her voice rose an octave, sounding giddy.

She mentally slapped herself.

Elizabeth looked at her, perplexed. "Follow me, then."

Chapter 26

My phone chimed. It was a message from Birdie.

Taking care of something. Will text when you should meet me.

I pocketed the phone and realized that I had taken a wrong turn leaving the Court of O'Conor room. I found myself lost in the matrix of the castle.

The map was folded in the back pocket of my jeans, so I stopped for a minute to read it.

According to the grid, we were just steps away from the library. I thought of the book, folded upside down on the chair in the hallway outside my room last night, and of what Pearce had said about my mother reading a lot.

"Come on, Thor."

The big dog plopped down on the faded carpet, rolled onto his back, and wailed uncontrollably.

"You're being ridiculous, you know that?" I said.

He kicked his feet in the air and yelped.

"Fine. Wait here."

The pocket doors to the library slid open easily. Inside the mahogany-trimmed room were floor-to-ceiling bookshelves, a cozy fireplace, soft leather chairs, and the distinctive scent of brown-sugar-and-vanilla body spray.

My mother's scent.

For the first time since I had arrived, I felt her presence all around me like an embrace. If she hadn't been here moments ago, then it was definitely a place she spent much of her time. I set out to explore the space, touching every inch of the room, drinking in the essence of my mother, absorbing the energy she had impressed on the books. My fingertips danced over leather-bound volumes of Keats, Browning, Twain, and Shakespeare. Books of all shapes and sizes filled row after row of sturdy shelves, some with gold-embossed lettering, some with weakened spines. Some dusty, some brand new. There was an entire section devoted to Irish writers—James Joyce, Oscar Wilde, Samuel Beckett, Bram Stoker—and one whole wall cluttered with sources for witchery.

On that wall, one thick volume was protruding just a bit from the others. I went over to read the title. *Banishment Spells: Breaking Hexes, Curses & Ties to Malevolent Beings.*

Now, that was a book I could use right now.

Gingerly, I liberated the tome from its neighbors.

In a swift *whoosh*, the wall skidded open, revealing a secret room. Something beckoned me to step inside. I stuck the book in the doorway so it wouldn't shut, and followed my instincts.

My jaw dropped to the floor as I realized where I was. The photographs, potion bottles, body spray, a gold compact that once belonged to Maegan, even the pathetic little pottery bowl I made her one Mother's Day.

This was her room. My mother's room.

There was a stack of letters on a white desk, beside a journal. I crossed over to the desk, picked up the first letter.

It began, *My darling*.

Before I could explore any further, or even read the note, I heard a loud voice say, "What are you doing out here, Thor?"

Elizabeth.

I shoved the letter into my pocket and quickly slipped out the door, forced the book back into its slot, grabbed the one next to it, and leaped into a chair as the wall whispered shut.

Elizabeth stepped inside just as I cracked the spine. She eyed me skeptically, flicking her gaze to the book and then back to me.

"Hello, Miss Justice. I believe your dog may need to pay a visit to the grounds. He seems to be emitting a noxious odor."

I closed the book, thanked her, and got the hell out of there.

We had nearly made it to the front door with the help of the map when Thor decided he just couldn't go on. He collapsed onto a settee that probably cost more than my car and sighed.

Maybe I could coax him out of his funk with some treats.

I headed over to where the buffet had been, through one of the Gothic archways, to see if anything was left. John was standing there, stuffing bacon into his pockets.

"What are you doing?"

He looked up. "Stocking up on snacks."

"That's disgusting." I inspected the buffet. It was picked over, and nothing remained except for a few sad-looking scones and potato pancakes, a plate of peanut butter cookies, and a bowl of mints. I grabbed some of the cookies and mints and shoved them into my sweatshirt pocket.

"So, what do you know about these competitions?" I asked John.

He said, "Not a thing. I never had to do anything like that. I'll be there, though, rooting for you."

I explained about my plan to get it over with and go after the cauldron. John agreed with me that we shouldn't wait, stating he didn't want to stay here any longer than he had to, that he wanted to get home to his wife as soon as possible.

"I'll text you the details as soon as I know them. I'm going for a walk with Thor."

"You want me to come?" he asked, shoving an entire biscuit into his mouth.

I wrinkled my nose. "No, thanks. You reek of bacon. Probably attract every stray dog within a thirty-mile radius, and Thor is already on tilt, thanks to that Irish wolfhound. Besides"—I patted my sword, still dangling from my belt loop—"I've got protection."

I left him there, eyeing the potato pancakes, and went back to my lovesick pooch.

He was still lying there, singing the blues.

"Thor, hey, buddy, you want a cookie?"

One ear perked up, twisted toward my voice like a telescope.

I walked toward the massive front door. "It's your favorite. Peanut butter…"

He sprung up, sprinted for the door. Just as I was about to open it, I heard a giggle coming from the catwalk above.

I saw Gramps kiss Tallulah, then slip into a room with her.

What is it about this place that makes everything with dangly bits act like a horny toad?

I heaved the colossal door open, and Thor led the way through. We stepped out into dappled sunlight. There was a mountain range just beyond the horizon that I hadn't seen the night before. A blanket of mist shrouded it, and I couldn't help but think it had been carefully placed there by the gentle hand of a god.

I tossed Thor a cookie, and he jumped up to catch it. He scarfed it down, then rushed over to a fountain, scaring off a flock of squeaky birds.

The scenery was truly breathtaking, and I drank it all in as I searched for a footpath that would lead to the back of the castle. I wanted to see the courtyard where my mother—or the impression of my mother—had lingered earlier that day. Hopefully find a secluded spot to read the letter I'd stolen from her desk.

There were hedges fashioned into animal shapes all around the grounds. Unicorns, dragons, hawks, cats, dolphins—every totem you could possibly imagine guarded the castle. We passed flowering shrubs that should have long been out of bloom, still boasting blossoms. Lilacs, roses, and honeysuckle, planted in pleasing contrast with the harsh evergreens.

Eventually, I found a crushed-slate path that wound around to the castle's posterior. Here, the grass was clipped short into lush waves of green that stretched to the rocky shore of the lake bed. There were pathways all around it, trailing to more towers with threatening points and steps that seemed to lead to nowhere. To the right was a wide entrance through a forest, to the left, a steep embankment where the lake had lapped away the landscape.

Thor busied himself inspecting the plants in the courtyard for a while, until something caught his eye above and he howled.

"What?"

He sat down, threw his shoulders back, and bayed.

I looked up to see the object of his affection, staring out a window.

"Geez, Thor, can you please try to focus? I need you solid, my friend."

I tossed him another cookie, but he ignored it.

I sighed. "Just don't go diving onto any sharp objects, okay? I don't think Birdie and the aunts are packing that much power."

I left him to his depression and walked to the water's edge, whipped out my phone, and called Chance via video chat.

He picked up after the first ring. "Hey, baby."

"Hi, handsome."

"I was hoping you would call. I was getting a little worried."

"It's been pretty crazy, but I finally got a free moment. Here, look at this place." I held up the phone, did a slow, 360-degree scan.

Chance whistled. "Wow, that's amazing."

I turned the phone back to face him. "It's like nothing I've ever seen, that's for sure."

Chance cocked his head. "What's that noise?"

Thor was still going at it.

"That would be the wail of a lovesick puppy."

"I know how he feels," Chance said, smiling wistfully. "So, how are things going? Everything okay?"

I thought of the ghost that had tried to kill me, but decided that would be a story better left for another day, when this whole mess was over and I was back in his arms, safe and sound.

I smiled. "Everything's fine. I should be back—"

Suddenly, my throat clenched up. I coughed.

"Stacy? You okay?" Chance asked.

That was weird. "I'm fine—"

Then more tightening, squeezing, until I couldn't breathe. I dropped the phone to claw at my neck. I couldn't scream, the restriction was so tight; I could only kick my feet out until I fell backward on the muddy edge of the lake. I scrambled to get up, to wield my sword, but again I was seized, even more forcefully this time, by the throat. When I reached my hands up around my own neck, I felt invisible fingers.

I could hear Chance yelling my name, could see Thor, but I couldn't scream. Could only gag. Cough.

Whisper.

As my head slammed into the ground, I bucked, and the grip loosened for a moment. Long enough for me to say, "Pickle, Pickle, Pickle."

The clamp around my neck tightened as the murderous ghost grew angrier.

No one came.

I reached for the locket. Then I remembered it had been sewn into Thor's vest.

Chapter 27

Elizabeth guided Birdie to a far-reaching upper wing of the castle. The sun was penetrating through the windowpane of a crooked nook as they stopped before a double-doored suite. Soft music drifted into the hallway, and somewhere, someone was preparing Irish stew.

Elizabeth knocked once. Aedon called, "Come in," and Elizabeth nodded at Birdie, then slipped away.

Birdie smoothed out her jacket, took a deep breath, lifted her chin, and stepped into the room.

Aedon was gazing out a large bay window. He turned and smiled warmly at Birdie in that charming manner he had that crinkled the corners of his eyes. Even as a boy, when he'd had not a line on his face, his eyes had curled into question marks at the corners.

"Brighid, alone at last." He stepped forward, clasped both of her hands, and kissed both cheeks. "It's been too long. How many years?"

Birdie stiffened. "I suppose since the day you wed Tabby."

Aedon searched her face, sighed. "You still haven't forgiven me, have you?"

Birdie wanted to say that yes, she had, but she couldn't force the words to leave the tip of her tongue and exit her mouth. She had forgiven him. It's what you do when you love someone.

"I was a stupid, hormonal boy, Birdie. Surely, you can understand that."

Birdie broke free of his grasp. She *could* understand that. It wasn't the soured romance that had scarred her heart. It was that he had believed Tallulah's lies.

"It isn't that." She looked deep into his eyes, exposing all her sorrow, all her pain, all her loss. "You were my friend, Aedon, yet you spoke on her behalf at the hearing. How could you take her word over mine?"

Aedon winced. His voice was hoarse when he spoke a few moments later. "She had me under an enchantment spell, Birdie. For three months, every word from her mouth was truth to my ears."

Birdie knew that spell. After all, she was the one who had written it. It was in her notebook. Through the years, Birdie had filled journal after journal with original spells, often mailing them home to her sisters to insert into the Blessed Book. She had poured hours of painstaking research, practice, and heart into every potion, recipe, and charm she invented. She had suspected, once Tallulah stopped trying to destroy her work, that she was stealing it, only she could never prove it. Not even when the final exam came and Birdie performed every incantation and ritual from memory, while Tallulah had to reference her spell book. It didn't help that Tallulah's rigid father was a council member. The man was hard as a rock, and just as feeling, even when it came to his own daughter. She hadn't witnessed too many hugs or pats on the back, yet Tallulah often bragged about how powerful he was, how he would crush anyone who dared cross him.

And that's exactly what he had done to Birdie. She had been expelled for cheating when it was discovered that both girls were performing the same spell work. Naturally, the man took his daughter's word over Birdie's.

"Birdie?" Aedon was saying, shattering the distant memory. "Are you all right?"

The youngest Geraghty smiled. "Fine."

"Did you hear what I said?"

"I'm sorry, I was away with the fairies for a moment."

"I said, thank you for giving me the opportunity to redeem myself. I hope you will accept my sincere apologies. Perhaps you may even gain your rightful place on the council."

Birdie said, "I'm afraid I don't know what you mean."

Aedon stepped over to a service cart and poured himself a cup of tea. Offered Birdie some. She declined.

"The challenge, with Tallulah. I have a feeling I know who will emerge the victor. Not only between the two of you, but between your grandchildren as well."

Birdie cringed.

Aedon rushed to say, "Oh, don't get me wrong. All will be handled in the strictest sense of the rules. Only fair play, under my watch. I offer only one piece of advice."

"What is that?"

"Just use everything you used against her the last time."

Birdie nodded, understanding. Her phone chimed then, and she checked it. Chance was calling her.

How odd.

"Excuse me, Aedon. This could be important."

Aedon said, "Of course."

As Birdie hurried out the door, he called, "Just remember, Birdie, whoever wins the lead will be in charge of the quest. Your child's life in their hands."

As I lay on the muddy bank of the lake, I remembered that the goddess had told me to present an offering if I needed help from the Fae. She had said they liked sweets, so I reached into my pocket and tossed out a peanut butter cookie.

Instantly, I was sucked into the web.

I pried open my eyes to find Danu staring at me. "Hello, Stacy Justice. Have you found my cauldron?"

Pickle was sitting in a fluffy pink chair, eating his cookie. He smiled and waved at me.

I rubbed my throat, practiced a few deep breaths. "Not exactly," I coughed. "I will, but I'm having some trouble."

"What is the problem?" Danu was draped in a shimmery gown that changed colors with her every step, depending on how the light touched it.

"A spirit is trying to kill me."

Danu frowned. "I was under the impression you were a necromancer."

"Yes, well, apparently this one isn't...er...romanced by me." I lifted my head, pointed to my neck. "Are there marks?"

Badb crossed over to me, stroking a rabbit so white, it glowed. She was wearing a glittering black cape over a tight leather catsuit. She looked like one of the Avengers.

"They can touch you?" she asked, surprised, inspecting my throat.

"Yeah, it kind of freaked me out the first time it happened too," I said.

The goddesses shared a look.

Danu said, "Unusual, but not unheard of. There is something."

She crossed over to a wall of jars filled with potions. "Two drops of this, one in each eye, and no spirit will be able to touch you for one earthly sun rotation."

One day. I took a deep breath. "Great. Thank you. For some reason, I can't see the spirit either. Can you help with that?"

Badb said, "Why don't you just use your sword?"

"How?"

She looked at Danu and was about to say something, when I interrupted.

"I swear, Badb, if you say 'really, this one?' one more time, you'll never see that freaking cauldron again."

She smirked and waved her hand over my sword. It sparkled to life. "It's fully charged, always, so long as no one else ever touches it. Just wave it when the spirit is near, and the apparition will be visible to you."

"Thank you."

She answered with, "humph."

Danu grabbed the potion. "It'll sting momentarily, but that will pass."

"Okay."

She tilted my head back and dripped the juice from the vial into each eye.

"Aghhhhh! Holy nutfugget! That burns! A lot!" I rubbed my eyes furiously as I bounced around the room, searching for water to flush them out.

Danu said, "Perhaps it's harsher on humans."

"Aghhhhh!" I stomped my foot repeatedly until the pain subsided.

After what seemed like an eternity, I opened my eyes.

To nothing. I couldn't see a damn thing. "Oh my god. Oh my God. You blinded me." I was bumping into chairs, tables, and what was most likely Pickle, judging from the high-pitched scream and the peanut butter breeze that blew by me.

Danu said, "Do you think it expired, Badb?"

"What? What?" I screamed.

Badb said, "No. It's an occasional side effect. She'll be able to see when we send her back."

Danu said, "All right, then. Ready to return?"

"Are you serious? I can't see. You have to do something."

Badb said, "Nonsense, you'll be perfectly fine once your horse breaks through the barrier to your realm."

"Horse? What horse? I've never ridden a horse." Panic was setting in.

"Horses have the ability to pass seamlessly between worlds," Badb said. "He'll do all the work."

"We have you to thank for it, really, Stacy Justice. After the snafu we hit last time trying to send you back, Pickle suggested this method."

I heard the *clickety-clack* of hooves. "I've never ridden a horse," I repeated, louder.

"Not to worry. The horse will take care of everything," Danu said. "Lightning, meet Stacy Justice."

Lightning whinnied.

I said, "Lightning? Wait a second. Do you have one named, I don't know, Turtle or something?"

This made Badb groan.

Danu said, "Don't be such a baby. Lightning was one of our first recruits, and when he heard your name, he became rather excited."

Lightning pawed at the ground. Then he bit me.

"Ouch!" It was just a nip, not hard, but it startled me.

Then something flashed in my mind, a not-too-far-off memory.

I stepped forward, ran my hands along the body of the horse, and felt a familiar energy. "What does he look like?"

Danu described the ebony horse with the streak of white down his nose.

I couldn't believe it. "Mini Thor?"

The horse whinnied and licked my cheek.

"I'll be damned," I whispered.

This was my first familiar. He had been a Chihuahua then, but I had released his spirit from being bound to me, and he had chosen to inhabit the body of a horse.

The goddesses hoisted me onto the horse that was my first familiar, and tucked my sword under my right arm.

A thought occurred to me then. "One more thing. What if the ghost tries to harm me by throwing things? He likes to throw things." Like my own five-pointed star, for example.

There was a moment of silence.

Then Badb said, "Duck."

"Duck? That's all you've got? Duck?"

Five thousand years, and she tells me to duck?

I heard the slap of an ass and decided I should begin practicing their suggested defense strategy. I grabbed Mini Thor's mane and lowered my head, sword clenched at my side, as we headed for the boundary line between this world and the other.

Chapter 28

Chance had phoned Birdie six times in the last few hours, until finally she felt she had no choice but to lie to the lad.

Yes, she had told him, Anastasia was fine. She had had an allergic reaction to something she had eaten, and she was now resting comfortably. Birdie wasn't sure if he believed her or not, but at least he stopped calling.

So now where was the girl?

From the description Chance had provided—the manner in which Anastasia had clutched her throat, stumbling, gasping—Birdie feared that what her granddaughter had told her earlier about an odious spirit was true. There was only one way to dispel such an energy, and it required a handful of dirt from an ancient graveyard. Luckily, there was no lack of those on the island, and Birdie had sent Lolly off to fetch some.

When her oldest sister returned, however, Anastasia still hadn't, and the Mage challenges had already begun. Birdie had completed two rounds and was tied with Tallulah. Soon, the Seeker contest would start, and without both

Seekers, Aedon would have no choice but to call the games. Anastasia would be forced to forfeit.

Fiona was standing on the sidelines, monitoring the girl's familiar. The dog was thoroughly spent. Birdie presumed he was worn out from tirelessly searching the area for his witch.

The loudspeaker roared to life. Elizabeth's voice blasted through the air. "The next challenge is worth twenty-five points and will decide the match."

Tallulah cast Birdie a sinister smile. Her grandson was suiting up behind her, his horse saddled and ready for the Seeker's jousting match. Birdie and her sisters had every intention of preparing Anastasia for her contest, but the girl had simply vanished. Even if she were to return in time, she likely wouldn't have an inkling of how to defeat Tallulah's smarmy grandson.

The young man she was looking at didn't seem like the same one who'd slouched in the Court of O'Conor earlier. Ethan was stretching, examining his jousting stick, checking the horse's hooves.

He seemed determined. And that frightened Birdie.

Elizabeth unfolded a piece of paper and boomed, "Mages, here is your next challenge."

Birdie looked up toward the tower where Elizabeth stood.

Elizabeth said, "Without bringing harm to the intended, you must coerce another to do your bidding. Explain the challenge before you proceed. Scores will be based on ingenuity, degree of difficulty, and lasting impact."

Birdie swallowed hard and flicked a nervous glance to Fiona. She had no spell for bending another to her will. Her mother had taught her that such witchcraft was forbidden.

"Tallulah O'Conor will be the first challenger," Elizabeth said.

Tallulah stepped into the arena, waved to the council watching from the confines of the castle, and grabbed the microphone perched on the stand near her sideline.

"My intended is Oscar Sheridan," Tallulah said.

Birdie's stomach lurched.

So that was her plan.

"Oscar met me only this morning." Oscar waved enthusiastically from Tallulah's side of the field. "But I will prove that the power at my fingertips can turn a man's heart in an instant."

Tallulah waved back to Oscar. "Come, Oscar. Declare your undying love for me."

Birdie had never seen the man move so fast, not even in his prime. He scurried forward like a squirrel with a nut and joined Tabby.

She said, "Now, how will you prove your devotion to me, my darling?"

Birdie was not the least bit surprised when the twit she used to be married to bent down on one knee, produced a rock the size of Gibraltar, and proposed.

Incensed, but not surprised.

Tallulah shot a triumphant look at Birdie, then shifted her gaze to the top level of the castle, where the council was situated.

Her smile faltered, and Birdie turned to see that the remaining members of the council were not as impressed with Tallulah's display as she had expected.

Tabby recovered instantly. That made Birdie nervous.

She watched as her nemesis said, "You have me nearly convinced, Oscar. However, I may need further incentive to trust your devotion."

As if he had rehearsed, although Birdie knew that he had not, Oscar reached into his inner pocket, rose up, and stepped toward the microphone.

He said, "I, Oscar Sheridan, vow to offer all my worldly possessions to the council in exchange for the hand of this incredible woman."

Betrayer! Birdie thought. She nearly fell over where she stood.

Lolly did.

Birdie knew that the council needed money to operate. The work they did—protecting the ancient secrets of the island—was costly, and with Oscar's real estate holdings in their possession, they might have the option to reach across the pond, set up a satellite headquarters in America.

Were they above bribery? She hoped so.

Birdie saw Fiona rise from her seat, and put a desperate hand to Thor's collar, trying to lock on to Birdie's gaze.

Birdie felt the heat on her face. She concentrated on Fiona's stare.

What? The question floated through her mind.

Fiona flicked her eyes to Thor, back to Birdie, then again to Thor.

The dog had a leg flung over his shoulder and was treating his private parts like they were a pair of lollipops.

Then Birdie saw the faint impression of the locket sewn into his vest.

The spell—the one she had performed back at the family home to pull Anastasia out of the web—penetrated her brain.

Could it be? Was that where her granddaughter had gotten off to?

Tabby stepped out of the arena to the thunderous applause of the council. An idea formed in Birdie's mind.

Birdie watched as her old enemy walked off, a smug look on her face. Behind her, Ethan was already leading his horse into the pasture. She saw an attendant speak with him briefly at the gate.

Birdie knew this was her one shot. If she failed, she might lose her daughter—and her granddaughter—forever.

She took a deep breath, walked up to the microphone. She glanced one last time at her middle sister. Fiona nodded, not with certainty, but rather with hope.

Aedon's words ran through her mind as she stood there, gathering her strength. *Use everything you did last time.*

Well, that included honesty, didn't it?

"I have a confession to make," Birdie said in a steady voice. "My granddaughter Stacy Justice is a reluctant witch."

She paused as the council mumbled in shock and awe. Aedon gave a slight, encouraging nod.

When the murmurs subsided, Birdie continued. "She always had faith in her family, but not much else." Birdie looked right at Tallulah. "Especially not in being Seeker."

Tabby smirked, shook her head.

Birdie scanned the grounds, the arena. *Where are you, child? If you're out there, hear my call.*

She took a deep breath. "My intended is Stacy Justice. As you can see, though she is scheduled for a challenge, she is absent from these proceedings."

The council strained their necks to search the area. Birdie saw several members nod.

"It is my will that she will become not only a true believer, but a confirmed Seeker, within twenty-four hours."

At this, Aedon stood, Tallulah balked, and Lolly clapped.

Birdie motioned for Thor. Fiona whispered something into the dog's ear. He stood and swaggered over to Birdie like John Wayne about to mount a horse.

The dog sat near Birdie, ears pointed skyward, locket just below his shoulder. Birdie put her hand on the pendant, opened her third eye, and prayed to Danu to deliver her granddaughter to her side.

Then she waited.

If I hadn't ducked, my head would have clotheslined a low-hanging branch, and I'd be the headless horsewoman right now. So, turns out "duck" isn't bad advice.

Instead, I was plowing through a field on the back of my first familiar, heading straight for that asshat Ethan. My sword was still tucked tightly under my arm as we charged through the impossibly green landscape.

Ethan was suited up like Lancelot, gaping at me in disbelief.

That was about two seconds before my sword rammed into his armor. He flew off his steed with a look of pure shock on his face.

Mini Thor—or, rather, Lightning—reared up with a ferocious battle cry, and I was sure I was about to wind up on my ass too.

I hung on until he trotted to a stop and pivoted his huge frame.

There was some commotion then, cries of protests and cheers as the horse I was seated on bowed to the ground. I dismounted Lightning, kissed his white streak, and watched as he galloped off into the woods.

I scanned my surroundings, dazed for several moments. The sun was at its apex, higher in the sky than it had been just a short while ago when I was near the water's edge at the back of the castle.

Almost as if I had been gone longer than it seemed.

The clock on the far-left tower confirmed this. It was noon.

Is that what happened in the web? When Danu had pulled me in the first time, I hadn't even missed dinner. Now, I had lost an entire morning. Which meant night was arriving soon, and if I didn't return the locket, the ghost was going to come after me. Again.

I had to get the hell out of here. Had to find the cauldron. Had to end this.

I spotted Birdie a few yards away, beaming at me. Fiona was standing off to the side, and Lolly was whooping, hollering, and waving a cowboy hat like she was at a prison rodeo.

A loudspeaker screeched above my head, and I turned to see Elizabeth standing on top of a tower.

"Everyone remain patient as I consult with the judges," she said.

I had no idea what she was talking about, but Ethan was still lolling about on the ground, having a hell of a time trying to right himself, so I went over to give him a hand.

That's when Tallulah charged at me, far more swiftly than a woman her age ought to have been capable of moving.

As if in slow motion, Ethan's grandmother rammed both her hands into my chest and sent me reeling through the air. I skidded on my back about five feet, the wind knocked out of me.

Things pretty much went downhill after that.

Tallulah was on me in seconds, screaming about cheating and hurting her precious grandson. She pummeled my face, and I tried to grab her wrists, but the woman was freakishly fast. Birdie reached us a heartbeat later and, with one banshee wail, ripped her old schoolmate off of me and tossed her a car's length away. I couldn't help but wonder what the hell was in the air out here that lent old ladies the strength and stamina of the Incredible Hulk.

Soon Gramps arrived, screaming at Birdie about being jealous of his new love.

There was no time to process that disturbing notion before Lolly and Fiona joined the fracas, each giving Gramps a fair flogging for good measure.

Then Thor rocketed forward, intercepting Gretchen, whose teeth were dripping venom, just as she was about to sink them into my thigh.

I belly-flopped onto my stomach to see poor Ethan still struggling on his back like a kid in a snowsuit. I crawled over to him as everyone was still bitching at each other.

I coughed a few times before sputtering out, "Are you okay?"

"Ehh. Ow. Oy."

"I'm sorry. I don't even know what happened."

He gave me a cockeyed stare. Either because he didn't believe me or because the suit was pinching something important.

"My grandmother happened," he spit out. "She always happens."

I clambered to my feet, offered my hand. "I know what you mean. I've got one of those."

He scowled, but accepted the assistance, and I heaved him to an upright position.

We stood there, dumbfounded, staring at the mess, but not really sure how to untangle it.

Everyone was still screaming at each other, even the dogs were nipping and barking, when the loudspeaker pierced the air with a sound like metal scraping metal for an excruciatingly long time. The crowd clamped their hands over their ears. The dogs dove for cover, each securing purchase beneath a bench.

After a minute, Aedon, in a forceful, edgy tone, said, "Everyone report to the Great Hall at once!"

Chapter 29

There was simply no dignified excuse for acting like a three-year-old. Heck, Birdie hadn't even acted like a three-year-old when she was that age. No, she wasn't going to bother with justifying her behavior. Even if she tried, she knew Aedon wouldn't hear of it. Such a display was not welcomed at the castle.

It was just that when she saw the threat to her granddaughter, her animal instinct to protect the girl kicked into overdrive.

She stole a glance at Tallulah, who herself looked shame stricken.

If she were to be completely honest, Birdie had to admit that Tabby had probably reacted the way she had for the same reasons as Birdie, despite the fact that Ethan's fall had been an accident. Suddenly, she didn't feel so different from the woman anymore. Not that she would ever tell her that.

Birdie decided it best that she stew in her embarrassment, take her scolding, and get on with the mission.

They were all seated at a round table in a massive room with twenty-foot ceilings and life-sized paintings of gods and goddesses along the wall. Dagda was there with his cauldron, Lugh clutching his spear, Badb, black wings stretched out wide behind her, and Nuada carrying his sword of light.

Birdie, Tabby, Ethan, and Anastasia were each nestled into plush red-velvet chairs with gilded legs. The two dogs were perched next to their respective sorcerers.

No one spoke. There was only the gentle hum of the radiator, and a faint aroma of licorice tea.

Aedon stepped into the room, looking disheveled. Tallulah rose to say something.

"Sit down, Tabby," Aedon snapped.

She did.

The head council member looked around the table. The silence stretched until Birdie thought she could no longer stand it.

Finally, her old friend said, "Never in all my years as a member of the council have I witnessed such a blatant display of disrespect, not only for this castle, not only for the initiative that we stand for, but for our fellow brothers and sisters."

He looked at each person pointedly. Anastasia bowed her head.

"Now, I understand that emotions run high during a competition, but have you all forgotten what we are doing here?"

Aedon paused.

Birdie shook her head. The rest followed suit.

Aedon spun around and paced back and forth for a moment. He ran a hand through his normally well-kempt hair. "The council is not pleased with your actions. They have decided to cancel the games, and they are tempted to revoke all of your nominations."

Anastasia fired a nervous glance at Birdie. The girl said, "What does that mean?"

Aedon said, "It means, young lady, that none of you is fit to find the cauldron."

Anastasia shot up. "No, please, you can't do that. My mother—"

"Is still up for her hearing in a month's time," Aedon said sharply.

Birdie said, "But the cauldron. Who will find it?"

Aedon said, "The Guardian had the plan in his Blessed Book. He, with the aid of the Warrior, will locate the cauldron." He looked from Tabby to Birdie. "A Mage has never been sent on a quest before, so I see no reason to send one now."

Tallulah looked relieved.

Birdie tensed. John had lied about finding the blueprint to search for the cauldron in his family's book of theology. Anastasia had received that information straight from Danu herself.

The girl looked around the room desperately. Birdie could sense her granddaughter was searching for a solution. Anastasia knew she had to be there. There was no other way.

"Very well," Aedon said. "You are all dismissed."

Then an unexpected voice said, "Wait. I'd like to say something."

Ethan stood up, tossed an apologetic look to his grandmother, and said, "I would like to withdraw my nomination as Seeker of Justice."

I couldn't believe it.

Neither could Tallulah. She jumped to her feet. "Ethan, don't be a fool. You've wanted this your entire life. You cannot quit now."

Ethan's eyes were soft as he smiled at his grandmother. "No, Gran, this is what you wanted. And to be honest, I'm not even sure it was for me."

He circled the table with sad eyes and took the old woman's hands gently into his own. "I'm not cut out for this. I think you've always known that."

Tallulah stammered. "That's preposterous. You're just afraid. Your mother was fearful of your gifts too, of what danger they might bring, but she's gone now, Ethan. It's time you grow into your own man."

"That's what I'm trying to do, Gran."

Tallulah scoffed. "So this is my grandson? A quitter?"

"That's enough, Mother," Pearce said from the doorway.

Everyone turned.

Aedon said, "Pearce, this is a closed meeting."

"A thousand apologies, Aedon." He strode forward, his long legs pointed toward me. "I was just coming to return the sword to Miss Justice."

He nodded at me and set it on a side table. I nodded a thank-you back. Hadn't realized I'd lost it.

Aedon said, "You are the boy's father, Pearce. What say you?"

Pearce passed his mother a look of remorse with his ocean-blue eyes. Then he turned to the lead of the council. "I believe my son knows his calling. Magic may flow through our blood, but some O'Conors have a potent gift, while others struggle to develop theirs. For many, it doesn't come at all." He was staring at Tallulah as he said this last part.

So he knew. He knew that his own mother was not the great Mage she claimed to be. Perhaps it skipped a generation in his family. Perhaps the power, or magic, or whatever the hell it was that drove witches to be witches wasn't fluid in their clan, as it was in mine, but rather, it zigzagged, touching only certain members of the family.

But then why was it so important to Tallulah? Why was she so driven to excel in this arena, if it cost her friends, loved ones, even her own dignity? She was a descendent of a high king, after all. Wasn't that enough?

Tallulah said, in clipped speech, "No, that isn't true." She shook her head manically, eyes darting all around the room. I got the distinct impression that she was afraid of someone. Or something.

But who?

Or what?

The woman shuddered, and a cold hand climbed down my back.

I twisted around in my chair. No one was there.

As I turned back, Tallulah's gaze met mine, held it for a single breath.

I was suddenly very aware that the locket was sewn into Thor's vest, and I placed a protective hand over my familiar, guarding the heirloom, and him. He nuzzled his big black-and-tan muzzle closer to me.

Aedon said, "Ethan, you may go."

"No, please, let me talk to the boy," Tallulah said.

Aedon cast a look of pity at Tallulah. However, when he spoke, he was all authority. "Tabby, let this go."

She clamped her mouth shut, even as she squirmed in her seat, lowered her gaze.

Pearce laid an arm over his son's shoulders. I watched as they left the room, Gretchen trotting close behind. Before the door swung shut, the older man looked over his shoulder and winked at me.

What the hell?

I tried to lock eyes with Birdie to see if she had caught that. Her mouth was set into a grim line. Her eyes were on Aedon.

Then I noticed something else. Something I had never seen in Birdie's face.

Admiration. Devotion. Longing.

Aw, geez, not her too.

Aedon pulled up a chair. "Now then, what shall we do about the two of you?" He looked from my grandmother to her old classmate.

Birdie looked at Tallulah, then at me. She said, "I have a proposal that may be in the best interest of us all."

Tallulah snorted.

Aedon ignored her and said, "Proceed, Birdie."

I looked around the table, realizing that between the three of them, they had about two hundred years more experience with all of this than I did. I also couldn't help but remember that I had encountered each of these sage elders at that tender age when life courses are set into motion.

Maybe I did belong here after all.

Then the gleam of my sword as the sunlight bounced off it through the open curtain caught my eye, and another, chilling thought crept through my mind.

Badb's words. *It's fully charged, so long as no one else ever touches it. Just wave it when the spirit is near, and the apparition will be visible to you.*

But Pearce had touched my sword.

Had it been an innocent gesture? Or had he known that his touch would neutralize the charge?

Chapter 30

The argument on the field had halted any further discussions regarding Birdie's confirmation as Mage, but Birdie knew that the truth was, Tallulah didn't want this mission. She wanted the prestige, the power of her status as Mage and council member, not the dangerous work it brought. While destiny, nominations, and confirmations were one thing, talent was quite another. It would take powerful magic to accomplish what they were asked to do. Deep down, Birdie was certain that Tabby knew she didn't have that. But her name—and her station—could prove useful. If only she would agree to Birdie's plan.

Birdie said, "I will accompany my granddaughter and the Guardian on this quest. I believe it best that Tallulah remain here. Should we need assistance from the council, Tallulah will serve us far better as our point of contact. Any decisions we make regarding the retrieval of the cauldron can filter through her." Birdie glanced at Tabby. "She also knows the ancient sites well, their locations, their histories. If the mission should take us into unchartered territory, Tallulah would be our navigational guide. With the clout

Barbra Annino

of the O'Conor name backing her, she may be able to open doors that we might not otherwise gain access to."

Tabby looked at Birdie, contemplating this proposal. She seemed pleased with the idea.

"What of Ethan?" Tallulah asked. "I would like him to join you."

Birdie looked at Anastasia. The girl shrugged.

"I believe that would be up to the boy," said Birdie.

Aedon agreed to the arrangement, and the three of them exchanged their cell phone information. Anastasia also jotted down John's number for them.

Aedon reminded them that the Warrior was unavailable until tomorrow. Then he gave them his blessing and left the room.

Birdie stared at her old rival. The two women sized each other up for a few beats, until Anastasia broke the silence.

She said, "Tallulah, do you really have that kind of pull? Was Birdie right about that?"

Birdie watched as Tallulah raised one eyebrow, a hint of a smile tugging at her lips. "Of course I do. I'm an O'Conor."

Anastasia said, "Excellent. We need you to break out the Warrior."

Tallulah frowned.

"Is that a problem, Tabby?" Birdie asked.

Immediately, the woman who was now romancing Birdie's ex-husband said, "Absolutely not."

Anastasia bounced over to Tabby. "Then it's settled. We leave now."

"Now?" Tabby asked.

Birdie's granddaughter sheathed her sword and said, "Don't worry, we'll bring you back a hat."

- 252 -

Birdie said, "And keep an eye on the girl's grandfather."

Tallulah looked as if she'd just been through a windstorm as Birdie and her granddaughter rushed out of the room.

A short while later, they were standing in the entrance-way of the castle. Lolly had just equipped Anastasia for battle. The girl was wearing a long leather coat lined with enchanted herbs and crystals, an athame strapped to her thigh, leather riding boots, with the broom tucked inside, and, of course, the sword.

She drew the line at the graveyard dirt.

"You're not dousing me with dirt, Aunt Lolly, especially not maggot dirt," she said.

Lolly explained what it was for, that Chance had called and told them about what he'd seen. Anastasia confirmed her experience with the malevolent spirit, and Lolly said that they wanted to protect her from it, and hopefully keep her from entering the web again.

She thought about it, then said, "Okay, but later, when we return. I haven't seen Ivy in a while, and I don't want her to lay eyes on a dirt dauber."

Ethan and John came in through the door then, arguing.

John said, "I always drive, kid."

Ethan said, "Have you driven in Ireland before?"

"I drive in Chicago. Trust me. This'll be a cakewalk."

"Have you ever been stuck in a roundabout?"

John knotted his brow. "What's a roundabout?"

Ethan crossed his arms. "Can you speak Gaelic?"

"No."

"Do they have sheep jams led by angry farmers toting shotguns in Chicago?"

John rolled his eyes. "Fine, kid, you drive."

Ethan grinned, tossed his keys in the air, and said, "Let the games begin."

Thor and Gretchen trotted happily alongside their witch and wizard.

John said, "Whoa, where do you think you're going?" He was looking at the dogs. Then he looked at Ethan. "Unless you got an RV, the pooches stay put."

Ethan said, "I was going to take the Escalade. It's quite roomy."

"I'm sure we could all fit," Anastasia said.

John balked. "Yeah? And if we find the cauldron, where the heck do you think we're going to put it? In the glove compartment?"

"Good point," said Anastasia.

Fiona offered to keep an eye on the familiars. Anastasia and Ethan both agreed, although Ethan eyed Thor and said, "Keep your paws to yourself, lover boy."

With that, three of the four corners headed off on a mission from a goddess.

I wasn't too happy about leaving Thor behind, with his raging hormones and broken heart, but there wasn't much choice in the matter.

Two and a half hours later, past miles of bright green pasture, endless sheep, and crumbled ruins, we arrived at the Academy of Sorcery, in Kildare, to collect Ivy.

I hopped out, jogged up the wide cement steps of the school, and pressed a buzzer.

"Yes?"

"Tallulah O'Conor called ahead. My name is Stacy Justice. I'm here for Ivy Delaney," I said into the small intercom.

The door hissed open, and I entered the mammoth stone building. The hall was smaller than the castle's foyer, but just as impressive, with elaborately papered walls, trophy cases, and portraits of graduating classes that spanned a hundred years.

Tallulah had texted me instructions to walk through a white archway, turn right, and knock on the third door on the left, so I did just that.

"Come in."

The woman sitting behind the desk was about 180 years old. Minimum.

She lifted her gaze, trained it on me. Her chin couldn't keep up with the rest of her face, so it sagged into a pile of paperwork for about two seconds longer than it should have.

I had been in a hurry before I opened the door. Now I just wanted to beat it out of there before she flatlined.

Ivy was nowhere in sight.

"Hello, I'm here to pick up Ivy Delaney."

The woman glared at me. I think she was trying to give me the evil eye, but she couldn't decide which one was stronger.

The left side won.

"No absences during exams! No exceptions." Her lips curled over her teeth like she had left something there for later.

"I'm sure if you check your notes, you'll see that Ivy is excused. She's needed for an important, er, mission."

I shimmied my sword at her.

The woman scowled, took about five minutes to stand, although she wasn't much taller after the effort, and croaked at me. "You think that sword gives you the right to break rules? Hogwash. I've given lickings to bigger witches than you, missy."

Where had I heard that expression before?

She pointed a gnarled finger at my boobs because she couldn't reach any higher. "Get out of my school."

Why was every old person I met so goddamn ornery? Where were all the matronly grandmothers who baked cookies and knitted scarves? If there was some sort of adoption program for that group of folks, I wanted a piece of it.

"Okay, look, Mrs...." I flashed my eyes to the nameplate on her desk. "Doherty. I only need Ivy for—"

Wait a minute. Doherty. Why did I know that name?

Before I could place it, she cracked me across the knee with a sharp wand.

"Yow! Jesus, lady. Take it easy."

I was doing a bee-sting dance when she came at me again. I blocked the blow with my right arm, and then something about her eyes, her hair, and that god-awful puke-beige pantsuit set off an alarm in my head.

Doherty. This was the woman who led the field trip to Tara. The one who threatened to strike Birdie.

I disarmed her and advanced until she was forced back into her chair. It wasn't as cool as it seemed in the movies. Mostly because she looked like Yoda and moved like a freight train at a cross light.

I leaned in. "Mrs. Doherty. We meet again."

"What?" she squawked. "I don't know you." She gnashed her teeth.

"Sure you do. Take a good look." I held my head steady, because her eyeballs looked wobbly.

She squinted at me. "Nope. Maybe if you hand me my glasses."

Oh, for crying out loud. "My name is Stacy Justice." I said it very slowly, a shroud of danger in my voice. "I told you that if you so much as touched the hair on another kid's head, I'd be coming back for you." I cocked my chin, and a flint of recognition sparkled in her eyes.

"No," she whispered. "It can't be. You…you look exactly the same."

"I moisturize." I unsheathed my sword and said, "Now get me Ivy or I call in my flying friend."

Horror settled into her face for an extended stay. She moved a lot faster then, punching buttons on her phone, signing paperwork, all while keeping her good eye on me, making sure I didn't lunge, I suppose. Within minutes, Ivy was by my side.

I waved to Mrs. Doherty on the way out of her office.

She still looked mystified.

Ivy hugged me as we got to the front door. She shoved her way through and bounded down the steps, hopped into the car.

Once inside, she was all business.

"What's the plan, people?" she asked.

Birdie handed her a spell that she and the aunts had constructed earlier to sync our psyches so that we could better connect to the image, or, rather, the messages, the cauldron would hopefully send once we were on top of the mound.

"There are a few things we need to do first, before we head to the hill," I said.

I explained that Ivy needed to get to the spear at the Royal Irish Academy, and that John would have to visit Howth Castle for the sword.

Ethan said, "I believe the place is closed for renovations. It's a private residence, mostly; they only open to large groups."

I frowned, looked at John. "Call Tallulah, see if she can get you in. If that doesn't work, mention Grace O'Malley."

John gave me a sly smile.

Ivy said, "So we're splitting up?"

"I think that's best. The Stone of Destiny isn't far from here, so Ethan can drive Birdie and me there. You and John can pair up, take the train from Kildare to Dublin, hit the Academy, then head north to Howth on the DART rail."

Ethan said, "'Tis Saturday. The Royal Irish Academy is closed."

I looked at Ivy, questioning.

She patted her bag. "Piece of cake."

The kid was equipped with all kinds of measures for breaking and entering.

"Call Tallulah if you get into a jam," I said.

Ivy gave me a thumbs-up.

I took a deep breath. "Okay, so whatever sort of spell you need to connect with your treasure is up to you guys. You don't have to bring them with you or anything; just set your power in tune with your talisman." I flicked a glance to Birdie. She gave me a cool stare of confidence. "Right. So, John, Ivy, you good with that?"

"I think I can handle it," John said.

Ivy said, "Roger, sister."

"Perfect." I checked the time on my phone. "We'll pick you up from the train in three hours."

Ethan whistled. "Not a lot of legroom there."

That was true. It would take them forty-five minutes to get to Dublin alone, but I wanted this over and done with tonight.

John saw my concern. "We've got everyone we need. All the power running at full throttle. We'll get it done."

His confidence seeped over to me.

But what he didn't know—what none of us realized until it was too late—was that when the spell broke, one of the four corners would be dead.

Chapter 31

Traveling from the Academy in Kildare to the Hill of Tara, Birdie couldn't help but recall the class trip she had taken there as a young girl. She stole a glance at her granddaughter, who was gazing out the window, her leg rattling nervously.

She had always hoped that she would be the one to escort Anastasia to this sacred site. She just never imagined that it would happen under these circumstances. She wondered if they should have at least liberated the locket from the vest of the girl's familiar. Would it have grounded her? Washed away the jitters that seemed to be overtaking her now?

No use worrying about it, she decided.

Ethan's steady hands guided the car through the rich landscape, expertly manipulating the wheel to avoid a flock of sheep that had spilled onto the road. The air was calm in Meath. Almost too calm, Birdie thought. She couldn't wait for this excursion to be over.

When the car finally hummed to a stop, Birdie stepped out, drinking in the scenery. There was a souvenir shop that hadn't been there when she had last set foot on this land, a closed sign banging over the rickety door. She spotted a few benches, a few new fence posts, and recently planted shrubbery, but other than that, Tara remained the same.

It felt like home.

Anastasia said a few words to Ethan and joined Birdie next to the car. They walked together in silence, toward the Stone of Destiny.

When they reached the engorged roots of the ancient oak that guarded the cemetery, Birdie stopped short. She stiffened. She could hear ghostly laughter, taunting, coming from the tree where Tallulah had ripped the spell from Birdie's first book many years ago. Up above, the branch that had caught the page dangled, beckoning the old witch to step closer.

Anastasia shifted uncomfortably next to her.

Birdie said, "I'm all right. I'm just...remembering something."

"We should go, Birdie. We don't have much time."

The girl tugged on her sleeve.

"One moment."

Birdie stepped closer to the tree, and instantly a vision emerged of herself as a girl. Her full lip quivered, but Birdie's young self tried to appear strong. Then a preteen Tabby's head poked out from behind a headstone, holding Birdie's work hostage. She was teasing Birdie, along with three other classmates, playing keep-away with her work.

And that hideous rhyme they were singing. *Brigit is a dimwit, a stupid twit.*

It was the reason Birdie had adopted her nickname. Thinking about it now made her Geraghty blood boil. The fact that the name she had been so very proud to carry had been ripped from her by a stupid childhood bully.

No, Birdie thought, Tabby hadn't taken that from her. No one can hurt you without your permission. She had allowed it.

It was the last time she had allowed anyone to wield such power over her.

From behind her, Birdie heard a faint shout. "Girls, enough!"

She whipped her head around to see a hologram of a young woman approach the children of her vision.

Present-day Birdie smacked her head. *That's right! The chaperone.* Birdie couldn't recall her name, but she remembered what the compassionate woman had told her.

Stay true to yourself, my dear, and you'll never go wrong. She had lived her life by that motto. She hoped she had instilled that same value in her children and her grandchildren.

The older Birdie flicked her eyes to Anastasia for a moment. "I learned a lot here." Then she glanced back at the veiled young woman approaching the childhood Tabby. She couldn't quite make out her face, but she could see the determination. It emitted from her core, a fiery red wave of resolve. That's when Birdie remembered what had happened next.

She looked at Anastasia. "You know, the only time I saw the Seeker's locket…"

Suddenly, her granddaughter rushed forward, grabbed Birdie's arm, and said, "We have to go."

But it was too late. Thunder clapped in the sky, and a jolt surged from Anastasia to Birdie.

A flash, an image.

And she knew.

Of all the moments to stroll down memory lane. Geesh.

"Birdie, we have to go. Now," I said again, as firmly as I could.

My grandmother swallowed hard, her green eyes cloudy. She nodded and led us up the hill toward the Stone of Destiny.

I was ever so grateful for that, but I could see it in her face. A recollection, or some distant memory, had just washed over her. I only hoped I wasn't in it. Not because I feared what might happen if she knew, but because I feared what might not happen. I needed her strong, I needed the full power of my grandmother for what we were about to do. If there were any doubts in her mind, even a hint of haze about the person she was and how she got that way, well, let's just say I knew from experience those nigglings piss off the fairies.

We trekked up the hill the short distance to the stone. Birdie seemed to shake off whatever had just come over her by the time we reached it.

"Stand back," she instructed.

I did.

She took a deep breath, raised her long arms to the sky, and began moving her lips so rapidly, not only could I not make out what she was saying, but I wasn't even sure she was speaking English.

And maybe she wasn't.

Her voice grew louder with each passing second. The wind picked up velocity in tandem with her words.

"Cumhacht de an tulach…"

Definitely not English.

Her eyes were closed, her feet planted, and her arms flexed as she continued to chant to the heavens.

The sky cracked open, and a streak of lightning hit the stone just as she laid her hands on it. The bolt ricocheted off the rock, and I dove for cover, tumbling down the hill in a fast-paced spiral.

After a moment, the wind died down and I heard, "Anastasia?"

"I'm okay."

She popped her head over the crest and said, "Quit fooling around. We have work to do."

Chapter 32

I pulled out my copy of the spell and studied my role on the drive from Tara, crunching on a granola bar Birdie had given me.

It was a watchtower call. I was to be east; Ivy, west; John, south; and Birdie, north. Each of us would weave a different chant, the idea being that our magic, the power of the gods, and the assistance of the ancestors would all link together to form a powerful pull that would call to the lost cauldron, requesting that the treasure reveal its hiding place.

On the way, we picked up John and Ivy from the train station. They both assured me there were no glitches in their treasure connections and they were ready to cast the spell.

We arrived at Fourknocks early in the evening. We left Ethan in the car, and I and the three other corners hiked to the top of the towering ancient mound the gods called the Hill of Summoning.

We clasped hands, each cloaked in a veil of grounding white light. Birdie gave the signal, and she began to chant first.

"Watchtowers of the north, come forth. May the gods come out to aid our course."

Ivy was next. "Watchtowers of the west, send your best. May the ancestors assist us on this quest."

John stepped forward. "Watchtowers of the south, come out. Cauldron, pave a path to your route."

Then me. "Watchtowers of the east, all meet. Unite the magic in our hearts and below our feet."

Instantly, the mound shook and shuddered, and a surge of electricity shot between our fingertips.

Birdie shouted, "Keep the flow going as it was written."

We broke, still chanting, each of us moving backward step by step, first to the edge of the mound, and then, once there, we all turned to face the crest of our corner. I slowly descended the hill, as instructed in the spell. The circumference of the mound was vast, and Birdie had concluded that by encompassing the entire curvature of the landscape, the spell would be all the more efficacious. The ground was still rumbling, so I half jogged, half slid down the hill, somehow dislodging my sword in the process.

Birdie had warned us not to break the circle of energy, so I kept chanting, finally reaching the bottom of the mound, where I turned and kneeled toward its belly, eyes closed, willing the image of the cauldron to come to me.

The image of the cauldron flashed, briefly, along with a street sign.

Then, another image.

A man I recognized from somewhere, though I couldn't place him, sneering at me with hatred so vehement, it had a heartbeat.

I mentally shoved him out of the way, and focused again on the cauldron, my eyes squeezed shut.

It flashed again, several times, and I knew exactly where it was.

I was about to stand to head back to the car, when a gloved hand clamped over my mouth. Another pinned my arms to their sides.

The ethereal voice of the riddler ghost curled through my brain. *Beware of the wrath of a rival, and the one who will betray.*

Panic flooded my gut. Who was this? Ethan? John? Was it the rival or the one who would betray?

I kicked, tried to bite, scratch, scream, even as I was being dragged away from the mound. I had a sinking feeling that my companions could not see me, nor I them. The instructions had been that when the spell was over, when we all felt like we had emptied our well and no more information would come forth, we were to meet back at the car. Would they be able to spot me from the roadside?

I looked down. Black gloves. Couldn't tell if it was a man or a woman.

Goddess, please don't let it be Ivy.

The dagger was strapped to my thigh. I wasn't sure I could reach it, even if I could wrestle my arms free.

But then the sword called to me. Actually *called* to me. A low hum buzzed in my ears, the tiniest of vibrations, but I somehow knew what it was. I focused on it, the three-muses grip, the shiny shaft that glimmered when Badb had blessed it. The sharp point of the blade.

As my feet knocked into dirt and rocks, and I was still being hauled off to Goddess knows where, I honed my mind's eye and pictured the sword in my hand. Imagined that I wasn't simply calling on Badb, but that her spirit was within me. That I was the embodiment of the warrior goddess herself.

I managed to elbow my attacker, freeing my arm. I stuck my hand out, and without hesitation, the sword flew into my grip. I swept it behind me, swift and low, taking out the legs of the person who had held me.

Free from the grip, I whipped around, the sword hot in my hand, and faced the one who would betray.

Aedon was already back on his feet.

"Hello, Miss Justice."

I was completely confused. He was the one who had called me to this quest in the first place. "What are you doing?"

He tightened his gloves. "I think it's time you and I had a private chat."

"About what?"

"Your reason for being here, of course." He stepped forward. I felt a wave of anger swell from him.

What was that? Why did he hate me? Did he know about the web? About my chaperoning the field trip?

But I hadn't done anything to Aedon.

"I don't think so." I whipped out my cell phone.

"I wouldn't do that if I were you," Aedon said. "After all, the spell is incomplete. Should you call to them, or phone them, you'll break the enchantment and the cauldron will never be found. The council would frown on that, I believe. We wouldn't want to upset them with your mother's release so close."

I smirked at him. "That's where you're wrong, Aedon. The spell worked. I already know where the cauldron is. I'm sure the council will be pleased with my work."

He feigned surprise. "Is that so? Do tell. Where is the treasure?"

The horrific realization of the message behind his sarcasm hit me like a brick. "You already know, don't you, Aedon? Because you put it there."

But why? Why would he steal the cauldron only to call me to look for it? Was this about Birdie?

He widened his eyes in surprise. "Why would I do that?"

"I don't know. But I'm sure the council will force you to tell them when I drag your ass in."

Aedon scratched his chin. "Well, this I must hear. How do you plan to drag me in, as you say, Miss Justice?"

I gave him a *duh* look and rallied my sword.

Aedon slid his eyes over my sword and paused for a moment, as if contemplating. I could tell he was enjoying this like a cat plays with a mouse before it pounces. He was powerful, that was sure. He had a lot of years behind him to perfect his craft. But I was swift, my muscles toned, my heart pure. And my mission stemmed from love, not hate.

Aedon said, "While that is an impressive tool, I wouldn't put too much stake in it. It's not the instrument that holds the power, but the person who wields it."

We were far from the mound. They wouldn't hear me if I called. Best to handle this jacknut myself. I pocketed the phone.

Gripping the sword with both hands, I took two strides forward and snapped my leg behind me in a twirling midair launch. I twisted the sword, intending to slam it flat against Aedon's back to knock the wind from him.

What happened instead shocked even me.

The sword leaped from my hands toward Aedon.

I crumbled into a heap on the ground, recovered, then reached out, attempting to will my sword back to me. My energy was focused only on that as I concentrated on the blade. It hung in the air for several moments, as if trying to decide which side to choose.

Damn you, Pearce, for tainting my weapon! Was he in on this too?

Aedon flicked his wrist, and the sword Birdie had given me long ago snapped in half and flung itself into some far-off shrubs.

Uh-oh. That was a new trick to me. I whipped my head to face Aedon. Climbed slowly to my feet.

He gave me a sinister smile. "I graduated at the top of my class. Telekinesis was my specialty."

Of course it was. I should have maimed the kid when I had the chance.

There was a pocket full of herbs and a pouch of crystals in my coat, but nothing more powerful than that. Except the athame. There was also the broom, charged with the power of generations of my clan.

I decided to keep both hidden for the time being, lest they follow the fate of my sword.

I reached into my pocket.

"Don't touch the phone, Miss Justice."

Could I reason with him? His eyes were fierce, but the rest of him was stoic, still.

"This is insane, Aedon, I don't know what's going on with you. I'm calling Birdie."

"You do that and I do this." He pulled a remote control out of his pocket.

I just stared at it, a new wave of panic passing through me.

"You know that cauldron you flew all the way over here to find? Well, this"—he wiggled the device—"is linked to a bomb beneath its belly."

Oh crap. Oh no. No, he wouldn't do that. He couldn't. I shook my head, tucked the phone away, and hit what I hoped was the record button. Pulled my hand back out of my pocket and held it up. "No, Aedon, you couldn't. I know you couldn't."

He stepped forward and said, "My dear, you have no idea what I am capable of." He added, in a frighteningly steady tone, "And if you truly know where the cauldron is, then you know what will happen if I detonate the bomb. Not only to all those people who will likely starve to death, but to the one thing you truly came here for."

I swallowed hard, a chill rippling through me.

My mother.

He said, softly, "Boom."

"You're mad. You would blow up your own castle?"

"Not if you leave this between you and me."

"What do you want from me, Aedon?"

"What I want," Aedon said, a vein throbbing in his temple, "is an eye for an eye."

He advanced on me.

"I don't know what you mean," I stammered, stepping back, scanning the landscape for the other three corners. "I've done nothing to you."

"Revenge, my dear, can be a complex emotion." His eyes were dark, focused, burning a hole through me. "It's true what they say. It really is best served cold."

"Revenge? For what?"

"For the life your mother took from me. My only son." He removed his gloves, tossed them on the ground. "Now, I shall take her only daughter." He shrugged off his coat, carefully placing the detonator on top of it, and crouched into a karate stance. "Right before your confirmation and her release. Poetic, don't you think?"

This could not be happening. He seriously wanted to fight me?

"If it's revenge you want, then why not just kill me?"

"What would be the fun in that?" He circled around me like a shark. "I intend to deliver your body bruised and beaten as my son was delivered to me."

"He was going to kill me. She was only protecting me."

I sidestepped closer to the hill. *Birdie, if you can hear me, tell John to get his gun. Tell him I'm just beyond the hillside, near my watchtower.*

I wasn't sure if John had brought his firearm, but I never knew a cop to travel without one.

Aedon snapped, "That's a lie. My son was sent to retrieve the locket. He was there on orders."

The locket. Had my mother given it to my father to hide? If so, where had it come from? Had it been hers? And how had Aedon's son known she had it?

"Whose orders?" I asked.

"That is not your concern."

Suddenly, I remembered the letter I took from the secret room in the library. I hadn't had a chance to read it yet. It was still folded up in my pocket.

Aedon said, "Did you know I was once a Warrior?" Then he cracked his knuckles.

Perfect. I was going to get my ass handed to me by Clint Eastwood.

"I'm not going to fight you, Aedon." The detonator was still behind him. If I could get him to circle farther away from it, I could reach it. Remove the batteries or something.

"You will, or I will kill not only you, but your family as well."

I turned, scoped out the hill. Where was John? Birdie? Ivy? Ethan?

"Come on, then. Let's get on with it," the old man said, stretching his legs.

I faced the man who wanted me dead, suspecting he was a pawn in a much larger game.

Who had sent Aedon's son to steal the locket?

The head of the council was growing impatient. "Come on, then."

There are about a dozen pressure points in the head and neck that can kill or paralyze an assailant. I knew this from my training. I suspected Aedon knew it too, because he had no weapons that I could see.

I crouched into a fighting stance, circled with him. It wasn't going to be easy to maneuver in this coat, but there was a vial of deadly nightshade in my pocket and a dagger strapped to my thigh, so I wasn't about to give up that insurance.

The remote was still a few feet away.

Aedon delivered a swift kick to my chest that sent me reeling. I lay on my back, dazed, for a moment, until he came at me again. Quickly, I reached my palms behind my head, flattened them into the earth, and bowed my legs, jumping into a kip-up. I delivered two swift roundhouse kicks, one to his stomach, one to his neck.

The one to the neck stunned him, and I dove for the remote. He came from behind me, chopped at my neck, but I squirmed away, flipped over, and head butted him. We somersaulted together into a pile of dead wood, and I somehow lost the remote. I didn't see it anywhere and had no time to hunt, so I advanced on Aedon.

Going for the kill shot. A quick, explosive jab just under the nose.

Before I reached him, he waved one arm in my direction, and I was airborne. I crashed into a tangled briar patch.

So we're going to play like that, are we? If he was going to use telekinesis to incapacitate or injure me, I'd have to be a lot faster. And deadlier. With the force of his strength, Aedon could easily snap my neck. I couldn't give him the chance.

I unsheathed the athame, tucked it into my sleeve. Then came out of the brush, crouched low.

"You're better trained than I thought," Aedon said. A trickle of blood ran down his cheek from where I had connected with my skull.

"You seem to have an unfair advantage." I took a few deep breaths and charged in a whirly pattern, kicking his head and sending a slew of uppercuts to his gut.

He collapsed and I grabbed the athame.

"That I do." Without warning, he catapulted up and rushed forward. He chopped the air with his hands in quick successive motions, focusing so intensely that his wound split wide open.

I screamed, tried to scramble away as my ankle twisted grotesquely until it finally broke. It made a hideous popping sound like a burst balloon. Then my index finger bent all the way back to my wrist until it snapped too, and I dropped the dagger. I thought that pain was unbearable until my knee shattered. I may have passed out for a moment then, because the next thing I knew, my shoulder was dislocated, my nose was gushing blood, and Aedon kept coming.

I prayed my neck wouldn't be next.

"Stop," I whispered. "Please, Aedon."

"Begging for mercy," he tsked. "Not very Seeker-like of you."

With my good hand, I reached for the broom charged with generations of Geraghty power and held it up, hoping to deflect the next blow.

To my surprise, it did. Aedon flew back and smacked into a tree, and whatever body part he had planned to break in me next was broken in him. It looked to be his arm, judging from the way he clutched at it, screaming.

Then I heard someone call my name. Aedon swung his head in that direction.

And I knew it was my only chance.

Chapter 33

Ivy, John, and Birdie stood outside the car, comparing notes.

"We all saw the same thing?" John asked, incredulous.

"It would appear so," Birdie said.

Ivy said, "Well, that was easy."

Birdie looked at the young girl. Something tugged at her mind, something just out of her reach, which was understandable given the amount of energy she had just exerted. Still, it seemed important.

"Yes, it was," Birdie said. She looked at John. "A little too easy, wouldn't you say?"

John raised an eyebrow. "What are you saying? That you don't think the cauldron is at the castle?"

Birdie suddenly felt very weak. She leaned against the car.

"Where is Stacy?" Ivy asked.

John looked around. "She had the farthest point to cover. I'm sure she'll be along any moment."

Birdie put her head down, focusing on a single blade of grass, trying to decipher what her instincts were telling her.

Ivy was buzzing with the thrill of the quest. "We head back to the castle now, right? We tell the council that it's there?"

John frowned. "Not sure that's a good idea." He looked at Ethan, who was craning his neck to see what they were doing. "Obviously there's a breach. A rogue member. Nothing gets in or out of that place without a council member's knowledge."

Ivy ran that idea through her mind. Then she brightened. "Maybe it's a test? To see how well we work together? Maybe they want to confirm us, but they wanted to make us do one more mission first, so they staged it."

John said, "This was staged, all right. Just not for the reasons you think." He approached Birdie. "What do you think?"

She was about to say that perhaps the spell hadn't worked after all, but then a pain shot through her head. She bent over.

John reached out to her. "You all right?"

"Birdie?" Ivy asked, a quiver in her voice.

"Quiet, both of you," Birdie said. Once they stopped speaking, the message came through clearly.

Birdie's head snapped up. "She's in trouble."

John didn't hesitate. He reached inside the car, grabbed a bag, and pulled out a handgun. "Stay here," he barked.

Ivy said, "No. We're in this together."

Birdie grabbed her arm before the teenager could chase after John.

Hold on, Anastasia. Help is coming.

I grabbed the athame and, in one swift move, launched it into Aedon's back.

He screamed in agony and collapsed forward, and I said, "Sometimes it's the instrument, dickhead."

I hauled my broken body up.

Then I heard Birdie whisper to me in my mind. She said they were coming for me. I didn't know if I had killed Aedon or just wounded him, but I decided it wasn't a good idea to stick around to find out.

John called my name again, and I said, "Here!"

My right leg was no use to me, and my left shoulder was dangling from its socket, but my will to survive was stronger than the pain. Inch by inch, I made my way forward until I saw John. I nearly bawled at the sight of him.

He faltered for a split second when he laid eyes on me. Behind him was another man. The one from the vision before the cauldron appeared. The one I couldn't place. He moved forward, a sinister look on his face.

"Behind you!" I shouted.

John whipped around. "Where?"

The man was moving toward him slowly.

I pointed. "He's right there!"

John said, "Where? Stacy, I don't see anyone!"

He waved his gun in the direction of the man, whose face was twisted into a ferocious snarl. As I tried to point him out again, the man disappeared.

Who was he? Was he a spirit? Had he died here in battle?

John rushed forward, ignoring my warning, and I saw Birdie and Ivy rounding the hill.

Relief I desperately welcomed washed over me.

Then I heard Ivy scream, "No!"

I shifted to the left, following her gaze. That's when the athame—my athame, which had been planted in Aedon's back—pierced my heart.

John charged forward, caught me just before I dropped. I looked at the dagger protruding from my chest, then over to where Aedon still lay, facedown in the grass.

How?

The answer came in the form of that same man. A spirit, I realized, hovering over me.

He vanished, without saying a word. Without my knowing who he was.

As I felt the life force drain from my body, I managed only one word.

"Mom."

Then the world blackened and I drifted away.

John lifted Anastasia's body carefully. Birdie watched as the man walked toward her, carrying her granddaughter in his arms, her head lolled back, her legs dangling like those of a puppet.

Lifeless.

He walked toward Birdie, who was still frozen in shock by what she had just seen.

The dead can't hurt you, she had always told the girl. She thought it an important lesson for a young necromancer just learning her skills. She didn't want her granddaughter to grow up fearful of her spirit guides. She had always taught her that the spirits were there to help her, and she them.

It had been a deadly false lesson, Birdie now realized, as a lump rose in her throat. For the blade had been pulled from Aedon's back as if out of thin air.

Aedon's back. Aedon, her friend, her ally.

Her betrayer.

What had he come here to do? What was his purpose for attacking Anastasia?

More importantly, whose invisible hands had plunged the blade into Anastasia's heart? That large heart that once beat with love and compassion for all who knew her.

Now still.

Guilt poured through Birdie. Her granddaughter had tried to warn her, tried to tell her that there was a malicious force following her. If only Birdie had insisted they perform the graveyard spell. If only she had never brought her here at all.

As John reached her, Birdie gasped at the sight of the mangled girl, her grandchild. The sweet young girl she had raised, cared for, taught.

The lump burst forth, not in the form of tears, but in a ball of anger that shook Birdie's core.

Birdie pumped her fist to the sky, wailed to the gods. "I trusted in you."

Why hadn't they protected her?

Then again, why hadn't she?

Ivy was shaking, crying.

Ethan jumped out of the car, yelled, "Bloody hell! What happened?"

He whipped his coat off and was about to drape it over the body of her deceased granddaughter, when Birdie intervened. She slapped the coat away and said, "No. You don't touch her. You don't go near her!"

She was fueled by rage, her thoughts a jumble of images, conversations, memories.

How had it come down to this? All that she had devoted to the council, to her heritage, to her people.

How could they have betrayed her?

How could they hurt this precious child? Anastasia didn't deserve this. All she wanted was to bring her mother home, and to please Birdie.

Anastasia had trusted Birdie, and she had failed the girl.

Ethan squeaked, "You think I had something to do with this?" He snapped his head back and forth, looking at all of them. "No, you can't believe that. I never left the car."

John told Ivy to open the door to the backseat. She did, and he gently laid Anastasia's body inside. He covered her with his coat. Then he spun around and punched Ethan in the face.

"You better tell me everything you know, pal, or the next slug will come from my Glock."

Ethan was doubled over, clutching his right eye. "I swear on my life, I've no idea what is happening."

"So you didn't see the head honcho come around the bend?" John growled.

"Who? You mean that tosser Aedon? He's here?"

Ethan seemed genuinely perplexed. Birdie stepped forward and rested a hand on John's shoulder. "There's one way to know for sure."

Birdie had seen Lolly pack deadly nightshade for Anastasia. She reached into the girl's pocket, kissed her forehead gently. When she emerged, she held the labeled vial out for Ethan. "One taste, and you'll be forced to tell the truth."

"Or I'll be dead. Isn't that stuff poisonous?" Ethan asked nervously. "How do I know you aren't the bad guys?"

John flashed his gun. "I will be if you don't do what she asks."

Ethan reluctantly opened his mouth, and Birdie placed a drop of the herb onto his tongue.

She waited a moment, then asked, "Did you know Aedon was after my granddaughter?"

Ethan's eyes were as big as the moon. "Aedon did this?"

Birdie said, "He's telling the truth. Everyone get in the car."

John cuffed Ethan to the passenger-seat door handle. "I'm driving, asshole."

Ivy sniffled. She crawled into the first backseat, put her arm over to where Anastasia's body lay. "Are we going to the hospital?"

John shot Birdie an uneasy glance.

Birdie said, "It's too late for that. We're going to the castle."

She looked out the window at the ancient mound, hoping upon hope that for what she was about to do, she would be forgiven.

Chapter 34

It was eleven p.m. when they arrived back at the castle. Come midnight, it would all be over.

One way or another.

"All right," Birdie said with much more conviction than she actually felt, "does everyone know what they are supposed to do?"

Ivy nodded despondently.

John said, "Ten four."

Ethan said, "Aye."

John leaned in to whisper in Birdie's ear. "You sure about this guy?"

Birdie said, "Not unequivocally." She glanced at Ethan. "But we'll need him."

John nodded.

Ethan said, "Would you please uncuff me now? I'll do as you ask, believe me." He shot a disgusted glance at the behemoth stone structure. "I want nothing more to do with the O'Conor name after tonight."

John unlocked the handcuffs and said something in Ethan's ear that Birdie couldn't hear. Ethan rolled his eyes, and John shut the car door.

Birdie paused, took a long look at the car that held the broken body of her oldest granddaughter. She allowed a single, fat tear to slide slowly down her cheek. Then she locked up her grief, wiped her cheek, and said, "Let's do this."

The Guardian, the Mage, and the Warrior approached the castle. John tried to open the front door, but it was locked. He was about to ring the bell, when Birdie stopped him.

"They mustn't know we're back. Not yet. There may be questions about Aedon, and we've no time for inquiries. We don't know how deep this goes; it may involve the entire council."

Luckily, Ethan was privy to a private road that led to the grounds. They hadn't needed permission to open that gate. As an O'Conor and Tallulah's grandson, he held a key to the separate entrance.

John looked at the imposing door, stepped back, and said, "How do you break into a fortress?"

Ivy snapped her fingers. "Through the roof." She tugged on John's arm. "Follow me."

As they crept along the side of the building, hugging the stone wall, Ivy explained that her class had toured the castle once. It had been a very informative tour, and, being the inquisitive girl she was, she had asked many questions.

"You see those towers?" She pointed to four massive stone structures that stood to the rear of the castle. "They all connect on the roof, and to the second floor via tunnels, so sentries could pass from one part of the castle to another. The guards would work foot patrol up top, monitoring for invasions. If an enemy attacked, they could quickly move to whatever section needed protecting by scaling the towers."

Birdie was impressed.

Ivy licked her lips, looked at Birdie. "There's, like, a hundred steps to the top, at least. You up for that?"

"Don't worry about me."

Ivy smiled. They each took a tower and agreed to meet in the middle of the roof.

As Birdie climbed the stone tube, the letter she had found in Anastasia's pocket ran through her mind.

The letter written in her daughter's hand.

It had read:

> *My Darling,*
>
> *I hope this note finds you in time. I know that they have called you on a mission and that you are coming to the castle. I fear for your safety. As sure as the sun shines and the moon glows, I feel it in my bones that there is a conspiracy underfoot. I don't know who is behind it or why, though I suspect that my upcoming hearing, and the man I slew, may have something to do with it.*
>
> *I still don't know who he was, or why he intended to harm you. All I know is that there is just one within these walls whom I trust. One whom you will need, who will believe.*
>
> *Trust no one else. The name of our ally is*

And that was all. As if she had been interrupted before she could finish writing.

Whom was her daughter referring to?

Birdie glanced up. She was halfway to the top. She picked up speed, pulling herself through the length of the tower one narrow step at a time.

Finally, she saw the opening. She crawled out of the tower and scanned the roof. Ivy and John were frantically searching for a passageway.

John said, "I can't find a way in."

Ivy looked confused herself. "It's here, I know it is."

A large, angry bird landed near the girl, and she shooed it away with her foot.

The bird hopped back and pecked at Ivy.

Birdie rested for just a moment. "What time is it?"

"Ten after eleven," John said.

The bird flew to the tip of the tower Birdie had just emerged from, and swooped down. It squawked near Ivy, pecking the ground around her feet.

"Shoo!" the girl said.

As it flew past her once more, Birdie realized she recognized the bird.

"Ivy, hold still a moment."

The young Warrior flicked her eyes to Birdie.

Birdie stepped toward the winged creature. "I think I know this bird."

She recalled a bird her granddaughter had befriended over the summer. It was a predatory bird, very large, very smart, Anastasia had told her. There was a picture in the paper of the bird after its owner had died. The old man who ran the junkyard.

This looked like that same creature. Birdie peered at the bird, who seemed to be encouraging her to say something.

"Liberty?" she asked. That was the name of the bird Anastasia had told her about.

The—hawk?—shrieked, then flew back to where Ivy stood. It blinked up at the girl.

John rushed over to where the bird was pacing. He flattened onto his stomach and put his ear to what seemed like solid stone, knocking his knuckles around.

"Bingo."

John struggled with the stone, trying to shift it this way and that. "There's a seam. I need a screwdriver, a knife, something."

Ivy tossed John a thick pocketknife. He flipped through at least thirty gadgets until he found the one he was looking for.

He traced an outline into the stone with a flat blade, while Ivy tried to loosen it.

They had their gateway.

John lifted the stone and shoved it aside. Ivy slipped through first. John stuck his head in the hole and said, "What do you see?"

Birdie leaned over the opening. Ivy took in her surroundings. "A lot of old crap."

"That doesn't help," John said.

"There's a painting of a woman with creepy eyes and a lot of armor."

John said, "That's near Stacy's room."

The girl wavered a bit at the mention of Anastasia's given name.

Birdie rushed to say, "Ivy, remember your task. Follow the map. Stay strong, and this will work."

It had to.

Ivy nodded and rushed off.

John slipped through the hole next, and Birdie followed, with his assistance.

"You know your way around without a map?" he asked, since Birdie had given hers to Ivy.

She nodded.

John called Ethan and said, "We're in. Meet us in the Dining Hall in five minutes."

It was twenty minutes after eleven.

John hurried down the hall while Birdie slipped into Anastasia's room. She grabbed her granddaughter's hairbrush, checked to make sure there were a few strands, pocketed it, then rushed out, smacking directly into Tallulah.

Tallulah said, "Back so soon?"

Birdie said, "Tabby, listen to me. I need you to take me to my daughter. It's urgent."

"No."

"This isn't a request!"

Tallulah blanched, surprised by Birdie's fortitude. "You know I can't do that yet. We must wait for Aedon to decide her fate. Once you find the cauldron, of course."

"The cauldron is here, and Aedon will no longer decide anything."

"Because you are a Mage? Please, Birdie, I didn't object to that little display of yours for the good of the council—"

"Anastasia is dead!" Birdie shouted.

Tallulah stepped back, shocked. "What?"

Birdie moved forward, grabbed Tallulah by the shoulders, and said, "Take me to my daughter."

Tabby's eyes were wide, and she glanced over her shoulder in fear.

"No. That's impossible. She called me not long ago."

It was Birdie's turn to look shocked. "What do you mean she called you? Anastasia? When?"

Tabby stammered. "I…I don't know. I've been too busy fending off your ex-husband to check."

"Where's your phone?" Birdie gripped her old rival more firmly.

"It's right here."

Tabby pulled the phone from her pocket. Birdie hit a few buttons, and Anastasia's and Aedon's voices trickled through the airwaves.

They heard Aedon speak of a bomb strapped to the cauldron, of his intent for revenge for the murder of his son. The locket, the orders from another to retrieve it, and a horrible fight.

Birdie powered the phone off. "Tabby, as a mother and a grandmother, I appeal to you. Take me to my daughter."

Tabby seemed stunned still. Although there was a nasty side to her temperament, Birdie knew the woman wasn't evil. "I can't believe it. Aedon really killed her?"

Birdie said, "Not exactly. I'll explain on the way. We must get to the cauldron before midnight."

Tallulah caught her meaning when Birdie flashed the hairbrush. "You think it will work?"

"It must."

The two women rushed down the hall together as Birdie explained about the ghost, and the attack on Anastasia at the mound.

"I don't know who he is or if he will return, but I've instructed the Warrior to work with my sisters on a binding spell."

Tabby swallowed hard, nervously. "I think I may know who he is. I just don't know how he escaped the castle."

Tabby's eyes darted all around as they made their way down the stairs with haste.

"Who?" Birdie asked.

"My father," said her old classmate.

Chapter 35

Tallulah explained that her mother had been the previous Seeker. That she, and only she, knew the power of the locket, and it had driven Tabby's father insane.

"Mother never broke the Seeker's code of silence regarding the locket, not once. When the time came for her to pass the locket along, he became obsessed with finding it. With keeping it in the family. He thought she would pass it to me, despite the fact that a Seeker is born every hundred years or so, but"—she looked crestfallen—"I could never meet his demands."

"We are who we are, despite what our families expect of us."

Tabby gave a weak smile. "I never knew she gave it to Stacy. Never knew my father sent anyone to harm her, but it makes sense now. What your daughter saw in her vision must have been true."

Birdie said, "If we don't bind him, he won't stop."

When they reached the lobby, Lolly and Fiona were performing a spell. Birdie handed them the hairbrush.

Ivy was there, removing the locket from Thor's vest. John appeared to be standing guard.

Ethan entered the castle, Anastasia draped in his arms. Tallulah gasped.

"Tabby, get my daughter. Hurry!" Birdie added when Tallulah hadn't moved.

Tallulah rushed off toward the library, and Birdie went to her granddaughter.

Ivy placed the locket around Anastasia's neck, a tear in her eye.

"Strength, Warrior," Birdie said.

A minute later, Tallulah returned, distraught. "She isn't in her room."

Fiona said, "Oh no." She shifted her eyes to Birdie. "We can't do it without her mother."

Birdie knew that, or feared it at least. The cauldron was powerful, that was certain. A symbol not only of sustenance, but of water, the womb, birth, life.

Resurrection.

It had been known to reanimate many a fallen soldier—especially those who fought to protect it. But without her mother to dunk her, would it work for Anastasia?

"Eleven thirty," Ivy said.

For it to work at all, the baptism had to be performed on the day the person died.

"Let's go," Birdie said.

"I'll keep looking," Tallulah said, and rushed off.

Fiona said, "Thor shouldn't be there. I don't think he's aware yet."

Birdie thought Lolly shouldn't be present either. "Wait upstairs, both of you. I'll call if I need you."

John, Ivy, Birdie, and Ethan headed for the Dining Hall. The sign posted on the wall read DANU'S DINNER GUESTS, THIS WAY. A mock street sign.

Birdie searched for a light switch as John helped Ethan place Anastasia gently on the floor beneath the portrait of the great goddess.

The cauldron was here, they were certain, based on the visions that filtered through to them on the mound.

They had discussed their plans on the car ride over. Everyone had a purpose, everyone was focused.

The lights flicked on, and Birdie thought Ivy had discovered the switch, until she heard, "Looking for this?"

She spun around to see Elizabeth standing near the golden cauldron, a gun in her hand. "Aedon told me you were here to steal the cauldron." She trained her gun on Birdie.

John asked, "What's that wire sticking out of the back?"

Birdie answered, "Didn't I mention the bomb?"

"No, but thanks for bringing me up to speed." John pulled his own gun out and said, "Look, Tinker Bell, I suggest you get your ass away from that pot before you blow us all to bits."

That was the last thing the Guardian said before a lamp crashed into his head.

Birdie watched, fury filling her belly, as Gary stood over John, the broken lamp in his hand. He discarded it and picked up John's pistol.

The youngest Geraghty turned to the tiny woman holding the big gun. "Elizabeth, don't be a dolt. Stop and think why the cauldron is here in the first place."

"Aedon said—"

"Aedon is dead!" Birdie said.

"I'm afraid that was just a rumor, Brighid."

Birdie whipped around to see Aedon, looking worse for wear, walk into the room, clutching his arm.

Birdie had no idea the capacity of her hatred until she lunged at him. With one wave of his hand, Aedon lifted the witch and tossed her through the air. She crashed into a serving cart.

"Thank you for your loyalty, Elizabeth," Aedon said.

The stupid woman nodded as Birdie hoisted herself upright.

"You will pay for what you have done, Aedon. I promise you that," Birdie said.

"I would warn you against threatening me, Brighid, but I suspect you have already seen the consequences of what happens to those who cross me," Aedon said.

Suddenly, Ivy came at Gary with the ferocity of a lion. She karate chopped his neck, and he slumped to the floor. The young girl grabbed the gun, looked at Birdie. "Twenty minutes until midnight."

"Ethan, get the water," Birdie said.

Aedon said, "Move, and Elizabeth will shoot you."

Elizabeth looked like she hadn't signed off on that order. In that moment, Birdie was certain Aedon was acting alone in his plan for revenge.

Birdie took advantage of the small woman's hesitation. "Do you see? Aedon is willing to destroy an O'Conor to satisfy his vengeance."

Elizabeth looked from Birdie to Aedon.

"Give me the gun, Elizabeth," Aedon said.

Elizabeth began to shake.

"Don't do it," Birdie warned.

The very walls of the room seemed to be holding their breath. *Please, let this woman be smarter than she looks,* Birdie prayed.

Ivy made the decision for Elizabeth when she shot the gun out of the woman's hand. Elizabeth shrieked and bumped into the cauldron, clamping her palm.

That's when the ticking started.

Elizabeth's fall must have tripped some sort of timer on the bomb. Birdie's priorities shifted. She couldn't let the cauldron explode.

She gingerly stepped toward it as Aedon focused on the small blonde woman.

"You should have done as I told you, Elizabeth," Aedon said.

Then he flicked his wrist and snapped her neck. Birdie watched as Elizabeth slumped to the floor.

Birdie said, "Aedon, please, don't do this."

Birdie's old friend ignored her. He trained his sights on Ivy and twisted his hand, and the gun she held opened, spilling its bullets across the floor. Ivy dropped the barrel.

"You don't have to do this. It was all a mistake. Liam O'Conor is the one to blame for your son's death. He gave the order to kill Anastasia," Birdie said. After what Tallulah had told her, it was the only explanation. He wanted the locket, and he wanted someone from his loins to be Seeker. Since that wasn't looking like it would happen, he must have decided to eliminate the competition.

Ethan used Birdie's distraction to escape the room. Aedon caught the boy's movements out of the corner of his eye. He waved an arm, elevating Ethan, and slammed him into a wall.

Birdie cringed.

The air in the room grew bitterly cold. Birdie looked at the cauldron, took another step toward it.

Then, as if summoned, an angry force swept through the dining hall, knocking everyone to the floor.

Birdie watched in terror as a spirit materialized. He looked familiar. Could it be?

The spirit looked at Birdie with disdain, then set his sights on Aedon.

Aedon groaned and rose to stand. He tossed a nervous glance toward Ethan, before he met the spirit's fierce gaze. "He's fine, Liam. I...I wasn't going to hurt him," Aedon stammered.

Birdie inched toward the cauldron, glancing at Aedon.

His focus was on the spirit of Ethan's grandfather.

Liam's face was contorted into a palpable furor.

Aedon lifted his hand, "Liam, please, you don't understand."

Birdie advanced another step toward the cauldron.

Liam roared and Aedon cried out, tried to duck. "Don't!"

Then the ghost of Liam O'Conor picked up a bullet, examined it closely, and sailed it straight through Aedon's skull. His body slumped back against a wall as the head of the council took his final breath.

Birdie was about to take another step toward the cauldron, when the ghost of Ethan's great-grandfather descended on Anastasia.

"Leave her alone!" Birdie shouted.

The man who was the cause of so much misery, both past and present, snarled at Birdie. Then he ripped the locket off her granddaughter's neck.

The cauldron tick-tocked.

Ivy whispered, "Ten minutes."

Ethan crawled to the cauldron. "I need something to cut the wires."

Ivy slid her pocketknife to him.

Birdie stood, keeping her eye on the locket as the ghost twisted it in his hand, inspecting it curiously.

"Which wire?" Ethan asked.

"We just studied this," Ivy said. "Cut the red wire."

Tick-tock.

Ethan reached in with the cutter.

Birdie said, "No, wait! Is there a black one?"

Ethan looked.

The ghost was still marveling at his trinket.

"Yes," Ethan said.

"That one. I know Aedon—he would think it poetic justice. Black is banishment."

Tick-tock.

"Five minutes," Ivy said.

"Ivy, get the water!" Birdie called.

Ivy rushed from the room.

Ethan said, "Here goes nothing."

He reached in and cut.

They all held their breath for a split second. The ticking stopped.

Birdie approached the spirit. He opened the locket, spun it around a few times, and frowned.

"I believe that belongs to my granddaughter, Liam."

The spirit sneered at her.

Ethan said, "Please, Great-Grandfather."

Ivy rushed back in with the water. "Three minutes."

Just then, Tallulah stormed into the room. "I couldn't find her mother"—she was out of breath—"but I brought the next-best thing."

She stepped aside, revealing an older woman who moved with great difficulty.

The woman bellowed, "Liam! Give me that locket. It doesn't belong to you, and it never did."

The spirit glared at the woman, and the room heated like a Florida summer.

"Honestly!" the old woman said. She looked at Ivy. "Don't ever get married. Husbands are nothing but a pain in the neck." She stepped forward. "Tallulah has informed me what you've been doing, and you should be ashamed of yourself."

Liam didn't look ashamed. He looked incensed.

"This kind of behavior is why I killed you in the first place." The woman turned to Tallulah, who was stunned. "Sorry you had to find out this way, dear."

Liam moved his lips, but only his wife, the Seeker, could hear him. Birdie assumed she must have been a necromancer.

"Two minutes," Ivy said.

"You want to see what it does?" asked the old Seeker.

The ghost of her husband nodded.

"Fine, but then you give it back."

He nodded again.

Tallulah's mother told her husband to open the locket. "You see that watch face? I want you to stare into it and concentrate."

He did.

"Sixty seconds," Ivy said.

Instantly, Liam was sucked into the locket. It hung in midair until Tallulah's mother grabbed it. She slammed it shut.

"That's one of its secrets," the old woman said. "When she wakes up, I'll teach the new Seeker of Justice the rest."

Ethan and Ivy lifted Anastasia, crossed the room, and laid her inside the cauldron. Ivy poured the water as Ethan draped the locket over Anastasia's neck. The spell was in place. It had to work.

They waited.

Nothing happened.

Birdie walked over to the girl, put a hand on her forehead, sending her energy, strength.

Anastasia's skin felt cold, brittle almost.

After what seemed like ages, Ivy said, "Why isn't it working?"

John's voice grumbled from the floor. He stirred. "Because we're too late." He was still lying on the ground. He groaned a bit as he held up a pocket watch. "It's five minutes past midnight."

Ivy cried, "No, that can't be." She looked at her phone. "We still have ten seconds."

Ethan checked his phone, met Ivy's eyes. "He's right."

"No!" Ivy wailed.

Birdie's knees gave way as her body numbed.

Chapter 36

Thor wouldn't stop howling at the loss of his witch. The entire room felt his agony.

Birdie and her sisters joined hands around the cauldron where Anastasia's body lay. Not quite ready for a release spell, they simply stood there, eyes closed, tears streaming down their cheeks, quietly.

Ivy broke into the circle. John followed, then Ethan, Tallulah, and finally Tallulah's mother.

"She was a good Seeker," the old woman said. "I don't know that there will ever be another like her."

The woman who was to pass the torch to Anastasia led them all in a prayer.

They held hands, chanting for several moments.

The water seemed to flow in tandem with their voices as Birdie heard a gentle lapping.

After several more minutes, Ivy whispered, "Something's happening."

Birdie looked into the cauldron to see the water ebb and flow around her granddaughter, as if stirred by an invisible hand.

The blood washed away from the girl's face. Anastasia's nose straightened. Color began to flood her cheeks. Her ankle untwisted itself, the swelling in her knee subsided, and her shoulder found its way back into its socket.

No one spoke.

They all stood there, listening to the gush of the water and the beat of their own hearts.

Or was that Anastasia's heartbeat?

Birdie flicked her eyes to the portrait of Danu, but the goddess was missing.

She flitted her gaze back down, and the girl's eyes popped open.

Anastasia looked up at all of them, her face a mixture of fear and confusion.

Fiona was the first to speak. "How are you feeling, dear?"

Anastasia darted her eyes around the circle, looked down at the cauldron, the water. "That depends. Are you planning to cook me?"

They told me I died.

That seems highly unlikely, since I was, the next morning, having breakfast with my mother. Birdie had this crazy theory that since I was killed by a ghost, it was easier to resurrect me.

I thought she was nuts. The dead can't hurt you.

Right?

She also said that Danu had a hand in my rebirth, which, after all I went through to get her precious cauldron back, seemed only fair.

"Stacy, dear, you look perplexed," Birdie said.

Stacy? That was weird.

"Well, first, I'm perplexed that you just called me by my given name." I slipped Thor some bacon under the table.

Birdie smiled. "Anastasia means 'resurrection.' Since you've already been through that, I think it best not to tempt fate, don't you?" Birdie sipped her coffee.

"Agreed. But actually, I was thinking about the spirit who kept coming at me with those riddles. They were like warnings, but I haven't seen her in a while." I drank some water. "Why do you suppose she didn't warn me about Aedon at the mound?"

"Because Aedon locked her up," said my mother.

I stared at her, awestruck. Pearce had found my mother in a remote wing of the castle under a binding spell in a locked room.

"You're the riddler?"

She frowned. "I wish you'd stop calling me that." She looked at Birdie. "No matter how many clues I sent, she didn't heed them well."

Birdie said, "Tell me about it."

"Hey! Getting sucked into the Web of Wyrd is the reason I'm alive, so you were wrong about that one."

My mother shrugged. "True. I left you clues that it was me, you know. The book on astral projection, Pearce telling you I was still able to perform magic."

"Oh yeah," I said slowly. "But why the disguise, why the riddles?"

She stabbed a forkful of eggs and said, "Liam was watching me closely. I didn't want him to know it was me. It had to look as if an ancestor, or a spirit guide, was coaching you."

Right. I glanced over at Tallulah, who was canoodling with Gramps. She had promised to break the love spell gently, but it didn't seem to be working. Pearce and Ethan were having breakfast at the table next to them. When I glanced their way, I couldn't help but notice the loving manner in which Pearce gazed at my mother.

I flicked my eyes to her and caught her staring back at him, smiling.

I put my fork down. "You're not coming home, are you?"

She sighed, gave me a coaxing look with those impossibly emerald eyes of hers. "I thought perhaps you could stay here for a while. We could catch up, spend some time together."

I wanted to, I really did, but I was needed back home. I couldn't leave Derek in the lurch that long. Goddess only knew how Monique's column was working out. Plus, with Cin pregnant, she needed help at the bar. Not to mention I missed Chance.

"I have a business, a relationship. Responsibilities," I said.

My mother said, "Tell you what. You can fly your boyfriend out here. At least stay through Samhain."

That was six weeks away, and this was the busy season for Birdie. I couldn't do that to her. Not after all she had done for me. Not after we had grown so much closer.

"I can't, Mom. I'm sorry."

She nodded. "I understand." She set her napkin down, folded her hands. "How about we come for Christmas?" She looked at Birdie, then at me.

Birdie beamed. "I would love that."

My grandmother excused herself, and my mother and I sat there for hours, talking. I told her about my father, about how his death wasn't an accident. She cursed his killer, said she had wondered about that. Said that "accident" never felt right to her. She told me about her life here, how Pearce had made the imprisonment bearable.

Suddenly she teared up, dabbed her eyes, and said, "I missed so much."

I put my hand over hers. "You gave me so much, Mom. You sacrificed your life, your freedom, for me. I know that, and I'm grateful."

She choked back a sob. "Promise me you'll visit often. And bring that man in your life. Birdie tells me he's wonderful."

"He is. You do the same."

"And promise that you'll be careful always. I don't care if you are the Seeker of Justice—you're still my baby girl."

Before breakfast, we had all attended a council meeting. Tallulah had been appointed head of the council, slipping into Aedon's place. She, in turn, had nominated Birdie to take her seat. The first order of business was granting Ivy two more nomination points. The second was freeing my mother. Last on the agenda was my coronation as the Seeker of Justice.

"I will. Just keep sending me riddles."

She laughed at that.

I hugged my mother close, wanting never to let go, the locket pressed between us like a conduit linking the past to the future. When I had asked Tallulah's mother about its power, she had pulled me aside and said only one thing.

"It does whatever you need it to do. It's only a tool. The power is within you."

I could get used to that.

THE END

Author's Note

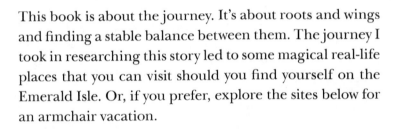

This book is about the journey. It's about roots and wings and finding a stable balance between them. The journey I took in researching this story led to some magical real-life places that you can visit should you find yourself on the Emerald Isle. Or, if you prefer, explore the sites below for an armchair vacation.

Hill of Tara, Meath: http://www.megalithicireland.com/Hill%20of%20Tara.htm

Heritage Ireland: Brú na Bóinne Visitor Centre Newgrange and Knowth: http:/www.heritageireland.ie/en/midlandseastcoast/BrunaBoinneVisitorCentreNewgrangeandKnowth/

County Kildare, Ireland: http://en.wikipedia.org/wiki/Kildare

Ashford Castle: http://www.ashford.ie/

Howth Castle: http://www.howthcastle.ie/

Mythical Ireland Fourknocks: http://www.mythicalireland.
com/ancientsites/fourknocks/

Tuatha Dé Danann: http://www.timelessmyths.com/celtic/
danann.html

Grace O'Malley: http://en.wikipedia.org/wiki/Grace_
O%27Malley

MABON

The story you just read takes place on the fall equinox,
called Mabon. Light and darkness are equal on this sab-
bat. It's a time when crops are harvested, daylight will soon
wane, and people are preparing for wintering. Rededication
ceremonies are common, as are feasts of thanks for the
bounty of the fields and the orchards. It's a good time to
smudge the home, invoke a protective spirit by ringing a
bell, and sweep out the negative energy with a broom. To
ensure a healthy winter, pluck a fresh apple (a symbol of
immortality) and cut it in half. Share one half with the
members of your household and freeze the other until
spring. Then bury it in your yard as a gift to the Goddess.

Irish Stew

When you visit Ireland, you are required to drink Guinness.
I'm pretty sure it's a law. Luckily, they export it to other
countries as well.

2 pounds stewing beef
2 pounds boneless lamb, cut into chunks
½ teaspoon salt
1 teaspoon pepper
2 tablespoons olive oil
8 large garlic cloves, minced
2 tablespoons butter
2 tablespoons flour
2 bottles Guinness stout beer
4 cups beef broth
2 large onions, peeled and chopped
3 large carrots, peeled and chopped
4 stalks celery, cleaned and chopped
8 red potatoes, quartered
2–3 sprigs thyme
2 bay leaves

Season meat with salt and pepper. Set aside. In a large stockpot, heat 2 tablespoons oil over medium-high heat. Add garlic. Cook for 30 seconds or until fragrant. Add butter, and brown beef and lamb. Sprinkle with flour and cook 3 minutes, stirring occasionally.

Pop open one bottle of Guinness and share with a friend. Add the other bottle to the pot, along with beef broth. Bring to a gentle boil, stirring occasionally. Reduce heat and simmer 1 hour. Add thyme and bay leaves. Remove from stove, cover, and bake in a 300-degree oven for 3 hours. Before serving, remove bay leaves and thyme sprigs.

Yield: 12–16 servings

Cheddar-Chive Biscuits

Irish cheddar is sharp, tangy, and nutty. A lot like the three Geraghty Girls!

2 cups buttermilk baking mix
$^2/_3$ cup milk
½ cup shredded Dubliner cheese
$^1/_3$ cup fresh-snipped chives

Preheat oven to 450 degrees. Combine baking mix, milk, and cheddar cheese in mixing bowl. Carefully blend in chives. Drop dough by spoonfuls onto ungreased cookie sheet. Bake 8–10 minutes or until golden brown.

Yield: 10 servings

Rosemary Roasted Potatoes

Plant rosemary in remembrance of a loved one.

2 pounds red potatoes, quartered
1 teaspoon minced garlic
2 tablespoons fresh rosemary
Pepper
Salt
¼ cup olive oil
4 tablespoons butter

Preheat oven to 425 degrees. Place potatoes in a large roasting pan. Sprinkle next six ingredients over potatoes and toss to coat. Dot with butter. Roast 30–40 minutes, stirring occasionally.

Yield: 4–6 servings

Green Isle Sauce

Fresh mint placed on an altar will call on the spirit guides to aid you in magic.

4 cups spearmint leaves, loosely packed
Water (just enough to cover leaves)
Sugar
Green food coloring (optional)

Place leaves in a saucepan and cover with water. Simmer 30 minutes. Strain mixture through coffee filter or jelly bag. Discard leaves and rinse pan. Return strained liquid to saucepan and add 1 cup sugar per 1 cup liquid. (So if you have 4 cups minted water, add 4 cups sugar.) Simmer 15 minutes or until sugar is dissolved. If desired, add a couple drops of food coloring. Chill 2 hours. Pour on ice cream or chocolate cake, or use to sweeten tea or coffee.

Yield: 6 servings

Hot Buttered Cider

In pagan cultures, the apple was a symbol of immortality and used in many love spells. For a simple love charm, cut an apple in half, remove the seeds, and share it with the one you adore. Then bury the seeds beneath a full moon for a long and prosperous relationship.

1 gallon real apple cider
6 whole allspice berries
½ nutmeg seed
3 cinnamon sticks
8 cloves
4 pats butter
Chamomile flowers
Suggested liquor: spiced rum

To a large pot, add cider and spices. Simmer 20 minutes. Strain, add rum if desired, then pour into a pretty punch bowl and dot with butter. Garnish with chamomile flowers and serve warm.

Yield: 12 servings

No-Sew Sweet Dreams Sachet

Valerian has long been used in sleep potions. Nestled alongside relaxing lavender and calming chamomile, you cannot help but drift into dreamland. The moonstone is there to stabilize emotions and promote lucid dreamscapes.

You can stitch this up, if you prefer, but this is the quick and easy method.

You'll Need:

2 3-inch fabric swatches
1 teaspoon each dried bee balm, valerian, chamomile, and lavender
1 moonstone
Hot glue gun

Instructions:

Put dried herbs in the center of one piece of fabric. Top with moonstone. Trace hot glue gun along all four edges. Top with the second piece of fabric and press ends together. Place at the head of your bed or beneath your pillow for pleasant dreams.

Acknowledgments

I'd like to warmly thank Terry Goodman for bringing me into this publishing family. Thanks to Danielle Marshall, marketing guru extraordinaire, and Jacque Ben-Zekry, who is so good at her job, she makes me feel as if she is my personal assistant. Thanks also to my tireless beta readers who read my work before the spit shine: George Annino, Leslie Gay, and Selena Jones. Your suggestions make a better storyteller out of me. Huge thanks as well to Alison Dasho for her editorial mastery and brainstorming sessions. Also to Annie Morgan, whose copy edit is just the right touch for this author.

This book was molded by the gracious people of the Emerald Isle who made my research trip even more enjoyable than it already was, especially Fiona, who was so much like Fiona Geraghty in beauty and charm (although not age) that I couldn't believe it. And to Carlos, the Italian import with the Irish brogue who offered us a very welcome ride across the country, and to John, who picked up a pair of rain-soaked travelers numerous times so that we could drink in every drop of County Kildare, home of Brighid Geraghty and the Great Geraghty Clan. You made a memorable trip magical.

Finally, endless thanks to my own clan. My grandmother, who left me a sign that she was with me in Ireland in the form of a penny. And my mother, who showed me long ago that strength often comes in small packages.

About the Author

Photo by George Annino, 2011

Barbra Annino is a native of Chicago, a book junkie, and a Springsteen addict. She's worked as a bartender and humor columnist, and currently lives in picturesque Galena, Illinois, where she ran a bed-and-breakfast for five years. She now writes fiction full-time—when she's not walking her three Great Danes.